Never Say Die

"Dammit!" Cooper suddenly screamed into the intercom. "There won't be any of us left! I've had it with this shit! They send us out on these suicide missions over and over like they're trying to get rid of us all!"

"Cool it, Coop!" Ryan barked.

"No, sir, I won't cool it! This is nuts! Let's just go back. All this for one guy? Come on, sir, just turn us around!" Cooper shouted.

Ryan paused, and then in a calm voice, "Sergeant Cooper, I need your help. I need you. You just hang in there, we'll get out of this." Ryan had no idea how, but he hoped he was right.

NIGHT STALKERS

MICHAEL HAWKE

BERKLEY BOOKS, NEW YORK

THE BERKLEY PUBLISHING GROUP
Published by the Penguin Group
Penguin Group (USA) Inc.
375 Hudson Street, New York, New York 10014, USA
Penguin Group (Canada), 10 Alcorn Avenue, Toronto, Ontario M4V 3B2, Canada
(a division of Pearson Penguin Canada Inc.)
Penguin Books Ltd., 80 Strand, London WC2R 0RL, England
Penguin Group Ireland, 25 St. Stephen's Green, Dublin 2, Ireland (a division of Penguin Books Ltd.)
Penguin Group (Australia), 250 Camberwell Road, Camberwell, Victoria 3124, Australia
(a division of Pearson Australia Group Pty. Ltd.)
Penguin Books India Pvt. Ltd., 11 Community Centre, Panchsheel Park, New Delhi—110 017, India
Penguin Group (NZ), Cnr. Airborne and Rosedale Roads, Albany, Auckland 1310, New Zealand
(a division of Pearson New Zealand Ltd.)
Penguin Books (South Africa) (Pty.) Ltd., 24 Sturdee Avenue, Rosebank, Johannesburg 2196, South
Africa

Penguin Books Ltd., Registered Offices: 80 Strand, London WC2R 0RL, England

NIGHT STALKERS

A Berkley Book / published by arrangement with the author

PRINTING HISTORY
Berkley mass-market edition / January 2005

Copyright © 2005 by The Berkley Publishing Group.
Cover design by George Cornell.
Interior text design by Stacy Irwin.

ISBN: 0-425-19992-4

BERKLEY®
Berkley Books are published by The Berkley Publishing Group,
a division of Penguin Group (USA) Inc.,
375 Hudson Street, New York, New York 10014.
BERKLEY is a registered trademark of Penguin Group (USA) Inc.
The "B" design is a trademark belonging to Penguin Group (USA) Inc.

PRINTED IN THE UNITED STATES OF AMERICA

10 9 8 7 6 5 4 3 2 1

Also I heard the voice of the Lord, saying,
  Who shall I send, and who will go for us?
Then said I, Here am I, send me.
                                            —ISAIAH 6:8

People sleep peaceably in their beds at night
    only because rough men stand ready to do violence
        on their behalf.
                                            —GEORGE ORWELL

PROLOGUE

February 27, 1991
Medina Ridge
Iraq

The voice drove into his ears from the helicopter's SATCOM radio, "Roger, Talon 6, you are cleared direct to target. Large armored force, a brigade of friendlies already engaged, more than two-zero-zero enemy tanks."

MAJ Seth "Maniac" McCall replayed the number in his head, trying to imagine a real-world battle between two hundred enemy tanks and an American armored brigade. What would it look like through the Head Display Unit he wore? Standard doctrine would have his helicopter standing off, five kilometers away, and engaging targets like an airborne artillery platform. In the dark and the rain, in the chaos they were sure to find, how would he and his copilot ever sort enemy from friendly?

"This is Talon 6, good copy, on the way. Over," McCall replied.

"Let's do it," grunted his copilot CWO Len Gile. Gile sat forward of and slightly below McCall.

McCall advised, "Turning right," and pushing downward, he lowered the collective. Each of the rotor blades above changed their angle, grabbing less air with each rotation. He decreased the throttle very slightly, and pushed the stick, or cyclic, far right. The entire rotor assembly tilted. Next, stomping fully on the right pedal, the tail rotor allowed the ass-end of the bird to swing left. The nose came right, dropped, and the aircraft's body rolled right.

He pulled up on the collective, gave her a big dose of power, centered the cyclic, and eased off the pedal. The helicopter righted itself on its new course, racing northward, leaning into a run that would take mere minutes at a top speed of nearly 175 miles per hour. McCall's wingman mimicked the maneuver. The four other AH-64 Apache attack helicopters from 1st Armored Division's 4th Brigade followed in pairs close behind.

The Apaches were completely dark and, with less than one hundred feet of altitude, were screaming over the hard-packed Iraqi desert. Ground troops along the way, squinting against the cool rain, scarcely had time to process what manner of flying beasts were directly above before they were gone. The helicopters were a pack of giant, ravenous dragons, each one sixty feet long, seventeen feet across, weighing in excess of fifteen thousand pounds, and moving with unimaginable speed. Battlefield gods on their way to a rendezvous with Iraq's best soldiers.

Gile called out, "Inside!" letting McCall know that Gile's attention would be focused inside the aircraft for more than a few seconds. The copilot and primary gunner on the aircraft, Gile worked the targeting system, known as TADS or the Target Acquisition Designation Sight. He selected the "white hot" thermal sensor settings for visibility in the pitch-black night and through the sheets of pouring rain. Any object putting out heat would appear white against the darker background in his sights. While he had the option of letting the targeting system scan automatically, Gile began manually scanning. This suited McCall just fine. Gile was as good a copilot/gunner as could be found in the U.S. Army, and if he felt the mission would be better served by manual scanning, that was good enough for McCall.

Gile called, "Outside!" to McCall to let him know both men were focused outside the aircraft once more.

McCall was straining to catch every detail through his Pilot Night Vision System or PNVS. It was separate from Gile's targeting system, allowing him to scan independently from his copilot. Still, while concentrating on the mission, there was a piece of him thinking about what he'd left behind at home. He and Maggie had one of those rare marriages where both people felt they married above their reach. Maggie had always been the most striking woman he'd ever seen, with lovely, soft brown hair and remarkably green eyes. Their daughter Jeanie, who just turned sweet sixteen, was the perfect blend of tomboy and princess. She had been a gift from God from day one, beautiful and bright. The little girl had grown up making cookies with Maggie and then, letting them cool, she would throw a football around in the backyard with him. McCall decided a ski trip was in order; after all this endless sand and vast expanses of flat desert, a ski trip with his girls would be just what the doctor ordered.

"Target, twelve o'clock!" Gile shouted, snapping McCall back into full-mission mode. Up ahead, through the PNVS, McCall spotted it as well. A battle that stretched from horizon to horizon. Streaks and splashes of white heat filled the night sights. Approximately one hundred American M1A1 Abrams tanks and other vehicles from the Old Ironsides division were fully engaged and fighting tooth and nail with Iraq's Medina division of the Republican Guard. The Americans were incredibly outnumbered. It didn't look anything like tank engagements of old, with two lines of opposing armor, firing at each other in a battle of attrition. These tanks were moving in a deadly ballet at up to forty miles per hour. They fired on the move, tanks exploded, and tracer rounds from heavy machine guns tracked through the battle space. The sky alternated from black to white with each explosion and the sound was an unending and deafening roar. Thin-skinned U.S. vehicles such as Humvees—ambulances and intelligence soldiers mostly—frantically tried to stay out of the way of their sixty-ton armored brethren, much like a two-year-old child standing on the line of scrimmage in a professional football game, as linesmen and running backs tried to avoid crushing them.

McCall and the other pilots were closer than the five kilometers than SOP would have dictated, and they needed to be. There was almost no way to sort this out. The 1st Armored Division soldiers on the ground desperately needed their help and it was time to get their hands dirty. They were still on approach, about three kilometers out, but they could destroy a few of the Iraqi T-72 main battle tanks on the way.

"Ready to engage!" Gile advised. Gile had sixteen AGM-114 Hellfire missiles at his disposal and looking out at the battlefield, he knew he would go through them fairly quickly. He set them for LOAL, or Lock-On-After-Launch, so that he could fire the missiles before they had actually locked onto the laser target designators marking the targets. This would allow him to get more missiles off in a shorter amount of time, because in the LOBL, or Lock-On-Before-Launch, mode the weapon would not fire until it had acquired a lock on a target. It also meant they would not be able to get too close because the missiles needed time to lock on.

"Slide right," Gile instructed McCall, and the helicopter slid sideways in its track, never losing forward momentum. Smaller helicopters, OH-58Ds, were out in the battle "lamping" countless targets with laser designators. Gile flipped the protective cover off the left-hand grip trigger switch.

"Firing Hellfires left side!" Gile barked and pulled the trigger. Two five-foot, 100-pound missiles blasted loose of the Apache's left armament wing and came up to nearly one and a half times the speed of sound before streaking down into an enemy tank. The explosion was blinding and breathtaking as the turret and main gun were launched into the air as if made of lightweight plastic.

Around McCall's helicopter the other five Apaches, also approaching the battle at full speed, began launching their own Hellfire missiles. All over the battlefield, tanks were being ripped apart, both from direct tank fire and death raining from above. Through McCall's night-vision, the shapes of men were running this way and that. Survivors from destroyed vehicles looked like apparitions driven from hell, black silhouettes racing through flames and across the backs of fallen men, dropping to the earth each time their surroundings went bright with the destruction of another tank.

Still they drove on. They were close enough to engage with reasonable certainty of who was friend and who was foe, and they did not hold back. The Apache pilots completely focused on supporting the soldiers on the ground.

Off to the left, there was suddenly a series of flashes seemingly coming from deep in the ground.

"What the hell was that?" Gile asked.

On the thermal imagery, there was nothing there, and then again, bright explosions in a row of holes. Artillery rounds, by the dozens, rained down all at once on the American tanks and armored Bradley fighting vehicles. American infantry scattered and ran in all directions.

"Talon 4, this is Talon 6, go check out those holes. Expect artillery dug in. Looks like they have an entire battery of guns down in those pits," McCall called.

"This is Talon 4, on the way," 2LT Mike Ryan replied. One of the Apaches broke off, and his wingman followed. The remaining four dropped their airspeed to a near hover and continued to engage the enemy tanks out in the battle space.

Ryan's flight of two Apaches came down low over the pits. Another series of flashes and another barrage of rounds fell on the American troops. There was no need to identify friend or foe, they would come in hot on the first pass.

"Talon 3, this is Talon 4, go with guns on the first pass. Let's shoot 'em up and shut the sneaky bastards down," Ryan said.

"This is Talon 3, roger that," the response came.

Ryan lifted forward in his seat, as if in an effort to see into the holes a split second sooner. His gunner/copilot was actually in the front of the aircraft, so this was a fruitless bit of reflex. As soon as they cleared the lip of the first hole, they saw it. Each hole had a crew of five serving a towed, old Soviet 2B12 120mm mortar.

Ryan's gunner opened up with the M230 30mm chain gun mounted beneath the nose of the aircraft. As he turned his head, he killed with a look, the gun firing at whatever he had his eye on. Talon 3, the wingman, was just to the rear and left of Ryan's helicopter, and was employing the same weapon.

"Talon 6, this is Talon 4, we are engaging a battery of 120mm towed mortars pulled down into these holes. From the looks of how we're doing, this problem's going to be solved in one pass," Ryan called to McCall.

The huge rounds blasted into the holes, tearing up the guns and crews and setting off ammunition sitting in piles. Men and their mortars were blown out of the holes.

"Talon 4, this is Talon 6, understood," McCall said.

In Talon 6, Gile was still shouting out before each volley of missiles.

"Come up," said Gile, "slide left!" McCall complied with the adjustments his gunner/copilot was demanding and the Apache gained a bit of altitude and slid left until Gile said, "Hold!" His firing resumed. Two more Hellfires roared downrange.

Ryan and his wingman wheeled around for another pass, but as expected, there was nothing left in the holes to shoot at. The two Apaches pulled in to a hover beside the other four, and the helicopters were six abreast once more.

No sooner had they reassembled than the synthetic speech of the AN/APR-39 Radar Warning Receiver began its shrill call.

"Strobe! Four o'clock!" Gile yelled, "Break right!"

McCall was already doing it. The anti-aircraft battery had lain as silent as a desert scorpion, radars off, as the helicopters had passed. Now the launchers and their radar systems were awake, alive, and probing the skies for their prey. The Apaches. Having locked onto McCall's, they let loose one of the few things that surely can make an Apache driver's blood run cold. An anti-aircraft missile was on the way.

A cloud of chaff, comprised of foil strips, went flying behind the helicopter as it wheeled around in an effort to confuse the missile, but the rain was quickly knocking the countermeasures down.

"Watch it!" Gile yelled "Traffic one o'clock!"

As they were turning right, the other Apaches were also reacting to the new threat. In the gloom, McCall's Apache had turned right into the path of his wingman. Both helicopters, already trying to avoid a missile, now dodged each other. McCall held his breath, made his turn tighter, and half-expected to feel the impact. He swore as the rotors of the two helicopters overlapped. The other aircraft passed so close to their nose, Gile instinctively pulled his feet back.

There was no time for a sigh of relief; having narrowly missed the other helicopter, they turned to face an oncoming missile that had closed more than half the distance already. There was chaff, rain, scrambling helicopters, and yet through it all, McCall saw it coming, the heat of the rocket motor looking like a signal flare in his thermal sights.

The missile was corkscrewing up at them with all the reason and mercy of a rabid dog. McCall raced toward it, or more precisely, toward its source. The SA-15 anti-aircraft battery sat behind the missile, five vehicles in all. Four launchers and a command post vehicle. More chaff spilled from McCall's helicopter as he juked up and down, left and right, hoping to be as tough a target as possible. What he wouldn't give for a knoll or a stand of tall trees to duck behind, but here in the Iraqi desert there wasn't a single terrain feature in any direction for hundreds of miles.

"Firing Hellfires, right side!" Gile yelled, and two missiles streaked from the helicopter's right armament wing. Another Apache, there was no telling who at this point, let loose a couple of their own Hellfires.

The anti-aircraft missile still came. The Apache rose and the missile rose, and still it came. Eight hundred and fifty meters per second. Forty pounds of high explosive. The missile could make 30-G turns and could reach the Apache as high as 18,000 feet. There was no way to outrun it, hide from it, outmaneuver it, or out-climb it. They would need to beat it with chaff and luck. The main focus for McCall wasn't beating this one missile. The missile was either going to get them or not. No, his primary concern was that each of those launchers could carry eight missiles and if they did . . .

As if reading McCall's worst fears, the four launchers seemed to wake from a stupor and each fired. Five in the sky.

"Dammit!" McCall hissed. Sweat beaded on his forehead. There was more than just the smell of adrenaline in the cockpit now. The scent of fear filled the space. It is a wholly different smell that only warriors know. Fear is a place that helplessness takes a soldier, one small step past exhilaration.

The first missile was in a critical stage, and McCall focused, "Breaking left!" The helicopter rolled left and banked hard, throwing out one more load of chaff. The twin General Electric engines screamed under the load, pulling the helicopter through the air with all their might. The anti-aircraft missile almost seemed to hesitate with indecision, and then luckily, chose badly and headed for the chaff. The proximity fuse harmlessly detonated the warhead in the midst of the foil cloud.

Still, there were more to worry about. It was surreal watching the Hellfire missiles from the helicopters pass the four anti-aircraft missiles from the ground in mid-flight. McCall wanted to drop his aircraft, to try some fancy flying once more, but it was Gile who was lamping the targets with a laser. They had to maintain line-of-sight contact with the anti-aircraft missile battery vehicles. He could jump up and down, slide right and left, but there was not going to be any dramatic breaking one way or the other. This time, it was a race. Would their missiles hit the vehicles and leave the aircraft enough time to try to avoid the incoming? It was like a sick game being played at hundreds of miles per hour, and it was certainly one of life and death. The missiles racing up at them were being guided by the radar on the vehicles that fired them. In an environment where chaff and radar jamming were present, the missiles could be guided by television cameras mounted on the launchers, but in this weather, those weren't much help. No, this was all about the radar systems on the launchers being knocked out before the missiles streaking up at the flight of Apaches could knock them down.

"Firing Hellfires, right side!" Gile announced, although everyone knew that this engagement would likely be over before this flight of Hellfires reached their targets.

"Winchester on the Hellfires," Gile added. Winchester meant all the Hellfires had been expended. McCall's Apache became a platform for the 30mm chain gun.

The SA-15 missiles were closing the distance extraordinarily fast. The six Apaches danced around the sky, two of them desperately trying to keep their laser designators lighting up the targets. Closer still they came, and farther the Hellfires went. Sweat fell into one of McCall's eyes, but he did not blink it away. Intensely, he concentrated on the targets, as if willing the Hellfire missiles to both find their mark and to hurry. It looked like the slower Hellfires had enough of a head start on the speedier anti-aircraft missiles, but it was going to be damn close.

When the first of the Hellfires streaked down into the SA-15 launcher on the far left, a flash of white-hot light filled the night-vision. The four Hellfires hit their targets within the span of a second or two, but McCall was so amped up on adrenaline that it seemed like four very separate and distinct events. It also signaled they were free to avoid four largely unguided and yet still deadly missiles. McCall decided to climb with everything the helicopter had. His Apache roared straight into the sky. A missile with his name on it flashed through the space he and Gile had just occupied. Its warhead detonated in the chaff below them. His wingman banked hard right and down and avoided the missile that had locked onto him, but one of the other missiles, flying wild, suddenly turned downward and went right through the tail boom. The explosion ripped the tail off, and the helicopter helplessly crashed to the ground in a fiery wreck. McCall wheeled at his new altitude trying to see where the remaining two missiles had gone, and banked just in time to see one spiral into the desert floor. The last detonated midair without striking a helicopter directly, but the explosion was close enough to one of the helicopters' tail assembly to damage it. Ryan was immediately heard over the radio: "I've got strong vibration in the pedals." The tail rotor, whining loudly, suddenly broke itself apart with a stomach-turning crunch. The helicopter was still up, but without a tail rotor, it began an ever-quickening spin.

"Mayday, mayday, we're going in," came Ryan's voice over the radio. McCall jumped on the SATCOM. "This is Talon 6, we need SAR, Search-and-Rescue, at the following grid," and relayed their present location. McCall should have waited to see if there was any hope of survivors before calling for rescue, but he knew Mike Ryan, and if anyone could pull through something like this, it was this tough, young lieutenant.

The broken Apache spun downward, the remaining four helicopters watching helplessly above. Ryan struggled to keep his aircraft upright as it slammed into the desert and then slowly fell over. The rotor blades tried to chop into the desert floor, as hard as concrete, and they splintered.

McCall kept whispering to himself, almost in prayer, "No fire. No fire."

Finally, there was no movement below. Everything was still.

"Roger, Talon 6, SAR is on the way," the SATCOM chirped into McCall's ear, letting him know the team would soon be at the crash site to aid any survivors.

After one more pass, the battle loomed large once more in the night-vision sights.

"Alright boys, let's get back in the fight. We are Winchester with Hellfires, so we're going in with cannon. Expend any remaining Hellfires you have and follow us in. Form up tight as lead and wingman; I'll be Tactical Lead, key off me. See you on the other side. Let's get us a few more of the bastards," McCall said.

"Hold up," came a pilot's voice. "We're basically out of missiles and you want to make gun runs through that? We're not going to do any good in there. That battle stretches for fifteen kilometers in each direction."

"Who the hell is that?" McCall asked Gile.

"Peterson, I think," Gile said.

"Talon 9, this is Talon 6, there's a bunch of Iron Soldiers down there in the middle of that 30-klick battle that need whatever little help we can give them. I didn't come all this way to watch two Apaches get shot down and then go home. Close it up and let's go," McCall answered.

"This is suicide, just more of your cowboy heroics, Mc-Call. You won't be happy until we're all lying on the deck," Peterson replied.

"At ease that, and let's form up. That's an order," McCall said.

The four helicopters came up on a staggered line, leaned forward, nose down, and began their run. They launched and then chased the four remaining Hellfire missiles into the fray.

The cannons on all four Apaches began spraying armored-piercing death, 30mm high-explosive rounds moving at more than twenty-six hundred feet per second. They chewed a wide path through the vehicles on their first pass. The Iraqis fired in terror and desperation at the four aircraft. Iraqi armored vehicles exploded and men fled as the Apaches came streaking through. Still, the helicopters took a hail of ground fire; all four canopies had several holes punched into them. One of the helicopters trailed smoke.

"Talon 6, this is Talon 9," McCall heard the call come in. "That's it, we've done what we can here, let's head back."

"Talon flight, I'm going back through, any of you that want to follow me, come along. Those of you who don't have the guts for it, stay out of the way. Form up again for another run, over," McCall said.

All four helicopters formed up once more, including Peterson in Talon 9. They began another run, with their cannons stitching another line of death through the Iraqi ranks, but this time the Iraqis were waiting. RPGs, or rocket-propelled grenades, came up like a wave.

"Breaking right!" came Peterson's voice and his aircraft banked hard right.

"Watch it! Traffic!" came a terrified voice, as an Apache tried to get out of Peterson's panicked path. While Peterson banked and climbed free, an RPG struck the other aircraft. Out of control, it slammed into the body of the aircraft beside it. The two Apaches twisted together and McCall's ears were filled with the screams of his brother pilots as the helicopters tumbled to earth.

"Dammit!" Gile hissed, and then all was chaos in McCall's cockpit; shards of the instrument panel and cockpit canopy, smoke, and then Gile slumped over as blood sprayed above his head.

"Gile! Gile! Len! Can you hear me?" McCall shouted. He looked up and saw Peterson's Apache pass overhead. His nostrils stung with the smell of burning electronics and coppery blood.

"Mayday, mayday! I'm going down!" McCall called as his controls became more and more sluggish and the flight of his Apache became more erratic. The sounds around him were all wrong. Whining, sounds of metal snapping, sparks of electrical arcing, and then one of his two engines quit. His aircraft lurched over, and he careened toward the ground nearly inverted. In that split second, he thought back to Maggie and Jeanie, knew how hard it would be on them, and was profoundly sorry for it.

The helicopter erupted into a fireball as it hit the ground.

Peterson banked once again and headed south, headed for safety. "Roger, this is Talon 9, Talon flight is down, no survivors, I'm returning to base," Peterson called on the SATCOM.

"Talon 9, roger, you mean no survivors other than your previous call? SAR is on the scene and says they have a survivor at previous grid," the SATCOM replied.

"This is Talon 9, that is correct, aside from earlier grid, we have multiple aircraft down but no survivors. Talon 9 is the only returning aircraft from Talon flight, over," Peterson called.

There was a lengthy pause, followed only by, "Um, Talon 9, that's a good copy, come on home."

Peterson sighed with relief. His copilot, CWO Murphy, was wracked with guilt, "Hey man, those two birds collided because of us. And we don't know for sure everyone is dead."

"They're dead!" Peterson snapped, "Nobody could have survived that. And they did not collide because of us. We were all up there, and we all reacted in our own way. They collided because those pilots made bad decisions."

"They had no where to go because you panicked," Murphy said.

"These things happen in combat, Murphy. That's how I'm going to put it in my report. You better back me up," Peterson said.

"And what if I don't?" Murphy asked.

"Look, it gets around pretty quick when a copilot doesn't back up his pilot. No one will believe you anyway. I've got more time in the chow hall than you have in the army. Trust me, these things happen. It's tragic, but it isn't my fault," Peterson said. "It's mostly McCall's fault. He was a nutcase. You hadn't flown with him for long. Trust me, he was a cowboy with a death wish, and tonight he and his people paid for it," Peterson said. Murphy sat silently and Peterson said nothing else.

"This is Uniform 39, I say again, we have one KIA and one WIA on board," the SAR pilot called. His name was CPT Jack Hartman. In the dark and the rain, it had been more than a little challenging finding the downed Apache. He had flown his UH-60 Black Hawk very low, trying to avoid whatever unseen monster brought down an Apache. If it was able to knock down such a formidable aircraft, it would make short work of a Black Hawk.

In the back of his helicopter, a medic was zipping a body bag closed over a young warrant officer's face. The wounded pilot, Ryan, appeared to be in shock. He clearly wasn't able to process everything that had just happened. There was no devastation at the loss of his copilot nor was there relief by his rescue.

"Lieutenant Ryan," a medic said, "Lieutenant Ryan, are you in pain? Are you nauseated?" The medic applied direct pressure with a pressure bandage to the side of Ryan's face. A long jagged gash was torn into his cheek. The bleeding was beginning to slow, but the medic worried the young officer might have a concussion. Ryan wasn't answering. He was thinking of all the life he had yet to live and had very nearly just cashed in: A beautiful girl named Lydia, who would soon stop dropping hints about a ring if he didn't hurry up and propose. The kids they might have. Fishing with his dad on weekends, listening to the same stories week after week. The faucet in his apartment that leaked around the base when he turned on the water. His one and only plant that he left with a friend. Balancing his checkbook.

CPT Hartman flew the Black Hawk just a few yards above the ground, working to stay below radar. The driving rain lightened, then was gone. In its place was something worse. Just as rain is a regular February occurrence in the Iraqi desert, as reliable as clockwork, fog consistently follows it. The aircraft was soon plowing through a thick fog with zero illumination. There was no light and Hartman's night-vision equipment was rendered useless in the dense cloud, so he flew strictly by instruments.

Even with the visibility worsening, Hartman hugged the ground with the aircraft just the same. He had his heading, trusted his instruments, and would do his best to get them back in one piece. Hartman spoke into the intercom, "Hey, Sergeant Mann, how's our guest doing?"

SGT J.J. Mann, one of the crew chiefs on the helicopter, looked over his shoulder at Ryan and replied, "I dunno, sir, he's white as a ghost, bleeding from the face, and looks catatonic. Other than that though, I suppose he's fine."

"That'll do, Mann," Hartman said sternly, his hands too

full with the aircraft and the fog to have much of a sense of humor at that moment.

"Sir, yes, sir," Mann answered. He couldn't see even a few feet into the fog racing by and the flight felt twice as long because of it. Frighteningly, they were low enough that Mann saw the ground, but it was completely without feature. Just a green solid mass beneath the mist, whizzing by until . . .

"Sir," Mann called in the intercom, "Are we off course?"

"Why?" Hartman asked.

"I could swear I just saw a road or an MSR or something pass beneath us," Mann answered.

"Out here? A road? Come on, Mann, I—" the copilot began, but Hartman cut him off.

"Was it a road or an MSR?" Hartman asked. An MSR, or Main Supply Route, could be as simple as the ruts left behind by hundreds of army supply vehicles passing through the desert. A real road, a paved way, would mean something totally different.

"Sir, I'm not sure. Maybe just an MSR," Mann replied.

"How could you have even seen it in this fog?" the copilot asked. Before Mann could answer, the pilots spotted a massive tower directly in their path, and suspended from it, several power lines.

"Damn!" Hartman growled, attempting to climb and bank away in time. Barely missing the tower itself, the bottom of the tail boom struck, and then the tail rotor bit into the long cables. There was a horrible wrenching sound and the helicopter came crashing to earth in a spin. Fire erupted inside the wreck and Mann found himself lying on the floor. When he tried to sit up, pain tore though his left knee, and he fell to one elbow. He grabbed at his leg while the fire around him grew more intense. He looked around, spotting the body bag first. There was no sign of the medic, or the wounded pilot. The fire raged hotter, and Mann could feel the skin on his face tightening against the heat. Pain or no pain, time to get out, he thought.

Mann pulled himself a few feet, his teeth clenched. The

pain was unbearable, with each move the intensity of it blew rational thought out of his head. The fire was singeing his eyebrows. He dragged himself another few feet, almost to the edge of the aircraft floor. The right leg of his flight suit caught fire and he felt the skin begin to heat and then sear. He pulled with everything he had, just trying to get himself out of the helicopter, when the cargo door slid fully open. Mann looked up into the eyes of the pilot they had rescued, LT Ryan.

Ryan grabbed the injured and burning crew chief and yanked him completely out of the wrecked Black Hawk. Mann fell to the ground, and screamed in pain as his ruined knee twisted. Ryan pulled him away from the crash and smothered the burning flight suit against the wet ground.

Leaving Mann there, he ran to the copilot's side of the Black Hawk. The man was clearly dead, with most of his head missing. Ryan moved to the pilot's side, and saw Hartman struggling to get himself out. The aircraft's skin and frame buckled and the pilot's door was jammed. He was not able to get out through the window or through the windscreen and the fire was closing in. He could not get out the back either, while flames were licking their way into the cockpit area.

"It's stuck!" Hartman shouted, "Pull on it!"

Ryan yanked hard at the door, but it barely moved. Hartman was throwing his weight against the inside, while Ryan pulled from without. The fire framed Hartman and Ryan was unable to see anything else behind the pilot but flames. Ryan was sure he was about to watch and listen to a man burn to death. Hartman grew desperate, repeatedly thrusting himself against the door with ever-increasing speed. Ryan pulled with all his might, his foot against the aircraft. Hartman began a long roar of rage, hitting the door again and again and again. Then, as if someone unlocked a child's car door, it simply popped open. Ryan went sprawling to the wet desert floor and Hartman came out, smoking, on top of him.

Hartman looked back up at his seat, flames consuming it, and then turned back to face Ryan. Ryan looked up at the captain and said, "Sir, I'm glad you got out and all, but could you get off of me?"

As the men scrambled to their feet, Hartman asked, "Did anyone else make it out?"

"Yeah, the short crew chief," Ryan answered, "I have no idea where the medic is. You lost your copilot, but the crew chief, the blond-haired kid, is on the other side."

"Mann? Is he hurt?" Hartman asked.

They ran around to Mann, who had not moved from where Ryan had left him, "His left knee is pretty bad. He has a few burns on the other leg, too. He's not going to die, but he's not going to hurry anywhere either."

"Hey, Mann, how're you doing?" Hartman asked as he knelt beside his crew chief.

"I'm okay, thanks to him," Mann said, pointing at Ryan, "But my knee is bad."

Hartman looked around, "Where's the medic?"

Ryan scanned the area, too.

"I think they flew out when the spinning started, he can't be far," Mann said.

"They? . . . He?" Hartman asked.

"The medic and the lieutenant," Mann said nodding at Ryan.

"You were thrown out?" Hartman asked. "Did you see what happened to the medic?"

"No, like I said, I have no idea where he went. I never saw him. I was in the bird, then I was on the ground. When I opened the cargo door, Mann was on fire," Ryan shrugged.

"Pull Mann farther away from the aircraft," Hartman said, nodding toward the growing fire and concerned about a possible secondary explosion, "I'll take a look around."

Ryan nodded and positioned himself behind the crew chief, gingerly taking him under the arms. Hartman jogged out in an ever increasing spiral around the downed helicopter. Finally, about half a kilometer behind the Black Hawk, he found the medic. He sprinted over and took one knee beside him. He was all cut up. One leg had been severed below the knee, and his abdomen had been cut wide open. Must have struck the ruined tail, thought Hartman.

He rolled the body gently and freed the small frameless medical backpack the soldier was wearing. He stood over the dead medic for a moment and then scrounged around in the debris for a couple of splints. Finding two roughly three-foot lengths of composite fiberglass, he jogged back to Ryan and Mann.

Hartman dropped the pack and the splints next to Mann's leg and knelt beside it all.

"Is he dead?" Mann asked.

Hartman nodded without speaking and opened the pack.

Ryan and Mann peered inside, as if there was some magical elixir within that might enable Mann to suddenly stand and walk. Hartman took out five olive-green cravats. Picking up the jagged-edged fiberglass pieces, he laid one on either side of Mann's broken knee. He then tied a cravat around the leg, pinning the splints in place, tying a knot on the outside of the thigh. Hartman tied another just below it, and then two more around Mann's calf. Taking the fifth cravat, he passed it down between one splint and the knee on one side. Mann hissed in pain as the cravat made contact. Hartman then looped it behind the knee itself, and passed the other end up between the knee and the other splint. Taking both free ends, he passed them both down on the outside of the splints, and tied them tight together. This last cravat would further support the knee, cradling it from behind, across the hamstring.

Hartman sat back and studied his work. Ryan nodded his approval and looked at Mann.

"How's that feel?" Hartman asked.

"I think you fixed it, sir," Mann answered, wincing.

"Always a smart-ass," Hartman said.

"Is there some painkiller in there for me, sir?" Mann asked.

Hartman dug around inside the pack passing over the morphine and codeine, and wrapped his hand around a small, white bottle. This he handed to Mann.

"Tylenol," Mann said, disgusted. "Seriously? Tylenol?"

"Not such a smart-ass now, huh?" Hartman said, "We might need the morphine if one of us gets really hurt. Let's start thinking about how we're getting out of here. No mayday went out. We weren't on radar, obviously. So we're on our own," Hartman said.

"Problem is we don't really know where we are," Mann said. "Those power lines weren't supposed to be there. That means we aren't here in the there we thought here was." The crew chief winked as he breathed some of the pain away, and then added, "No one will be looking for us here, wherever we are."

Ryan stood and said, "We're in Iraq." He pulled Mann to his feet.

"Easy, easy," Mann grimaced. He tested the splint job. He couldn't put any weight on it, but at least the leg was immobilized. "Yeah, in Iraq, with a handgun each." He popped the Tylenol bottle open and took out six tablets. He tossed them back and worked them down his throat without drinking anything, the last of them sticking briefly before going down. He gagged a bit, and Ryan couldn't help but snicker.

"Yeah, real funny, laugh at the hurt guy," Mann tried to joke, but with the pain he was obviously in, Ryan immediately felt bad about laughing. He walked over, pulled Mann's arm across his shoulders, and turned to Hartman. "Which way? We should get going. This fire can probably be seen for miles, even in the fog, and will attract attention."

Hartman looked back toward the power cables and the road. "I want to get away from the lines, but when the sun comes up in a few hours, we'll still be visible to anyone on the road."

"How about we walk until we run out of night and then we dig in, hunker down until dark again? We work our way southwest until we reach friendlies," Mann suggested.

"That sounds good," Ryan agreed, looking at Hartman.

"It's not a bad plan, but built into it is us hoping to bump unannounced into an American unit's perimeter in the dark," Hartman said flatly.

"We'll just tell them who won the last World Series," Mann said.

Hartman looked at him for a moment. "Who was that? Was it the Red Sox?"

"Yeah, if it were like 1918. Do us a favor, sir, let us answer those types of questions," Mann said. He started to laugh, but then winced in pain again.

Hartman supported Mann by his other arm, and the three of them, linked together, began walking slowly, incredibly slowly, toward safety.

"I have to rest," Mann said after a couple miles. It had taken nearly two hours to travel the distance, and Ryan and Hartman were nearly as exhausted as Mann. They carefully lowered him to the sand, and Ryan let himself fall beside Mann. His face had stopped bleeding for the moment.

Hartman remained standing and looked back at the Black Hawk wreckage. Two miles in the flat Iraqi desert is not far at all, and although the fire had largely burned itself out, he could still see the flickering light through the substantial fog. The sun would rise in about three or four hours. That meant at their current rate, they might put six miles between them and the crash site. On a clear day, one could see for fifteen or twenty miles in every direction in this desert. It was devoid of terrain features, with not so much as a sand dune to hide behind, and the surface was packed, flat sand. Hartman looked down at Mann who immediately read his expression.

"Just leave me here," Mann said. Hartman was already shaking his head.

"Listen, sir, we can dig me in, hide me, and you guys go get help. I promise not to go anywhere," Mann said.

"No, we're not leaving you behind. No one gets left behind," Hartman said.

Ryan looked up at Hartman, saw his face, and knew he was serious and beyond convincing otherwise. Not that Ryan wanted to change the man's mind.

"Sir, it doesn't make any sense, you have to go!" Mann said, getting frustrated.

"Sergeant, I already gave you my answer," Hartman said sternly. "Now at ease that, or I'll take your Tylenol away." Hartman managed a smile. Mann didn't return it. He was sure that his injury was going to slow them all enough to get them captured.

Ryan stood and held out a hand for Mann, who hesitated and then took it. Pulled to his feet, he hooked his arms around the two officers, and they set out again. And then the rain returned. In torrents, the water drove against them. Their clothing was completely soaked through and the heat was wicked away from their bodies. Mann fought to free the sharp ends of his splints from the saturated sand after every step.

As the sun lit the horizon, with only scattered clouds in the morning sky, the three settled into the shallow trenches they had dug. Just wide and long enough to lie down in, they had spread the sand as evenly as they could. As the sun heated the air, the temperature climbed its way up to almost seventy degrees, but the chill of the wet sand was tough to shake off. The urge to lift his head just enough to look back at his aircraft was almost overwhelming, but Hartman resisted.

Iraqi soldiers swarmed around the aircraft, looking for some clue, some trace, some sign as to possible survivors but the shallow footprints left by Hartman, Ryan, and Mann had been washed away by the night's rain.

The Iraqis set a perimeter around the downed and charred aircraft and waited for an officer to arrive. A young conscript stared out at the desert in the exact direction of where the three Americans lay hidden.

Hartman could tell Ryan and Mann were sleeping from their even breathing, with one of them even occasionally snoring. Hartman was awake, but he knew that he, too, should sleep. He couldn't, half-expecting an Iraqi soldier to walk up on them, or one of the other two to awaken, sit straight up, and give them away.

Darkness fell.

"Ryan," Hartman whispered.

"Yeah, I'm awake," answered Ryan.

"So am I," said Mann.

"You ready to get going?" Hartman said. He had been waiting for what seemed an eternity since the sun had set. During the day, he thought the night would never come, but then sunset had been a false end to the wait. It did not truly become dark for hours afterward.

"I'm not sure I can even get up," Mann admitted.

"We'll get you up," Ryan said.

Ryan stood and stepped over to Mann. Hartman joined him. Their muscles and joints were sore from the cold and the damp, and facing the night, they all knew there was no way to get warm.

Suddenly a flash of light swung across them, and the men looked up to see a vehicle in the distance turning. They fell to the ground as the vehicle stopped abruptly. It backed up, swinging its headlights in their direction once more.

"Don't move," Hartman whispered.

They watched, knowing that if the driver of the vehicle decided to investigate, there was no way they could escape. They lay there, not moving, not breathing, waiting.

The vehicle did not move, and its lights remained pointed at them.

"We've had it," Mann said. "That truck looks like it could hold a couple squads."

"Or food," said Hartman. "Just stay cool."

The truck sat there, and then the lights swung away to the right as it began to roll.

Ryan was immediately relieved. "That was close."

But Ryan had spoken too soon; the lights swung back their way, and the vehicle approached. It was closing the distance fairly rapidly, and the whole time the three of them prayed it would turn away. It did not. It took a grueling fifteen minutes, but eventually the truck was only fifty meters away.

"What do we do?" Mann asked.

"Nothing, sit tight. Make them come to us," Hartman said. He pulled his handgun and worked the slide back, chambering a round. Ryan saw this and then did the same.

"This is suicide," Mann said, pulling his own handgun from its holster.

The driver's door opened. They couldn't see the driver beyond the bright lights. He climbed down and approached the Americans, entering the light, clearly exposing himself.

Hartman was confused. A soldier would not do such a thing, but this man was wearing an Iraqi army uniform.

The driver yelled something in Arabic. The Americans said nothing. He came closer still, until he was a mere twenty meters away. Hartman jumped up and rushed the driver, who began shrieking in Arabic. Hartman tackled him, pinning him to the ground. Ryan helped Hartman rise and lift the driver to his feet, and the two held the terrified man in front of them as they approached the truck. Hartman whipped the door open, and the front was empty. They cautiously worked their way to the rear, and Ryan dropped the tailgate. Hartman lunged forward with his handgun and scanned the bed of the truck. There was no one there. The driver was alone, perhaps just as lost as they were. Hartman climbed into the truck bed, and motioned for the driver to follow.

"Ryan, can you drive this truck?" Hartman asked.

"Yes, sir, I can. You want Mann with you back here or up front with me?" Ryan asked.

"Have him ride shotgun. Let's put some real miles behind us," Hartman said, the tone in his voice finally optimistic again.

"Sounds good," Ryan said. He moved forward and helped Mann to his feet and into the passenger's seat. Mann propped his leg as best he could and left his handgun in his lap. They headed southwest, turned off the headlights, and drove away. The gears made a terrible grinding sound while shifting from second to third, and the Iraqi driver, even with Hartman's gun pointed at his chest, clapped his hands to his head in despair for his poor transmission.

Hartman grinned ear to ear in spite of himself.

Ryan drove mostly by dead reckoning. Every now and then he stopped, jumped down, and took a bearing on a 210' azimuth. Then he hopped back into the truck and tried to stay driving in that general direction. There were no landmarks to aim for, and no GPS. He would wing it. They didn't know exactly where they were headed anyway.

The Iraqi, who was apparently exhausted, was the first to fall asleep. Mann was next, and then Hartman simply faded off. Ryan, fighting to keep his eyes open, drove on.

The truck came to a sudden, sliding halt. Hartman and the Iraqi were thrown across the bed. Mann was jammed awake against his splints. He screamed in pain.

The engine shut down. Hartman leaned forward, next to Ryan's window. "What's up?"

"Look," Ryan said simply.

There was the barely perceptible silhouette of a 577 armored personnel carrier. An American vehicle often used as a command track. It was a shadow against the black, but it was there.

"How did you see that?" Hartman asked quietly.

"I didn't," Ryan answered. "Someone over there put a tracer round over our vehicle and then another in the dirt directly in front of us. They know we're here."

"What do we do?" Mann asked.

Suddenly the Iraqi began yelling in Arabic.

"Shut up!" Hartman barked at him. The Iraqi sat down, silent.

"All that Arabic they just heard should be helpful," said Mann sarcastically.

A voice came from the perimeter, "Who goes there?"

"We're from a downed Black Hawk. We were on a Dust Off mission to rescue a pilot and we went down ourselves. What is this unit?" Hartman yelled back.

There was a moment of silence and then the voice called back, "Brandy."

"Listen, we don't know the correct answer. We're lost Americans. My name is Captain Hartman. Let us in. We need to use your radio." He hoped it would be that simple.

There was another pause and then, "Who won the last World Series?"

Ryan, Hartman, and Mann roared with laughter. The Iraqi was twice as frightened, thinking his captors had suddenly gone off the deep end.

The sentry heard the laughing and was not amused. "Turn back to where you came from. Do not approach this perimeter. Follow my instructions exactly."

Mann had had enough. He stopped laughing. "Go wake your CO, you dumb-ass. We're not going anywhere. My leg's busted. I've got two officer pilots and an Iraqi in this truck. Have some pity. I feel like a Special Ed teacher with a limp."

Silence again, and then the faint sound of laughter from the perimeter.

"Thanks for that, Mann," Ryan whispered. "A Special Ed teacher?" Mann shrugged and grinned.

The sentry's voice again, "Get out of the truck and come on in. Do you need a litter?"

Ryan called back quickly, "Naw, ol' teach can walk just fine." It was Ryan's turn to grin.

1

May 18
More than a decade later
Bekaa Valley
Lebanon

CW3 Jeanie McCall looked out into the twilight. The sky ahead was filled with other MH-60M Pave Hawk helicopters, an improved and enhanced version of the trusty Black Hawk, exactly like hers, with the legs of adrenaline-cranked Rangers hanging out of large, open cargo doors.

A platoon of the Pave Hawks had been upgraded to DAPs, or Direct Action Penetrators. The DAPs were Pave Hawks made into gunships, carrying either 30mm chain guns, Hellfire missiles, grenade or rocket launchers, or 7.62mm Gatling guns.

Interspersed in the smoky blue-and-orange sky among the Hawks were AH-6J and MH-6 Little Bird helicopters. The former were attack helicopters in their own right, and the latter carried operators from B Squadron, 1st Special Forces Operational Detachment-Delta, more commonly known as Delta Force. The Delta operators rode on long seats on the exterior of the nimble MH-6s, checking their weapons one last time as nonchalantly as if they were sitting on park benches.

The Rangers and Delta operators were customers this evening of 6/160th SOAR, the 6th battalion of the 160th Special Operations Aviation Regiment, a regiment known as the Night Stalkers, and without question the best helicopter pilots on earth. The Night Stalkers were a unit with a proud history that stretched from Grenada to Panama, from Desert Storm to Mogadishu, where their struggle made the words "Black Hawk down" familiar to millions of Americans. They served in Haiti in 1994, in Operation Enduring Freedom in Afghanistan to rid that country of the Taliban, and in Operation Iraqi Freedom ending the rule of Saddam Hussein. Interspersed between those missions were countless covert operations, unseen and unread about by the American public.

Sitting beside McCall was her copilot, CW2 Ken Willet, a quiet professional with a thick moustache and a receding hairline, who seemed an almost psychic navigator. Two soldiers in the back rounded out her crew. SSG James Hill, a street-tough from Chicago's Southside, and SGT Luis Arroyo, a proud native of Puerto Rico.

Hill was enormous, his skin the color of coffee, his hair shaved away. He had a serious nature that came of growing up too quickly. He had seen his best friend murdered and it had driven him out of the Southside. He had found what he was looking for in the military, in the army. It was a meritocracy, where hard work and success were impartially rewarded. More important, he had found a new family.

Arroyo was short, with thick black hair and eyebrows, and very quick with a gag and a laugh. He was always looking for an angle. Never anything blatantly dishonest, nothing that would hurt anyone, just always looking to get that one extra bit he could. He was honest, but opportunistic. He didn't trust easily, and within the unit he only really had respect for Hill and McCall.

Soldier-customers sat in the back of McCall's helicopter keyed up, nervous but ready to fight, anxious to get on the ground. The center row of troop seats had been removed from all the Pave Hawks. In addition to her crew chiefs, a FRIES, or Fast Rope Insertion/Extraction System, master waited with ten Ranger-ropers who intended to slide down a rope into hell. Six ropers, sitting on the floor, were tied down using three and a half feet of tubular-nylon webbing running through the cargo tie-down rings on the floor of the aircraft.

When they were over the target, two thick ropes would be thrown out and these would hang from a FRIES bar extending outside the aircraft above the large cargo doors. The FRIES master was secured into the bird by a safety harness. The crew chiefs were at their door guns. The last four Rangers sat side-by-side, seatbelted into the aircraft's aft row of seats.

The mission was to hit a training camp in Lebanon's Bekaa Valley, an area long known to host terrorists. This mission's target, however, was even more sinister than just a camp that turned young boys and girls into fanatic suicide bombers. Intelligence indicated that the long-sought weapons of mass destruction that escaped from Iraq in 2003 had been smuggled from that country, through Syria, and into Lebanon. Iraqi generals had passed the weapons on to Syrian government officials who knew they were too hot to keep within Syrian borders. The Syrians, with Iranian help, put some of the weapons under the care of their puppet organization within Lebanon, called the Party of God, or Hezbollah. This reportedly included nerve agents such as sarin and perhaps biological agents like weaponized anthrax. Most important, there were reports of a low-yield nuclear weapon. Reports credible enough to send the 160th SOAR into Lebanon carrying some of the fiercest ground troops in the world.

Hezbollah, wildly popular in Lebanon because it had driven the Israelis from Lebanese soil and for the hospitals and schools it ran, was still, at its core, a terrorist organization. While hiding behind its position as a bona fide political party within Lebanon, it continued to act at the behest of its two main benefactors, Iran and Syria: Innocent Israelis were shelled as they slept, the families of suicide bombers were promised and given money, it was sympathetic to groups such as Hamas and Islamic Jihad, and there were reports of Hezbollah working with Al Qaeda itself. With W.M.D. in the Bekaa under Hezbollah's control, the Middle East, and indeed the world, had become a much more dangerous place.

The soldiers were to be inserted, confirm the target or targets were in fact present, photograph whatever they find, and destroy in place. A high-altitude airstrike would not be good enough. Washington wanted confirmation, and proof, that the weapons, and especially a nuclear weapon, had finally been found and destroyed.

Willet's voice came in over the intercom, "Five minutes."

McCall looked over at him, nodded, and looked at the horizon. The light was fading fast. The transition to night-vision equipment would happen just as they arrived on target. She wondered why they were attacking at dusk. Why not do this in the wee hours of the morning, at oh-dark-thirty? She didn't write the op-order, so she'd probably never know, but it gave the impression that the decision makers thought time was of the essence. That if they waited even a few extra hours, it may be too late.

SSG Hill looked over in the fading light as the FRIES master tugged on one of the ropes. There was no real purpose in doing this, but like all good FRMs, he would not stop checking and double-checking the equipment and his work until the men were inserted. Hill could just barely make out the FRIES bar attached and extending out above the door, nor could he easily see the hefty rope as it jumped in response to the pull. Hill looked back into the face of the FRIES master, who stared back at him impassively from behind the headset mike. Hill turned to the door and watched the dusk grow darker still. It was cooling a bit, a welcome relief in the humid May air. The feel of it—the rush of it—was not unlike summer evenings spent sitting on the roof of the State Street housing projects, the air fresh somehow compared to the stale stillness on the ground.

Willet's voice came once more and the FRIES master put one hand to his headset. He rose, and the Rangers watched him. He held up one finger, and shouted, "Stand by!"

The four Rangers who would rope first rose to their feet and began performing final checks on their equipment.

McCall saw her target, a cinderblock building with a tin

roof, and saw the other helicopters fanning out to their targets. She came in to the north side of the building, at about thirty feet, moving at around eighty-five miles per hour. Just as she arrived at the structure, she performed a smooth, controlled termination to a hover. She flipped her NVGs onto her face, turning them on, and the world went monochromatic green and yet more detailed. Structures she had seen only in silhouette appeared in a grainy new view. She scanned the structures, knowing an enemy muzzle flash would be that much more noticeable in the NVGs. So far, nothing. She called back through the intercom, "Deploy ropes."

The FRIES master threw the ropes out, watching as they fell uncoiling to the ground below. He gave Hill a thumbs-up and Hill responded to McCall with, "Ropes deployed."

Pointing the way out, the FRIES master shouted, "Go!" The first two Rangers exited the helicopter, rotating their bodies at least ninety degrees to make sure their equipment cleared the aircraft. They placed the fast rope between the arches of their feet and descended into the dusk. As he saw the first of the men leave the aircraft, Hill said into the intercom, "Ropers out." The rotor wash blasted down on them as they went, buffeting them as they descended.

They slowed their descent a little more than halfway down. The other Rangers began following at one-second intervals.

It was as the first ropers hit the ground and hurried to clear themselves of the ropes, aware that the next men would surely drop on top of them if they did not move, that all hell broke loose. With men hanging from ropes on either side of the helicopter, and with many of the D-boys already inserted on the ground and rooftops, the seemingly abandoned camp sprang to life. Suddenly from every window and doorway, from streets and even the backs of trucks, weapons began firing. There was not a single aircraft that was not taking fire. The Delta operators on the ground immediately began returning fire in the target-rich environment. The doorgunner crew chiefs of the Night Stalker Pave Hawks also opened fire with

their M134 7.62mm, 6-barrel, air-cooled, electrically operated Gatling miniguns. The Rangers in the doorways flinched
at the zipper-like report and flash of what seemed like a solid
stream of tracers. The rounds passed way too close to the rope
for the Rangers' comfort.

McCall tried with all her might, while shouting to Willet,
to maintain the hover.

The FRIES master had been here before. "Go! Go! Go!"
he roared, pointing straight out at the ropes.

The remaining Rangers hurried out the doors and out of
sight. Hill and Arroyo continued to fire, brass and links fell
everywhere. Enemy rounds punched up through their helicopter. The FRIES master moved to the door, grabbed the rope
himself, turned to Hill and thrust one hand, pointing to release
pins in the FRIES bar. Hill paused firing long enough to nod
vigorously, and then the FRIES master was gone.

Hill looked down and watched the man clear the rope, and
said into the intercom, "All ropers away."

"Jettison ropes," McCall immediately answered.

Hill pulled the two pins holding his rope as Arroyo did
the same on his side. They fell limp and coiling to the
ground below.

A bullet hole appeared in the Pave Hawk's windscreen to
the left of McCall's face. She yelled into the intercom, "Come
on, Hill! Set me free!"

"Ropes clear!" said Hill forcefully.

"Rope clear," agreed Arroyo.

A tracer passed Hill's head, disappearing into the ceiling
of the aircraft. He flinched involuntarily and then jumped
back on his gun.

"Arrow 42 coming out!" McCall called into the radio,
across the air net, letting the C2, or Command and Control,
aircraft know she had delivered her customers and that she
would be climbing to her assigned flight pattern above the
fight. She would fly in a lazy oval, waiting to be called back to
extract the men she had inserted.

Aboard the C2 helicopter, sitting in the rear, LTC Jack

Hartman, the commander of the 6/160th, couldn't make out anything coming over the SATCOM radios.

At age thirty-three, he was still in great shape. He could run well for a man who could bench press 375 pounds for eight reps, putting in at least ten miles of roadwork per day, even on weekends. His face was weathered and belied a deep strength, but it was not unkind. His soldiers, pilots and support alike, respected him deeply, knowing he would never expect them to do something he was not willing to do himself. Since that night in Desert Storm, he had held command in several types of units, and in conflicts around the world, and was now commanding a battalion of the best that army aviation had to offer.

But on this mission, the Night Stalkers were not able to communicate. He could hear the broken voices of his pilots occasionally, however none of the information was getting through. The VHF radios that would have been used as backups were even worse, spewing nothing but steady white noise. McCall's call on the SATCOM had been garbled.

"Say again, Arrow 42. This is Arrow 6," Hartman called. He only knew it was McCall because she was the first and only female pilot in the 160th SOAR. None of the words had come through, but the voice had unmistakably been that of a woman. The radio crackled, but Hartman couldn't even make out a call sign. On the intercom, he instructed his pilot, CW3 Glen Arsten, to climb and circle wide. Hartman slipped on a pair of NVGs. How was he supposed to direct the fight? He could not even contact Zeferin, the military base in Israel from which they had launched this assault.

"Arrow 5, this is Arrow 6, over," Hartman tried again. Nothing. He was pretty sure he was watching MAJ Mike Ryan's, now his executive officer, helicopter circling lower and closer to the fight.

It was obvious to McCall that the fight on the ground was intense. There were great flashes of light, with tracers zipping in all directions, fires dancing inside windows, and vehicles burning. There was a dedicated and capable enemy force here, and it was putting up one hell of a fight.

The Little Bird attack helicopters whizzed back and forth up the main street, unable to engage. Whatever was going on with the radios was preventing the troops on the ground from coordinating air support from the AH-6s. Then, all at once, between two large buildings, everyone saw it. Flashing strobe lights. McCall lifted her NVGs away from her face and could no longer see them. She lowered the goggles once more and they were as bright as day. The AH-6s saw them, too, and they formed up for runs. The bursts of light from the infrared strobes revealed many men on the ground between the buildings, firing at the circling aircraft and at the American ground forces trying to take their perimeter. Then an RPG streaked up out of the alleyway past a Pave Hawk that was providing covering fire for the soldiers on the ground, just barely missing its rotor blades.

The strobe lit up the lingering smoke trail once, twice. The smoke hung there, and then they came. The Little Bird attack aircraft came out of the night sky strafing the ground with their guns blazing. The space the men occupied was churned up, and then a successive run was made, and then a third. The first of the helicopters had come in so low, its rotor blades passed below the lowest point of the rooftops on either side of it. Its speed had been nearly twice the speed of the other helicopters making the runs. McCall knew it had to be Rick. 1LT Rick Sirois had a reputation for being reckless, a cowboy. The same words she had often heard used to describe her late father's flying. It was probably one of the reasons why she was drawn to Sirois's company. She watched him cartwheel around for another pass, and she smiled in the dark.

After the last run was made, and the dust and smoke cleared, there was nothing moving below. Whatever resistance had been there was silenced.

There was a flash off to her left and a radio communication tower fell to the ground. Immediately, McCall's ears were filled with chatter, rather than the white noise and the choppy voice-sounds she had been hearing since the shooting began. Tracers arced up in her path and she juked left.

"This is Arrow 5, to any Arrow element, can you read me, over?" MAJ Ryan called, his voice betraying the frustration he felt.

"Arrow 5, this is Arrow 6 actual, I read you, let's get some SITREPs and see where we're up to, over," LTC Hartman called back. The radios came alive with pilots updating their leaders with conditions and situations.

Hartman switched over to the other net, the ground net, where he could communicate with the operators on the ground. "Hammer 12, this is Arrow 6. SITREP over."

"Roger, Arrow 6, this is Hammer, we have just secured the primary target building. We are searching it now. Over," the reply came.

"Roger that, keep me advised, Arrow 6 out," Hartman answered.

Inside the primary target building, Hammer 12, the call sign of CPT Kyle Norris, and his team of Delta operators were searching room to room. They had already been through every door in order to clear and secure the building, but now they were retracing their steps looking for the weapons they had come to destroy.

Moving in pairs, they treaded back down a long hallway, kicking in doors and entering each room. They moved quickly, each man carrying an H&K MP5A2 9mm submachine gun, highly customized by H&K. Much like a professional athlete would get shoes or golf clubs or a pair of skis customized by a sponsor, so did the Delta operators. H&K and other manufacturers would send people to Fort Bragg and measure arms, fingers, necks, eye positions and then customize the weapons to perfectly fit each soldier.

Norris entered a room filled with metal cases. They carefully pulled one open. Inside were row after row of nerve agent tubes, glass containers that would be fitted into special artillery rounds for delivery.

"Take pics, then set this all to burn, thermite," Norris ordered. The team members around him started prepping the room. Thermite charges do not explode but instead burn at around four thousand degrees Fahrenheit for about forty-five seconds. A small thermite grenade could burn straight through the engine block of a large truck. These chemical weapons would be buried in thermite to ensure they were cooked away.

A voice came through on Norris's headset, "We've got it here. First floor, main hallway, third door on the left when you are walking south."

"Roger, sit tight. I'm on the way," Norris said. "I want everyone to converge on that room. Set up security in the hallway. No one else goes in until I get there. Leave the device alone."

There were no responses. Everyone had heard, and this was Delta. There would be no list of call signs calling back to indicate an understanding of the instructions. The orders were already being executed.

Norris turned to the men setting the charges. "Set this to burn, twenty minute fuse, wait for my order to ignite, and then get out to the extraction." The men answered in unison that they understood.

Norris then moved quickly to join the others. As Norris entered the first floor hallway, he moved around operators already stationed at the third door. He lowered his weapon and entered the room. Inside he found two pairs of operators spread out around the room, behind the cover of wooden crates, watching the door. All of the crates were stacked. All but one. An ordinary wooden box, much larger than the others, sat by itself, set intentionally alone. On its side was the international three-piece symbol for radioactivity. In French and English, on the crate was stenciled, "Medical Equipment." It stood four feet high and wide and was eight feet long.

"Alright, let's get it open," Norris said. Two operators ran to the crate from their positions. One pulled a handheld drill from a pack and bored a hole through the side of the crate near one corner. He withdrew the drill bit and was passed a snake camera. Looking like a cable with a bulge about eight inches from one end, the other end was attached to a small video screen. The loose end, which had a small light and a lens only a quarter of an inch across, was fed into the crate. The image was immediately shown on the small screen and the operator manipulated the camera to get a look inside. There was something large and metallic inside, just as expected. He gave Norris a nod.

Norris nodded back, and the process continued. Turning the cable in his fingers, the lens swung up, allowing the Delta operators to see if the crate was wired to explode on this corner. There was no sign of anything there except wood.

They pulled the camera out of the crate. Lifting a small pry bar from his bag, the D-boy began to loosen the boards on the small end of the crate. They were pretty sure there was nothing to worry about along this edge, but there were a total of four edges that were about to be pried loose.

One board at a time, painstakingly slowly, the operators pulled the corner open. With each board, more light spilled into the crate, revealing a bit of one end of the contents. It looked to be steel, just as expected.

Another board was pulled free, and then another. The operator worked his way down to the floor, and pulled on the last board. It didn't look right, Norris thought. He expected it to be shiny new metal, but this was older; it even appeared to have grease or soot on it.

The operator thought so, too. "What the hell is this thing?" He yanked the last board open and exposed a small digital timer. A countdown of five seconds began.

"Move! Move! Move!" Norris roared.

Operators ran out into the hallway with Norris right behind them. They dove for cover, but when there wasn't any, most of them just fell to the floor. And then they heard it. *Pop.*

Norris raised his head. *What the hell?* He got to his feet and moved back toward the room. "Everyone stay where you are." Creeping in slowly, he gently lifted the timer. It had run down to zero. He followed the wires leading out of the small black box. They ended in two separate, and charred, ends.

Norris felt around the edge of the metal object inside the crate and felt something give. Shining a mini-mag light, he peered in. Fixed to the side of the steel was a chunk of Semtex plastic explosive nearly the size of a football. Norris whistled in spite of himself. This would have easily killed them all and probably thrown this 2,000-pound steel monstrosity right through the wall. Half the building might have come down.

"Get in here, check this out," Norris said into his mike. Half of the men in the hallway moved into the room, the others maintained security.

Norris held up the charred wire ends. "Someone set this to blow but forgot to put the cap in the explosives. There's a huge wad of Semtex here on this thing. More than needed to be there. We're dealing with real amateurs. Who would give a nuke to these people?"

After a moment's pause, Norris said, "Open this thing up." They stopped being careful with the crate, and ripped it open.

"Damn," was all Norris could say.

It was clearly not a nuke. It looked more like an oil burner for a large furnace.

Small arms fire pinged above the helicopter's cargo door nearest Hartman. He flinched, and then looked up without rising, checking for damage.

"Arrow 6, this is Arrow 5, all aircraft accounted for, so far four wounded, no KIAs," came MAJ Ryan's voice.

"Roger that, let's keep it up, primary target building secured, sweeping it now," Hartman replied. "Let's make sure . . ."

An RPG came rocketing up at Hartman's bird and the pilot flared the helicopter suddenly to avoid it. Like a horse rearing up, the aircraft stood on its tail as the rocket passed in its path. The quick move more than likely saved the helicopter, but in the jolt, Hartman was thrown against his harness and the wind was pressed out of him.

"Sir, are you alright?" Ryan's voice came through.

"Just fine, Arrow 5, Glen is just over here showing off again," Hartman said. CW3 Glen Arsten, Hartman's pilot, grinned behind his NVGs.

1LT Rick Sirois passed beneath Hartman's helicopter on a gun run on his best-guess position for the RPG gunner. His guns tore up a small building and he climbed just in time to miss it himself.

"Bullet 13, this is Arrow 5, was that you that just made that run beneath Arrow 6?" Ryan called to Sirois.

"Roger that," Sirois voice. McCall was listening and could almost hear the smirk.

"Bullet 13, there might have been friendlies down there for all we know. Take it down a notch, over" Ryan ordered.

There was a pause. Ryan came on again, "How copy over?"

"This is Bullet, good copy over," Sirois's voice was flat, mechanical, almost mocking.

McCall couldn't help but chuckle at his tone. She had met him while she was flying for the 10th Mountain Infantry Division, stationed at Fort Drum, New York. She and a few others from her division had gone to Fort Campbell for training in advanced Air Assault Insertion techniques. Sirois had not been a Night Stalker at that time either, but was flying for the 101st Airborne. He was one of the instructors, and McCall couldn't stand him. He was so egotistical, so cocky. It was his indisputable skill as a pilot that won him some of her respect, however. She had been a Black Hawk pilot for over a year at that point, and Sirois was sitting in the copilot seat beside her on a training run. The back of the aircraft had been full of air assault troops from the 101st, and he instructed her to insert the soldiers in a particular clearing. It was an odd spot. Unlike all the meadows and fields of tall grasses and shrubs, this LZ had nothing at all. It looked like a landing zone on Mars. McCall descended quickly, as she had been taught and had done dozens of times. When the rotor wash reached the ground, it

seemed the entire surface of the LZ lifted into the air. Sand
swirled around them, and visibility was less than a couple of
feet. McCall decided to abort. She pulled up gently on the collective and gave the aircraft more throttle. Sirois was shouting, "No! No! No! You're committed! Just land!" Too late.
They could not see a thing. Flying a helicopter is a balancing
act; it is an effort tantamount to juggling with all four extrem-
ities, with both hands and both feet. For every control movement a pilot makes, there is a counter or cooperative
movement that must go along with it. You cannot change anything in a helicopter in isolation without risking dire results.
As the aircraft rose, it lifted clear of the brownout, and Mc-
Call immediately saw what everyone on board suspected.
They were spinning. The increased grab of the air with the additional throttle had produced torque that McCall had not
countered with additional pedal. Sirois demanded, "Give me
control." McCall gave it to him. He stopped their spin almost
immediately and then landed, in the middle of a second
brownout. When he lost visual reference, he felt his way,
keeping everything the same. They bounced slightly on the
Black Hawk's landing gear, but they were down. The soldiers
piled out, and Sirois lifted off once more. All was sand and
then they were free and clear, soaring into the blue. What surprised McCall most was that he never teased her about that
day. He went over it with her, calling it a "teachable moment,"
and never mentioned it again. For all his arrogance, he was a
professional. She had learned from him that day and more
than a few times since joining the 160th SOAR, where she
found him waiting, flying an AH-6. Normally, a gifted Black
Hawk pilot would have ended up flying a Pave Hawk, but he
had switched to the nimble Little Bird at his first opportunity.
He was always looking for the next thing in which he might
excel. When she heard his sarcastic response to being admonished for hotdogging, she couldn't help but laugh under her
breath. Even while being shot at.

Hartman watched outside his door as one of the Pave

Hawks went down into the fight to pick up a couple of critically wounded soldiers. They would then be immediately flown back to Israel. As the helicopter rose back into the night sky and pivoted south, the radio next to Hartman, the ground net, was suddenly and furiously chirping with traffic.

"Arrow 6, this is Hammer. We've got chem weapons here; they're set to burn, but no joy on the big prize. The crate is here, but it contains what looks like an old boiler. We're coming out, over."

"Hammer, this is Arrow 6, roger. Grab a few prisoners, and let's get out of here. All ground units should move toward the fallen radio tower for extraction," Hartman replied.

"Arrow 6, this is Hammer, roger that, we'll build a perimeter there around an LZ. Once the perimeter is set up, we'll toss infrared strobes out to mark it. Over."

"Arrow out," and then flipping to the air net, "All Arrow elements, this is Arrow 6, prepare to extract ground elements. Hold current patterns until called in. Load your helicopters completely full; we'll leave no one behind. They will set up an LZ near the fallen tower. All Bullet elements, provide ground support, when sure of targets, to protect ground force perimeter and LZ. The outer edge of the friendly perimeter will be marked with infrared strobes. Over," Hartman ordered. He knew this would be a dangerous time. Patterns are always dangerous and there would be a clear and simple pattern of helicopters coming down to pick up ground troops.

McCall made yet another wide turn. The enemy was firing scattershot into the air, and she couldn't hear it, but bursts of tracers would zip past her windscreen sporadically. Hill and Arroyo had a much better view of how much fire they were taking. McCall could hear them curse in surprise again and again in the intercom as another burst of enemy fire put holes in her aircraft.

The infrared strobes on the ground started to flash. Each time another was thrown out, the circle was more neatly defined around the friendlies below. The AH-6s were making run after run. The fire McCall had been taking subsided a bit as the Little Birds took their toll.

"This is Arrow 6, Arrow elements queue up and let's get those guys out of there, over" Hartman called over the air net.

McCall watched as the Pave Hawks began to take their turns, the first approaching the ground. The ground fire intensified once more, concentrated on the helicopter coming in to extract. A return volley from the friendlies on the ground was followed by yet another run by the AH-6s.

The first Pave Hawk lifted away, its belly full of Rangers, and turned south to head for the rally point where they would regroup for the flight back to Israel. McCall waited her turn. Two more RPG rounds leapt into the dark sky, almost straight up, not really coming close to any single helicopter. The Night Stalker aircraft were charcoal-gray against a blue-black background and not easy to pinpoint. The rounds fell back to earth, exploding harmlessly.

The enemy then finally grasped the obvious. As the next Pave Hawk came down to pick up its load of men, two more RPG rockets screamed across the ground into the perimeter. The first fell short of the helicopter, detonating among the men waiting to board her. The second passed in through one cargo door and out the other without striking a thing. McCall watched as the minigun in the door paused its firing for a moment while the doorgunner was surely collecting his wits and offering a prayer of thanks after such a close call. Men clambered aboard, dragging their dead and wounded with them, and the Pave Hawk leapt into the dark sky.

It was McCall's turn. "Arrow 42 coming in," she called as she pushed the cyclic forward. The nose dipped a bit and the powerful helicopter was quickly over the LZ. It never hovered, but instead flared, tail down suddenly with nose high, to bleed away its forward momentum, and then it was on the ground. Men scrambled to get aboard. Hill helped soldiers secure two litters, each with a wounded man, into clips along the inside wall. They were one over the other, not unlike bunk beds. If not secure, one man could fall onto the other. In training, the clips holding the litters made an audible click, but with all the chaos, a freight train passing through the helicopter would not have been heard. To Hill it seemed as if small-arms fire was hitting every inch of the aircraft. Remarkably, he could feel himself getting irritated at the amount of maintenance work it would take to fix all the damage he expected to find once they got back. It never occurred to Hill that they would not make it.

For Arroyo it was a different story. He was nearly convinced they would not make it home, and he was determined to take as many of the enemy with him as he could. His mini-gun was ablaze and he swept it back and forth across the shapes just outside the perimeter. An AH-6 added its fire to Arroyo's and it seemed that not even a cockroach could have survived in the kill zone. Tracers tore up the open space and the building beyond. Dirt and building materials flew into the air, tracers ricocheted and went off at strange squiggly angles, and men fell. Yet, when he stopped firing momentarily, a fresh round of enemy fire came in, throwing friendly soldiers to the ground and showering him in sparks and debris.

"Let's go! Let's go!" McCall's voice came through, barely heard on the intercom. It was all the pilot could really do at this point. She was dependent on her crew chiefs to protect the helicopter and get it loaded.

Hill pulled one more man on board and squeezed him in, the helicopter already overloaded. "We're full, let's go!" he shouted into the intercom. McCall's muscles seemed to react to Hill's voice more than to her own brain. They had been waiting, aching, to pull the helicopter up and out of there. Hill's call set them free. She pulled the collective up smoothly, increased throttle slightly, gave it left pedal swinging her view left, and as the aircraft rose she dropped the nose. The helicopter was up and out of the LZ and headed south toward the rendezvous.

As the last of the Americans were extracted, the thermite ignited. The entire room, once a storage area for a prized cache of deadly chemical weapons, became twice as hot as any blast furnace in any steel mill. The air itself caught fire. Cinderblocks exploded. The weapons were vaporized. Still, it was the nuke they were after, and they had missed it.

2

May 18
Beirut's southern suburbs
Lebanon

He looked from his office window to the street named for his martyred son. Sayyed Hussein Nasballah, the Secretary General of Hezbollah, was sleeping moments before when the phone rang. Hamed Druha, his principal deputy, was calling and the news was not good.

"*Samahet ash-Sayyed*, they came in large numbers, heavily armed, and we suffered many dead," Druha's voice was steady, but intense.

"Is the battle ongoing?" Nasballah asked.

"No, they have withdrawn. The Syrian army also lost many men, hundreds. Why would the Zionists put commandos on the ground?" Druha asked.

Nasballah thought for a moment, "You say they came in helicopters, but there were no fixed-wing aircraft? No F-15s? The Zionist Jews won't go to the market for bread without cover from the F-15s, sounding their sonic booms, rattling windows to intimidate. Just helicopters?"

"Those were the reports," Druha answered.

"Find out if any of the dead were left behind," Nasballah said, "but I suspect that this may not have been the Zionists, at least not by themselves. Look into it."

"Yes, I'll look into it immediately," Druha responded. "Sorry to wake you, *maoulana*."

"No, you were right to. I'll expect to hear from you," Nasballah hung up and immediately placed another call. He rubbed the sleep from his weary eyes.

"Yes, I'll hold while you wake him," Nasballah said quietly. He waited and looked once more at the empty street. "He's not asleep? Yes, yes, I'll hold." This puzzled Nasballah. Why would this man be awake at such an hour?

He needed to know what they should do next, to know how bad the news really was. The situation may have shifted this night in ways he dared not imagine.

"Yes," Nasballah said suddenly into the phone, "there has been an attack in the Bekaa. What? Yes, but how did you know this already?"

Nasballah listened, again puzzled.

"I do not know yet if it was the Zionists because they . . ." Nasballah froze. "Americans? In Lebanon? How do you know?"

How had he gained so much intelligence so quickly? Nasballah knew that with his position, this man would have excellent sources, but he knew details that Nasballah did not yet know, and the attack was directed on Nasballah's people.

"All destroyed. And the Hand of Allah?" Nasballah asked.

Nasballah listened, his eyes squinted, and then he let out a long sigh of relief.

"Who gave the order to move it, and to where?" Nasballah asked.

"Yes, I understand, but where did you tell them to take it. I must know so I can protect it," Nasballah insisted. But then, "Oh, I see. If you need my assistance in any other way, please do not hesitate to ask."

Out of the country? Nasballah hung up the phone. They took it out of the country? But to where? It seemed such a dangerous course of action. Granted, the Bekaa had not proven to be safe. The Zionists had it under tight and nearly constant air reconnaissance and surveillance. Still, where could they hide such a thing? Afghanistan? No, that would not be prudent. Even if they hid it in the mountains along the border between Pakistan and Afghanistan, it would be very difficult to move it again, and communications to those guarding it would be sporadic at best. Maybe Tajikistan? Uzbekistan? Certainly not Syria or Iran.

Nasballah shrugged and scratched at his beard. The phone rang once more.

"Yes," Nasballah answered. "Yes, Hamed, I have heard this, Americans in Lebanon, but how do you know? Oh, from our men on the ground. They're sure of it? Yes, very well, thank you."

Nasballah hung up and walked out of his office, turning down the dark hallway, and headed into the attached residence. His bare feet were silent on the tile. Nasballah was graying, with a heavy beard, and thick glasses. His belly had rounded with age and comfort, but he was still generally healthy and robust.

He walked around a large chair and fell backwards into it. What was the next move? If the Americans were after it, then it was no longer a secret. Should they hurry? To do what? To employ? To hide away? In the name of stopping terrorism, the United States government had seized and occupied two entire nations. The Americans apparently knew Hezbollah, a relatively localized group, had had something much more deadly than even the victims of September 11 could imagine. He wondered, had the Americans begun a campaign against Hezbollah, or were we just holding the wrong item at the wrong time?

3

May 19
Before dawn
Zerifin Military Base
Israel

The helicopters came in, a few limping and smoking, and landed amidst a fleet of Humvee ambulances and other emergency and ground personnel. The landing gear beneath the Pave Hawk setting down closest to the hangars gave way, and the large aircraft fell to its belly. It began to list slightly to one side and then rolled completely over. The four spinning, massive, and deadly rotor blades, each more than twenty-five feet long, made contact with the tarmac. Shards of composite titanium and fiberglass flew in every direction. Men and women from the ground crews were cut down, many wounded and some obviously dead. Bodies and body parts were strewn about. The concrete was awash in blood. Surviving members of the ground crews rushed in to their aid, slipping on the slick tarmac. The cries and moans of the wounded rose above the sound of the rest of the aircraft landing around them.

MAJ Ryan landed, and did not wait for his rotor blades to stop spinning. He climbed out of the Pave Hawk's cockpit, a feat normally better suited to a contortionist, and jumped down from one of the large cargo doors. The rotor wash drove down on him. He ran to the nearest wounded soldier, a young PFC, and began checking her from her head down. No more than nineteen years old, thought Ryan. She was not moving, unconscious, but Ryan could not find anything wrong with her. Not a cut from head to toe. He began again, checking as carefully as he could, surrounded by the madness around him. Finally a medic ran over.

"What do you have here, sir?" the medic asked.

"Hell if I know. I can't find a mark on her," Ryan answered.

The medic ran his hands around her head, "I've got a pretty good bump here, sir, I think she might just be a cold duck."

"A cold duck?" Ryan asked.

"Yeah, these kids, they sometimes duck so fast, they hit their heads on the ground, and knock themselves cold," the medic said. "She should be okay."

Ryan nodded, rose, and ran to the next soldier.

"You alright, Sergeant?" Ryan asked.

The sergeant was kneeling and looked up Ryan. He said, "Yessir, I think I'm alright, but can you help me find these?" He pulled his left hand away from his right, exposing it, with all four fingers missing. They were diagonally cut off, with the index finger completely gone. His hand was bleeding heavily. Ryan pulled a pressure bandage from his vest and began applying pressure to the ruined hand without tying it on.

"Medic!" Ryan yelled, adding his own voice to the mayhem.

The same medic he'd spoken with before jogged over. "What's up?"

"He's lost his fingers," Ryan said without removing the bandage.

The medic traded places with Ryan, holding the pressure bandage tightly to the wound. He helped the soldier to his feet and began slowly walking him to an ambulance only a few yards away.

"Wait," the sergeant said absently, "we're forgetting my fingers. They're over there somewhere."

Both the medic and the sergeant looked back. On the blood-wet concrete, there were dozens and dozens of pieces of aircraft and pieces of soldiers that were finger-size. Because of the chaos, with soldiers in worse shape than the sergeant and the possibility of fire, the medic decided to lie. "We'll get them for you. You head to the hospital and we'll get them for you."

"Oh, okay," the sergeant said and climbed into the ambulance.

Ryan watched as they went. He turned and tripped over someone's legs. Legs no longer attached to their owner.

He fought off the swelling urge to vomit. Getting up, he scanned the scene for a place where he could help. In the corner of his eye, he saw motion off to one side. Someone had walked into a hangar across the tarmac. Ryan walked with purpose through the carnage, stepping around the wounded soldiers being triaged, and headed for the hangar. With each broken body he stepped around, he became angrier.

Ryan reached a gray steel door, grasped the handle firmly, and yanked it open. Inside, an NCO stood discussing the operation with a platoon of soldiers sitting on the hard concrete floor.

"Attention!" the sergeant yelled. All of his soldiers leapt to their feet, snapping to the position, backs ramrod straight. The sergeant, too, was at attention.

Ryan walked directly toward him, stopping less than a full step in front of the man.

"Sergeant Pettihorn, can you tell me what the hell you people do in this unit?" Ryan demanded, not quite a shout, but close. Ryan's knees and hands were bloody. SFC Joe Pettihorn's eyes did not drop to look at the blood, instead his gaze stayed straight and level, when he immediately answered in a clear West Virginia accent, "We are commo soldiers, sir!"

"And then why, Sergeant, can my people not communicate in the air?" Ryan continued. "It does tend to make things a tad easier when we can actually talk to the pilot in the helicopter next to us by some method other than hand signals."

"Sir, there was nothing wrong with the radios," Pettihorn began.

"Nothing wrong with them?" Ryan was shouting. "For most of the mission, we couldn't get even the simplest message transmitted. I was thinking about stringing a couple cans together. We've got the most high-tech commo gear in the world, and we can't use it. Or is that the problem, Sergeant, maybe the radios are more advanced than our commo people?"

Pettihorn had been holding his tongue, but this rotor-jockey had criticized his soldiers, and it was time to be angry. "Listen here, sir, these people are up around the clock making sure those radios work and they are the best at what they do!"

"Then we have a problem, because the best techs in the world can't keep the best radios in the world working," Ryan snapped back.

"What you don't understand, sir . . . !" Pettihorn could feel his face and scalp burning with rage.

"Don't tell me what I don't understand, Sergeant!" Ryan retorted. "If you can't get your heads out of your asses, we'll find people who . . ."

"Y'all were jammed!" Pettihorn screamed into the major's face, cutting him off.

Ryan paused, considered this for a moment, and then came back with renewed vigor, "A collection of Hez losers can't jam satellite comms. They wouldn't have the expertise, the equipment, the power. Maybe the VHF but not the SATCOMs. You'll have to do better than that."

Pettihorn squinted at Ryan, walked over to a gray metal rack holding various pieces of radio equipment, and tore a thermal paper printout from a squat olive-green device. Clutching the paper in his hand, he walked back to Ryan, and shook his fist in the major's face. "There was a sustained and powerful transmission of white-noise at 253 MHz. We were picking it up all the way back here."

"The guard channel?" MAJ Ryan asked, thinking. "But that by itself . . ."

"That's not all. They were cranking some serious juice up there, more wattage than a small commercial radio station would. They were spraying that RF across a very specific range, 235 to 410 MHz, covering the entire spectrum," Pettihorn said.

Ryan's face went white. The exact frequency range of the

SATCOM radios in their helicopters. "Where do they get this information?" Ryan growled. He was suddenly exhausted.

"The Internet. It's all there. Even Hezbollah has its own website. On unclassified websites, some hosted by our own military, you can find just about anything you want," Pettihorn replied. "We used to snicker and joke about it, but this time we got bitten right on the ass."

Ryan fell silent. This meant that the enemy not only had an unexpected level of expertise but that they also anticipated his type of unit as a possible threat. Enough so that they had spent what had to have been considerable treasure and sweat in preparing a defense.

"Now, the next time you have a problem, Major, maybe you can ask us about those things which you clearly don't understand before threatening to replace us. Your radios work, and you've always had good comms, because my people are the best. Don't you ever question their expertise or dedication again," Pettihorn said, and then he added a curt, "sir."

Ryan could have shut the sergeant up with a single barked word, but instead, he took his lumps. Turning to walk away he simply said, "Carry on, Sergeant."

Ryan exited the hangar into the predawn air, and took in a lung full. Slowly exhaling, he brought his left hand to his face and gently rubbed an old scar running vertically the length of his cheek. *Our dependence on our technology will be our undoing someday,* he thought, and then turned and walked out onto the tarmac. He still didn't believe Hezbollah simply did a search on Google for his unit's radio frequency range and then made a trip to Radio Shack for the parts to build a jammer. *Hezbollah must have had direct help besides just receiving cash from Syria or Iran. There were Syrian troops on the ground in the Bekaa; maybe they helped Hez build it. It would certainly support the intel that high-value targets had been there. Dammit,* Ryan thought, *they probably just missed the W.M.D. Next time, next time we'll get them.*

Ground crews were wheeling the helicopters into hangars.

Soon they would be loading the helicopters onto the massive C-5B Galaxy cargo planes for the trip back to Fort Campbell, Kentucky.

Ryan watched the large war-birds move silently into the lighted man-made caverns. Soldiers were hosing down the concrete, removing the dark blood left by the crash. The wounded were all evacuated and most of those uninjured were looking to get some sleep, although some had accompanied their friends to the hospital. The dead had been bagged, and parts were being sorted, matching legs, arms, heads and torsos. Ryan was ready to go home. He spotted LTC Hartman stepping around a Pave Hawk.

"Mike, let's talk," Hartman called, and he turned and headed for a small trailer set up on the edge of the tarmac. Ryan didn't answer, but picked up his step.

"We can't have these ground crews running up to the aircrafts until the rotors have stopped," Hartman said.

"Yessir," Ryan agreed.

"Be sure to get the word out. I want the ground personnel to wait until the rotors have stopped. The aircrews can exit before then, but only after they are sure the aircraft is down and stable," Hartman continued.

"Yes, sir, I will," Ryan answered.

"Mike," Hartman said as he pulled the trailer door open, "we lost a lot of good people tonight. I want you to find out what happened out there on the pad. It doesn't matter how important the mission is, when it comes to me sitting down and writing letters to mothers or visiting young families to let them know their loved one isn't coming home . . . and I especially hate it when we are sent after something that isn't there."

Ryan said nothing, he just waited for the instructions sure to follow.

"I want you to quietly get in touch with your friend at IN-SCOM and find out where this intel came from," Hartman said. Ryan frowned; this was a personal favor asking him to burn up some political chips with a buddy at the Army's Intelligence and Security Command, not an order, not something that could be commanded. Friends are always made to feel like less than friends when you are pumping them for information, and for that reason, you did not do it often. Hartman was asking him to do just that.

"What about Cat?" Ryan asked, looking for another option. Hartman stared at Ryan for a moment, and then lowered his eyes, shaking his head.

"Okay, sir, I'll try, but you're not asking for intel, you're asking for sources. The intel community would normally sooner compromise their mothers than their sources. No promises," Ryan said.

"Thanks, Mike," Hartman said.

Ryan turned and exited the trailer without saying another word. No one at INSCOM would know more than what Hartman could probably learn with a phone call, but Ryan decided he understood Hartman's reluctance to use his own source.

4

May 21
Hezbollah's Television Station—Al Manar
Beirut, Lebanon

He came into the television station like the star that he was.
People scurried in every direction, only half of them with a
destination in mind. This entire enterprise had been built with
money raised in the United States and Canada from organizations supposedly raising money for Arab charities and children. The U.S. Department of Justice had shut down a few of
the most lucrative and blatant groups, the more obvious ones,
but still the money was coming in. The large sources were
easy to spot, but the thousands of smaller sources would drive
them mad before they could shut them all down. You can dam
the river, but you cannot stop the rain, as his teacher had once
said.

Sayyed Hussein Nasballah stared into the oversized camera, frozen in its lens, waiting. His thick, graying beard had
been neatly trimmed and a black turban was atop his head.
Being a "sayyed" indicated he was a sure descendant of the
prophet Muhammad, and the color of his turban meant he
was a cleric or an Islamic scholar. It also meant power and
credibility.

A young man waved his hand from side to side and then
dropped it. Nasballah began his address, "In the name of Allah, most compassionate, most wise. All praises be to Allah,
the Lord of all. May peace and praises of Allah be upon our
prophet Muhammad, his pure progeny, his followers, and all

the martyrs and combatants for Allah's teachings, until the Day of Judgment.

"Brothers and sisters, the Zionists and the Americans have carried out an attack on a small village in the Bekaa. They did this only to humiliate us and to terrorize the innocent. The attackers damaged a hospital and destroyed a school. Several of our brothers and sisters were killed or injured, and a small number were snatched away into their black helicopters.

"We stand together with Hamas, Islamic Jihad, and al-Aqsa brigades in defiance of the Americans and the Zionists. As I have said we are facing American threats against Lebanon, Syria, Hezbollah, and the Intifada in Palestine. The whole world must hear our voice that we are not afraid, even if they threaten us with devastation and killing, even if they use all manner of terror against us, we say to them our martyrdom is granted to us by Allah. We also say to the United States and the Zionists, it is better to die, than be humiliated.

"Hezbollah will welcome the Americans with rifles, blood, arms, and martyrdom operations. When the Marines were in Beirut, we screamed, 'Death to America!' and today, as they return to the region, 'Death to America!' is and will stay our slogan."

The young man raised his hand once more, holding it high above his head as Nasballah sat motionless, and then the hand fell. Nasballah pushed his chair back and rose. Members of the crew came forward, smiling, excited about the speech. Nasballah kindly waved them back, nodding, as he stepped out from around the table and headed off with his entourage.

Not a bad speech and short, thought Nasballah, but the Americans won't be back for a while. They were probably after the Hand of Allah, not Hezbollah. They'll be back someday, but the immediate danger from America had followed the weapon to wherever it had been moved.

Nasballah stepped out into the street and was immediately ushered into one of three cars, each a black, late-model E320 Mercedes Benz. He did still wonder where the Hand of Allah had gone. Perhaps it was time to take a trip.

As the cars rounded the first corner, the lead vehicle suddenly exploded. Even sitting in the backseat of the second car, Nasballah shielded his face with his arms. His car skidded to a halt, blocking the road. The car behind them tried to stop in time but the two cars collided.

"The Israelis are hitting us with Apaches!" Nasballah's driver cried.

Nasballah had gathered his wits, "Don't be an idiot! We are in Beirut, not Gaza. It was a car bomb. Get out of the vehicle."

The men exited the car and moved to the sidewalk. Nasballah sent his driver to see if anyone had been blown clear of the car, or if any Lebanese civilian bystander may have been hurt.

"Do you think it was the Israelis?" the driver of the third car asked, joining Nasballah on the side of the road.

"It must have been," Nasballah said, but perhaps not.

"I'll call for a car," the driver muttered, dialing his cell phone.

A lot of people wanted Nasballah dead. The Israelis were at the top of the list, but if they had committed to the task, he would be dead. This was something else. Someone with resources, motive, and opportunity, but lacking in skill and execution. This was most likely the work of other Arabs. There was no shortage of enemies among that group either. But the timing was suspicious. Just as he was relieved of his responsibility for the weapon, someone had made an attempt on his life. Maybe knowledge of the weapon's existence, and who had it, were things someone would just as soon have die with him.

5

They were each 250 feet long. Their wingspans were 223 feet. They stood sixty-five feet tall and could fly more than five hundred miles per hour. The C-5B Galaxy cargo aircraft were the largest in the American military, and they were landing with the helicopters of the 6/160th inside their massive bellies.

The ground crews had spent only an hour preparing each of the Pave Hawks in Israel. They removed their rotor blades and loaded four of them onto each of the C-5Bs. On this end, if they had been in a hurry, they could have downloaded the helicopters and had them flying within two hours, but the Night Stalkers were home, and every aircraft would be inspected to the tiniest detail. There would be no rushing. It would be a painstakingly meticulous process.

The entire nose of each gigantic aircraft would rise in turn, and long aft ramps would drop, revealing the helicopters inside. The crews would pull the helicopters free, almost as if the C-5Bs were giving birth to the Pave Hawks, and then with some tender loving care, the war-birds would be combat-ready once more.

The pilots were off to endure yet one more AAR, or after-action report. They had had a less formal one in Israel, to ensure information had been gathered from the pilots while it was still fresh, but they would sit once again and go over the mission in fine detail. What went right, what went wrong, and what could be improved. Some of the criticism, while always constructive, could be withering.

Jeanie McCall sat across the room from Rick Sirois. As each pilot in the briefing took an opportunity to point out the mistakes they and others had made, McCall noticed Sirois looking her way. She returned his stare in a competitive way, seeing who would break the locked eyes first.

"Sirois," MAJ Ryan said.

Sirois hesitated, as if trying to determine some way to respond to his superior without losing the childish staring contest to McCall. He determined he could not and very grudgingly turned away.

"Yessir," Sirois said. McCall broke into a huge grin. Ryan looked at Sirois, and then suddenly looked at the smiling McCall. Her smile fell. She felt foolish.

Ryan turned back to Sirois. "You made a strafing run beneath the CO's helicopter without knowing whether or not there were any friendlies in that building."

"Well, sir, even if they were friendlies, they fired an RPG at the CO. Seems like that deserves some return fire," Sirois said, no hint of a smile on his face. The room burst into laughter.

"Sirois, do you think that's funny? Are you attempting to be amusing? You're a good pilot, but being a cowboy gets people hurt. I expect you to demonstrate some self-discipline. Are we clear?" Ryan demanded.

McCall's eyes fell to the floor. Ryan had flown with her father, but had never spoken of him. He had been there the night her father was shot down, accused of being reckless, a cowboy who got his flight shot down, but McCall had not yet brought herself to ask the major about that mission or her father. His comments to Sirois were too close to home, and she could not help but feel they were partially aimed at her and her dad. As if reading her mind, Ryan shot McCall a glance and then just as quickly looked away and continued with the debriefing.

McCall was not able to focus on the rest of the discussion, and when Ryan finally dismissed them, she rose quickly to leave. Many of the other pilots had a family to go home to, people impatiently waiting for them. They scurried out of the room, like anxious well-loved pets returning home. McCall watched them leave, not moving. A thick silence fell on the room until Sirois cleared his throat behind her.

"Hey, let's go to the Mae West and shoot some pool," he said.

McCall did not move at first, sadness mixed with anger still heavy in her chest, and then she slipped back into character. "You sure you need more lessons in humiliation from me?" A crooked smile spread on her face as she turned to face him.

"Loser buys the beer," Sirois retorted.

"Well, since we know who that's going to be, and the Mae West is BYOB, buy me a twelve-pack of Pilsner Urquell," McCall smirked.

"What's up with you and the Czech beer?" Sirois said, approaching her as she stood.

"Hey it's that or Moosehead Dry, and unless you're driving up to New Brunswick, you'll have to stick with what's available," McCall said.

"You wouldn't even know about Moosehead Dry if I hadn't brought you up to my old stomping grounds last summer," Sirois laughed.

McCall smiled, but looked suddenly weary. She was running out of steam for the normal playing and banter. "Just buy anything but Heineken. Only yuppies who don't know beer from Moxie buy that stuff. And don't get any of the new microbrew stuff either. Another curse of the yuppies. If it's a brewery they've never heard of, it must be good."

Both pilots laughed at this, a bit too hard, and as they turned to leave, Sirois slapped McCall on the ass. She straightened and froze, turning to look at him. Sirois's hands rose. "Sorry, forgot myself," he grinned.

LTC Hartman sat in his office. He had overheard everything the two pilots had said, heard the fun in their voices. They were going to a pool joint that was expressly off-limits to military personnel, but he really didn't care. After what his people had done and been through, it seemed a game of pool at a forbidden hole-in-the-wall was tame. He stood and walked to the door, looking across the briefing room to make sure they had gone, and picked up the phone.

He began dialing, paused, and hung up, cursing himself. He pulled out his wallet, fished out a slip of paper, and dialed once more. He waited, shifted his weight, standing as a child does outside a confessional, and then heard a recorded message.

"You have reached the office of Cat Hartman, Assistant Secretary of Defense for Intelligence Oversight. This line is insecure. If you feel you have reached this number in error . . ."

Hartman hung up the phone. "In error. That's right. Get past it, Jack." He shook his head, sat back down, and returned to writing his report.

McCall's Jeep Wrangler, soft-top nowhere in sight, pulled up in front of a small dive on Fort Campbell Boulevard. A sign loomed over them as they exited the vehicle. Sirois looking up read aloud, "Mae West, thirty exotic dancers, open four P.M. to question mark, even on Sundays. Sounds like a nice, family establishment, huh?"

"Why do you read that sign every time we come here?" McCall asked.

Sirois just smiled back, pulling two twelve-packs of beer from the back of the Jeep. One, the silver of Coors Light, the other, green and Czech.

"Think we can go somewhere sometime that serves alcohol?" asked Sirois.

"I like coming here. It's off-limits to soldiers. We can get away from the army for a while," McCall answered.

"What about the half-naked women parading around?" Sirois smirked.

McCall laughed, "They keep you from concentrating on pool. It's one of my many advantages."

They walked into the Mae West and were met by the smells of stale beer soaked deeply into the wood-plank floor, cigarette and cigar smoke hanging in the air, and sweat. Despite being early afternoon, it was dark inside. Immediately in front of them was a bar serving only soft drinks, ice and mixers, glasses, and snacks. The Mae West's windows had long been painted over. A topless woman walked by, her enormous breasts swinging as she went.

Sirois smiled, jabbed a thumb as she passed, and said to McCall, "Whaddya think?"

McCall shrugged, "Best boobs money can buy, I guess. Pick a table."

There were four pool tables in the Mae West, and only one had a game going. A stained-glass hanging-light cast a glow through the smoke down onto well-worn felt. From one corner a jukebox made to look like it was left over from the 1950s played CDs, and music came down on them from speakers hanging in every corner of the ceiling. Every other song was by Lynyrd Skynyrd. Once, an out-of-towner stopping in for a drink and not knowing he needed to bring his own beer, walked over to the jukebox and then turned to the bar, wondering aloud why there were no selections by the Dave Matthews Band. He was thrown out bodily. Crash.

As McCall and Sirois walked over to the table, "Hey Tonight" by Creedence Clearwater Revival was echoing around them.

Sirois broke, and a single solid-red ball fell. "Lows," he said and McCall nodded. Sirois called a shot, took it, and missed. McCall took a long pull on her cold beer and put the bottle down on the edge of the pool table, on top of many years' worth of bottle rings. She struck a match and sucked at the flame through a short cigar until the tip glowed red. She shook out the flame and picked up her pool cue. Walking slowly, hips twitching just a bit, she leaned over the table, lining up her shot.

Three townies stood behind her, off in one corner, leering and laughing, pointing. She called the pocket, "Combination, side pocket," and shot. As if on a rail, the ball went exactly where she said it would, collided with another ball, and that one sank. A half-naked dancer waved to Sirois, offering a personal dance from across the room. Sirois waved "no thanks" and looked back at the pool table. McCall saw this. "Hey, why don't you go get a dance there, Sirois? You won't get another turn in this game. I'll let you know before I break on the next one."

"Now, now, McCall, you know I only have eyes for you," Sirois said.

"You're gonna have a black eye if you keep that up," McCall said as she called a shot and sank it.

Sirois laughed, "I know why you get touchy, McCall. You get jealous. If I went over there, let her dance for me, you'd be out of your mind jealous. The reason I don't take her up on it is I'm sure you'd kick her butt."

"You think I'd fight over you?" McCall said, making another shot. "I'd turn you in at the pound if I thought they would take you. I only hang out with you out of pity. Miss Plastic Boobs can have you."

Sirois grinned broadly. She was tough and he loved that about her.

McCall swung around the table and bent over for her next shot. The catcalls from the three locals could clearly be heard as they cheered and gestured toward McCall. Sirois saw it, and they both heard it, but the pilots said nothing until Sirois asked, "Hey McCall, why don't you come out here on amateur night? I bet you'd win first prize. I hear it's a Tasmanian devil T-shirt to wear shopping at Wal-Mart, and some hair bleach."

McCall stopped aiming, looked up at Sirois's broad smile through cigar smoke, and with clenched teeth said, "And I always thought the term 'amateur night' was only used in reference to your sex life." She remained stone-faced, went back to lining up her shot, and took it. Sirois laughed and watched her shoot. Rough around the edges, but damn, she was beautiful. No make-up, baggy clothes, brown hair severely pulled back, blinking away cigar smoke, and she was still a knockout. Large oversized hazel eyes, high cheekbones, slender neck, and somewhere under all the clothes, great curves Sirois had only really seen through her flight suit. It was the most form-fitting thing he'd ever seen her wear.

As she straightened, one of the townies approached her from behind. He was huge, his rolling gut covered in an off-white, polyester, short-sleeve, dress shirt. Sweat stood out on his wide forehead, and he clutched a nearly empty bottle of Dewars in his left hand.

"Heads up," Sirois said quietly.

McCall did not turn around, but stiffened and gripped the pool cue a bit tighter, the stubby cigar tight between her teeth.

"Hey there, little miss thing," the drunk slurred. "Can I play with you?"

"Thanks, no, I have a game," McCall said, turning to face him.

"I don't want to play pool, girl. Let's go play in my truck," the drunk replied, grinning teeth covered with chew, his eighty-proof breath spilling into her face.

"Hey man, watch out now," Sirois warned.

"What are you gonna do about it, twiggy?" the drunk asked Sirois.

"Listen, man," Sirois's hands were up, "I'm not your biggest problem here."

The drunk laughed and looked back at his friends, got two thumbs-up, and turned back to McCall. "Listen here now, girly, let's just run off together, for twenty minutes or so," he said, his words turned into a barking laugh. He put his bottle on the pool table, McCall's eyes following his movements, and he stepped closer to her placing a big, greasy hand on each of her hips.

"Oh man, you've had it now," Sirois said under his breath.

"Come on, baby, don't make me keep askin'," the drunk said in a mock-pleading voice.

McCall pulled the cigar stub from her smiling mouth, and blew smoke into the drunk's sweaty face. He coughed a bit and then chuckled. She titled her head to one side, gave him her flirtiest grin, and then all was movement. The pool cue in her left hand, its thick end on the floor, went from vertical to horizontal in a flash. She gripped it, with both hands curling over it from the top, pulled it back, and drove the small end into the drunk's oversized gut. He grunted, released her, and bent slightly, arms still outstretched over her pool cue. She drove both fists skyward and back over her head, the thin end pointing down slightly, driving his arms off to her left. She relaxed her grip and spun her right hand so that the long maple shaft rested in her palm above her head, and bringing her right hand down to her left, swung the cue breaking it over the drunk's head. There was a loud crack, and Sirois wasn't sure if only the cue had broken. The drunk went down like a sack of potatoes.

His two friends rushed at McCall. Sirois jumped onto, and ran across, the pool table, diving atop one of the two approaching men. McCall had turned 180 degrees and was facing away from her attacker as he approached at a quick but stumbling run. She shifted backward on her feet and suddenly spun around. What was left of the pool cue came whistling in an arc around her, catching the second man in front of the left ear. His feet came up off the floor and he landed flat on his back, on top of his friend. McCall was then grabbed from behind. Her pool cue was no more than twenty-four inches long at this point, with a jagged, splintered end.

"You crazy bitch!" the man growled in her ear, his arms around her, gripping her, robbing her of breath. She jabbed back over her shoulder with the remains of the pool cue, catching the man in the mouth with the sharp wood. He released her and she spun to see him clutching at his ruined lips and lacerated gums, turning away from her. She jumped forward and kicked the side of his knee hard, and the man went down screaming.

Sirois sat up suddenly and, straddling his man's chest, began to punch the man in the face.

A strong hand gripped a fistful of McCall's hair. Before she could react, another man punched her latest assailant in the mouth, freeing her. He in turn was hit from behind. The fight immediately spread throughout the Mae West. McCall looked around, saw the club's two bouncers trying to swim their way through the brawl, and knew it was time to go.

"Sirois!" she shouted over the din, and a wooden chair crashed into the wall near her head. "Sirois!"

Sirois at last looked over, and she motioned for him to follow. She ran for the door while drinks, glass, and furniture were flying around. Sirois was right behind her when she suddenly stopped, turned, and ran back the way they had come. Sirois stood stunned as a whiskey sour exploded against the wall above his head. He ducked reflexively, and when he looked up again, McCall had returned with her hands full. "We almost forgot the beer!" she shouted. Sirois shook his head, and grabbed at the beer. She let his beer go, but stubbornly held on to her own, and then grinned. Sirois shrugged and turned once more for the door as a flying bottle passed between them.

They made it through the gauntlet and out into the fresh air. She took his free hand and they ran to her Jeep, hopped in, and drove off on Fort Campbell Boulevard just as the local police arrived. Looking back over their shoulders, they burst into laughter. As he laughed, Sirois reached for his split lip, wincing. McCall saw him and cackled that much harder.

"You were wild in there," Sirois smiled. "If you get that from your dad, no wonder people thought he was nuts."

The Jeep stood up on its front tires, screeching to a halt. McCall was no longer smiling. "Get out." She was looking straight ahead, out the windshield.

"Hey, I meant nothing by it," Sirois said, suddenly getting serious as well.

"Get out of the vehicle," McCall said, still not looking at him. They were stopped in the middle of the road.

"No, I'm not getting out here. Just calm down. I'm sorry I said it okay?" Sirois said. McCall turned her head, looked at him, and her eyes seemed to well up a bit. Then, all at once, she threw a fist. It caught Sirois in the mouth. His lips, already split, bled fresh. His head was rocked back.

"Ow!" he said, clutching his mouth. "What the hell?"

McCall glared at him. Sirois looked at her and said, "Yeah, you're really proving me wrong here, you're cool as a cuke you are."

McCall stared a moment longer and then burst into laughter once more. A pickup behind them honked his horn and went around them, the driver shouting as he passed. Sirois joined McCall laughing. She put the Jeep in gear, and they drove away.

Sirois said smiling, "You know, for a chick, you're a pretty cool guy."

McCall stopped smiling again, and looked at Sirois. He cringed, "You're not going to hit me again are you?"

McCall half-smiled, "No, I won't hit you, you wimp."

She looked back at the road. A pretty cool guy, she thought, and shook her head. When did I stop being a woman? she wondered.

6

June 25
IMU Camp at Sangor
Karategin Valley in the Pamir Mountains
Tajikistan

Ahmed Yuldash, an officer in the Islamic Movement of Uzbekistan, watched with stone-black eyes as an ancient flatbed truck came into the camp. Yuldash shook his head, amazed that anyone would be willing to try to drive a truck that size, its decrepit diesel engine sputtering the whole way, along the treacherous road. The narrow dirt path the truck had followed ran along a sheer cliff, far above a roaring river. The water below looked like a narrow stream at best.

"Yes, the trap is set and the bait is arriving now. I still do not think they will try to assault us here. A dozen men could hold off an army for months in this fortress. With how narrow the gorge is, we are relatively safe from artillery and high-altitude bombing. This leaves only helicopter assault, and what lunatics would fly helicopters into this?" Yuldash said into a satellite phone, gesturing to the camp around him. He nodded his understanding of the answer, and then, "Yes, the calls and radio transmissions have been made, without encryption, just as you said."

A dark man, a scar on his forehead, entered the room, picking from a handful of nuts he carried. Yuldash bowed slightly in the man's direction, and then spoke into the sat-phone again, "Yes, we gave so many clues that even American intelligence will guess the Hand of Allah has come here. We are waiting with many good men, well-armed, but I tell you they would be insane to assault us here."

The man with the nuts smiled slightly at this. He was the leader of the IMU, whom many thought had been killed in the American invasion of Afghanistan. Had it not been for Pakistan's secret help, he more than likely would be dead, but the Pakistanis had sent helicopters to rescue him in spite of publicly supporting America's efforts. His broad face beneath a neat beard made him seem much like the well-loved uncle in every family, but this man was a terrorist. He had once fought on the side of the Soviets in Afghanistan as a paratrooper. He was moved by the mujahideen resistance there and became a practicing Muslim. Switching sides, he founded the IMU in an effort to unseat the president of Uzbekistan and to form an Islamic state in Central Asia. Attacks and bombings began to rock Uzbekistan, and the man took a new name soon known throughout the region—Juma Nagami. They were driven first from Uzbekistan, and then from Afghanistan by the Americans, and they had since operated from Tajikistan. Nagami knew that superpowers never think that any military objective is insane, they only think of objectives as requiring a certain amount of resources. Apply enough resources, and any military target becomes reasonable, in the minds of the Americans. It was the same with the Soviets before them.

Yuldash hung up and turned to Nagami.

"They will come," Nagami said calmly, popping another nut into his mouth.

"As I told our friend in Tehran, then they will pay a heavy price," Yuldash said.

Nagami smiled and put a hand on the young man's shoulder, "You have hung out so much bait, they would be willing to pay a heavy price indeed. You have told them the Hand of Allah is here. They will come because they are afraid. It is not a feeling Americans are used to."

"We will be ready," Yuldash said.

"I want to stay with you," Nagami said while turning away and looking out at the camp.

"No, you must go. We cannot afford to have you martyr

yourself. The movement needs you alive still. Please," Yuldash said.

Nagami sighed and turned to face him once more, "Be careful, try to survive this one. The movement and I still need you, as well."

"The will of Allah," Yuldash shrugged and smiled. Nagami clapped him on the back, and the men walked out to the truck.

7

A Keyhole KH12 satellite passed silently over Tajikistan's Karategin Valley in the Pamir Mountains. The KH12 was fourteen feet in diameter and over forty-five feet long. It had tons of high-tech equipment, like a Hubble telescope pointed at the earth, moving at thousands of miles per hour in a low and near-polar, sun-synchronous orbit. It was only over the target for a few minutes. But it was long enough. The spy satellite took a series of images with its sophisticated optics, digitally enhanced them, and then passed the treasure to the National Geospatial Intelligence Agency via Milstar relay satellites.

"Hey Leitch, look at this."

Andy Leitch had worked at the NGA since it was called the National Imagery and Mapping Agency. He stepped forward and looked over the shoulder of a young imagery analyst named Joanna Cowan.

"What d'ya got?" Leitch asked.

Cowan was new at NGA, but she had that most prized of skills in the world of IMINT, or Imagery Intelligence. She saw in complete pictures when given only a few fragments. She could read between the lines, fill them in, and almost as important, she could make others see what she saw.

"We were hanging back pretty hard when we made this pass over Tajikistan," Cowan said. She circled a pen tip an inch from her computer monitor screen. Leitch took an enormous bite of his doughnut.

"Oh, the camp at Sangor? You haven't discovered a new terror training camp, Cowan, that's old news. That's an IMU camp. Sort of their über stronghold. Nice catch though, a lot of people would have missed it," Leitch mumbled around his food, turning back to his own station.

Cowan sighed and looked at her keyboard. "Does that camp at Sangor get large shipments of freight often? Because they are today."

Leitch spun, "What are you talking about?" He walked back and leaned in to see the screen as Cowan worked a large black knob. With each spin, the video ran back and forth. There, on a cliff-side road no wider than the vehicle itself, a large, flatbed truck could be seen working its way up the hill. Leitch put his doughnut down and picked up the phone.

"Get me Director Orff's office," Leitch said, watching the screen as the truck moved back and forth with the video. "Yeah, right now. Cowan might have found what Orff's been looking for." Leitch smiled, mouth dressed in white sugar, and patted Cowan's shoulder. Cowan returned the smile, and then checked her shirt for traces of pastry.

8

At least three or four times a year, the 6/160th SOAR tried to get out to Pennyrile Lake to blow off some steam. It was a small lake, fifty-six acres in all, but it made for some good largemouth-bass fishing and a small picnic area provided grills and some open space.

SGT Derek Cooper, a crew chief on MAJ Ryan's aircraft, threw a tight spiral. He had all-American good looks, with enough sandy hair to part on one side, and the personality to match the Eagle Scout award he earned only a few years before in Rowan, Iowa.

The football sailed thirty yards before falling into the outstretched hands of SSG James Hill. He caught the ball midstride, and then had to do some fancy footwork to avoid plowing over two young kids who came running across his path. A huge grin broke over Cooper's face, watching the gruff and tough Hill twist and dance in order to miss the preschoolers.

"Nice catch," he called to Hill.

"Nice throw," Hill yelled back, "but don't throw it into such tight coverage next time." Hill smiled and threw the ball back to Cooper. A Frisbee sailed beneath the arc of the football. Arroyo came jogging after it, a bottle of Modelo Negro in his hand. He waved the beer at Hill, smiling.

"Hey, Arroyo, what's a Puerto Rican doing drinking a Mexican beer?" Hill said.

"Puerto Ricans feel sorry for Mexicans, so we buy their stuff, you know, to help their economy," Arroyo replied, picking up the Frisbee and jogging back the way he came.

Hill and Cooper laughed, and the football was thrown once more. The ball still in the air, Cooper began imitating a sports announcer. "Elway lets the long ball go, it's a beauty, and it's caught! Touchdown, Denver!"

Hill froze with the ball in his hands, "Denver? If it ain't the Chicago Bears, baby, it ain't football."

"Chicago sucks," Sirois said as he walked up.

"You're still pissed because they whipped your Pats in the eighties," Hill laughed.

"True," Sirois said, "but we've won the Superbowl twice since then." He took a long sip of Coors Light.

A midnight-blue Honda Accord slowed and left the road, pulling up on the grass next to the variety of other vehicles. There was the sound of the handbrake being pulled, and then the door opened. Out stepped a long and toned woman's leg. Sirois stared, and tapped Hill on the shoulder as Hill threw the ball to Cooper. They watched as Jeanie McCall stood up out of the Honda. She was wearing a short sundress, held up only by strings over each shoulder with help from her gravity-defying breasts, and on her feet, sandals. Her hair was loose and looked more golden than brown. She held a small purse, looked down at it, and then tossed it back into the car.

The football thrown by Hill sailed down and struck Cooper in the head, who was also paying attention only to McCall. They'd never seen her dress this way before. As the first female pilot to be accepted into the 160th SOAR, the first woman Night Stalker, she had tried often to be one of the guys. This was clearly not the agenda today. Cooper was knocked off his feet by the ball, but rose to one elbow to continue staring at McCall.

She closed her door and looked out across the field. Every pilot and crew chief, every spouse, nearly every child, was gaping at her, not moving.

"What?" she demanded. As if she had pried loose a stuck

gear in some elaborate, German toy, the entire picnic began to move again. Cooper rose, and trying to get a bit of revenge, threw the football hard to Hill, hoping he would not notice it coming. Instead it went too high and long, and McCall broke into a sprint, jumped high with her arms above her head, and made a beautiful catch. In the effort, her dress rode up, exposing her underwear, the white briefs standing out against her tan skin. She landed and immediately tugged her dress back into place. Hill and Sirois stood shoulder to shoulder, mouths hanging open, gawking. Cooper and Arroyo were also frozen with what they had just seen. A few wives whispered jealously amongst themselves.

Arroyo spoke first. "Ma'am, that was about the coolest thing I've seen since I joined the army."

McCall blushed, and everyone was still frozen. She suddenly felt very uncomfortable. It was MAJ Ryan who saved her. He walked up, past Sirois and Hill. "McCall, you want hot dogs or hamburgers?"

She jumped at the open door he had provided. "Hamburgers, definitely, hamburgers."

"You want cheese?" he asked, gesturing for her to come into the crowd and mingle.

"Sure, cheese, that would be good," McCall said, relief in every word. She tossed the ball underhand to Hill.

Sirois and Hill snapped out of it, gave each other a knowing look, and separated. Sirois took a long drink of his beer. MAJ Ryan called back over his shoulder, "Mr. Sirois, get over here."

Sirois hesitated and then jogged over to catch up with the XO and McCall. The three walked over to a forest-green picnic table, the layers of paint over the wood too numerous to guess. LTC Hartman rose as they approached, wearing jeans and an olive-green T-shirt with "NSDQ" printed across his chest—Night Stalkers Don't Quit, the motto of the 160th SOAR. Lydia Ryan remained seated.

MAJ Ryan said, "Lydia, this is Rick Sirois and Jeanie McCall, a couple of our pilots."

"I'm very glad to meet you both finally," Lydia smiled, "I've heard so much about you, Jeanie."

MAJ Ryan stiffened as McCall shot him a glance.

"It's very nice to meet you, ma'am," McCall replied.

"Oh please, it's Lydia," she said.

Hartman and Sirois were left awkwardly halfway between sitting and standing, and when Sirois gave Hartman an uncomfortable look, the commander said, "Please, everyone, let's sit."

Ryan sat on one side with McCall and Sirois, facing his wife. Sirois sat on the other end, left for the most part one on one with, and across from, Hartman.

It was quiet again, and then Ryan asked McCall once more if she wanted hot dogs or hamburgers. She smiled and said, "I'll still have a burger, sir."

"Right, right, a burger. Be right back," Ryan rose and walked toward the grills. The four remaining watched him go until Lydia Ryan broke the silence.

"How does it feel to be the first female Night Stalker?" she asked McCall. "Has it been tough?"

Sirois and Hartman both turned to listen to McCall's answer. McCall shifted, and then answered, "No, I don't think it's been too tough on them. I think the guys are adjusting just fine."

Hartman's brow furrowed a bit and Lydia Ryan blinked once before breaking into a deep laugh.

McCall's tough-guy act felt odd inside the sundress however, and she tugged at the string running over her right shoulder.

"Good for you, Jeanie," Lydia smiled, "good for you. Do you and Rick both fly Black Hawks?"

"I fly a Pave Hawk," McCall answered quickly, "but Sirois flies a Little Bird." McCall was thrilled this woman was asking about helicopters and had not delved into some girly topic where she would have been totally lost.

Lydia Ryan nodded, but McCall was not sure if the XO's wife was familiar enough with helicopters . . .

"So Rick, you couldn't catch Jeanie no matter how hard you tried," Lydia Ryan smirked.

McCall and Sirois were a bit surprised that she knew a Pave Hawk's top speed exceeded that of the smaller helicopter.

Sirois recovered, "It's not all about top speed. Skill comes into it, too." He was a bit smug, teasing McCall. She wanted to punch him in the teeth again, but the whole sundress thing . . .

"Ah," Lydia Ryan said, "the seventh commandment of helicopter flying, 'Thou shall not let thy confidence exceed thy ability for broad is the way to destruction.' "

The younger pilots stared in awe at this middle-aged woman quoting from the Helicopter Commandments. Hartman chuckled and shook his head.

Lydia Ryan read their expressions. "Kids, I've spent more time listening to helicopter pilots than you have been on the planet. I've picked up a thing or two." She smiled warmly at McCall.

"It's true," Hartman added, "I bet she would check out on a Pave Hawk today if we let her try."

MAJ Ryan returned with two paper plates. One had a cheeseburger centered on the plate, the other had three hot dogs smothered in mustard.

He gave the cheeseburger plate to McCall and then offered a hot dog each to Hartman and Sirois. He took the last hot dog for himself. McCall looked at Lydia Ryan. "Won't you eat, ma'am?"

"Lydia, Jeanie, call me Lydia," Lydia Ryan said. "I had a big breakfast, but you go ahead."

Then it started. Like a wave moving across the picnic area. Hartman was up and moving to his vehicle before it reached their table. As if they were being overrun by a swarm of some sort of strange cricket, pagers were sounding loudly, spreading from one Night Stalker to the next. Men began giving quick kisses and hugs good-bye to their wives and children. McCall, with a mouthful of cheeseburger, stood, dropped her car keys on the table, and gave Lydia Ryan a quick half-wave. Lydia returned a well-practiced good-bye gesture and rose to hold her husband. MAJ Ryan kissed her forehead, whispered for her not to worry, and then he ran to Hartman's truck, leaving Lydia their car.

McCall sprinted, sundress riding up once more, beating Sirois to his motorcycle. She jumped on and listened as the powerful 1300cc engine of the Suzuki Hayabusa came alive. Sirois caught her and the bike just as the rear tire began to turn. He jumped on and grabbed her around the waist. Her long legs were exposed and her hair was in his face as they picked up speed very quickly.

"Don't you think I could have driven my own bike?" he shouted in her ear.

"No. I'd like to get there today," she shouted back.

She swerved to the left around one car and then slalomed around the second car to the right in the breakdown lane, approaching seventy miles per hour.

"Well I'd like to get there in one piece," Sirois yelled, gripping her more tightly. Beaming as only an adrenaline junkie seems able in times of self-created danger, McCall swooped down low, passing another car on a long curve, riding on the double yellow lines. If Sirois had reached out, he could have touched the car as they passed it. Then, coming the other way, a Ryder truck filled the opposite lane. The motorcycle, traveling better than eighty miles per hour, passed between truck and car, leaning low into a turn. Sirois could hear McCall howling with delight.

He, the veteran combat pilot who had been in amazingly tight and tough situations, closed his eyes, gritted his teeth, and waited for the ride to end.

9

McCall and Sirois, wearing flight suits and carrying clip-boards, took seats near the rear of the room. In front of them was row after row of metal folding chairs, for the most part empty, and in front of those, a small stage made of plywood wrapped in a gray commercial-grade carpet. A podium stood on the stage and a projection screen hung behind it.

"We beat everyone here, hmm, I wonder how that happened?" Sirois asked McCall sarcastically. He was still coming down off the adrenaline rush.

McCall playfully shrugged. "What do you think of Lydia Ryan?"

"I thought she was pretty hot, but I would never date a married woman," Sirois answered, teasing. McCall punched him in the arm. She had liked Lydia, a woman with whom she could connect and who was neither a soldier nor her mother.

Hartman and Ryan walked into the room and went straight to the stage. They looked deadly serious, having just been briefed themselves. They would pass the orders on, giving the Night Stalkers of the 6/160th their latest mission.

Pilots appeared, taking this chair and that, at first spacing themselves with chairs in between them until it was no longer possible, and every seat was filled. A few stragglers stood in the rear of the room. The doors were closed and locked, and everyone could hear the faint sound of Top-40 music playing in the hallways, further covering their discussion from potential eavesdropping. The lights dimmed and a photo appeared on the screen behind Hartman, who stepped up to the podium.

"People, these are satellite photos of trucks bringing in what intel believes is the missing W.M.D. from Lebanon. As you can see, this is a deep gorge, with overhanging ledges, and only one way in and out on the ground. It is too narrow for an airstrike, and we would want to confirm destruction of the W.M.D. in any event," Hartman explained. "So we will carry customers into this location, D-boys and Rangers. We expect this to be every bit as hot as the Bekaa was, with less room to maneuver. We will have to work our asses off to avoid flying into each other, let alone being shot down. As we speak, our aircraft are being loaded onto C-5s for the flight to Tuzel Air Base in Uzbekistan. The target is in Tajikistan. Intel believes it is the Islamic Movement of Uzbekistan holding the W.M.D. These will not be the ragbags of Hezbollah or even the Syrian army. The IMU has been at war for years, and its leadership is well trained, with conventional warfare experience against none other than the Soviet army. They have at least two helicopters, bought for them incidentally by Osama bin Laden, and their leader Juma Nagami is a brilliant tactician. Brilliant."

There was some murmuring in the audience. Hartman had not said much about the IMU that they did not already know. There were other terror organizations that were perhaps more cruel, more vicious, but none that were better soldiers. The IMU would fight like pros. Coordinated, controlled, and deadly. Better than the so-called legitimate soldiers of many third-world countries.

"You will be held here in iso until we return from the mission," Hartman continued, and a few pilots grumbled. Iso, or isolation, meant that from this point on none of them would be able to see their families or even make a phone call home. This would prevent anyone from letting even the smallest mission detail slip. It also got very tedious, especially if they spent days in iso, as they sometimes did.

"People, we will not be here long on this one," Hartman said as if reading their minds. "Are there any questions?"

"Sir," CW2 Mike O'Brien, Sirois's copilot asked, "why are we going to go in from Uzbekistan and not from the south, from Afghanistan? The flight will be pretty long from Tuzel, and we will either need to fly nearly the length of Tajikistan or fly over Kyrgyzstan."

"True, Mr. O'Brien, but it is believed that we will have a better shot at operational security and tactical surprise going the long way. Northern Afghanistan is filled with Uzbeks who are friendly to the IMU. If we fly north out of Afghanistan, folks on the ground will have a pretty good idea where we are headed. If we fly east or south from Tashkent, we could be going to a lot of places," Hartman answered. "But you will get to see Afghanistan, people. That is where we will land after the mission. After launch, we will initially fly east, then south through Kyrgyzstan, conduct the assault, and then fly southwest to Afghanistan where a FARP will be set up and waiting for us." A FARP, or Forward Arming and Refueling Point, was basically a remote gas station.

"Sir," CW3 Glen Arsten, Hartman's own pilot, rose to speak, "the width of the gorge looks too small to insert ground troops quickly enough to overwhelm an enemy. It seems that we will be taking turns dropping off a handful of guys to be shot up, one load at a time."

"Well, Mr. Arsten, Major Ryan will discuss the details of the assault tactically in a moment, but I will say that I share your concern, as do the ground commanders. This certainly won't be easy, and it is likely that some of us will not come back, but if those trucks are carrying what intel says they're carrying, I'm willing to take my chances with the IMU," Hartman said, "and with your flying."

The room broke into nervous laughter at this. Arsten smiled, and sat back down. Hartman then said, "Any more questions before Major Ryan gets into the details? No? Alright then. Major Ryan." He stepped away from the podium, and Ryan moved up.

"Alright, situation, we have a terrorist organization holding what intel believes is W.M.D. They are in the Karategin Valley in the Pamir Mountains. There is no way to assault this thing from the ground as this slim road is the only way in and out of the camp," Ryan said, tracing the projected image of the road with a laser pointer, the red dot running along the edge of a nearly sheer cliff.

"This also means there is only one way out for the W.M.D. Two AH-6s will circle here above the road and kill anything that tries to drive out," Ryan said.

"As far as the insertions are concerned, very few of us will actually fly into the gorge and drop troops into the camp itself. We'll have MH-6s do that. The rest of the customers, in Pave Hawks, will be dropped here," Ryan pointed to a ledge of rock forming the western wall of the camp itself, "and those folks will rappel down into the camp. As you can imagine, it is imperative that the defenders of the camp feel pressure from both sides at once. Either assault without the other will be easily repelled."

Ryan paused and let the significance of this sink in, and then said, "The men being inserted directly into the camp will be cut off and lost if the rest of us don't get our customers down on this ledge in force. The Rangers coming down the cliff need to link up with the Delta operators within the camp, or the whole mission is a wash."

"Where do the attack birds come in, sir?" asked CW2 Alan Vassel.

"You'll be making strafing runs, down the middle of the gorge, performing close air support. Do not take the width of the gorge for granted. Up around this bend it comes together at the top and becomes too tight for even the Little Bird rotors to fit through. You will have to climb out of the gorge to turn at speed, as I'm sure none of you will want to hover." Ryan paused for nervous laughter. "Be careful what you shoot at. It will be close-quarters fighting from the word go, so pick your targets carefully. If it shoots at us, or even looks like it will, you shoot at it. Watch out for RPGs and worse, they probably have SA-7s. Do not engage in close air support until it is coordinated from the ground. The chances of fratricide will be too high. Your specific assignments are being prepared now, and we'll talk to each of you in the next couple of hours, but people, eat now. I don't think we'll still be here come chow time. The next meal will be on a plane on the way to Tajikistan."

10

The crew mission briefing had gone just fine. Her copilot CWO Ken Willet had sat quietly, Arroyo had asked a few nervous and obvious questions, and Hill had as usual seemed anxious for the brief and the mission to just be over.

With the briefing concluded, McCall sat in her helicopter, Willet at her side and the crew chiefs in the back. She announced, "A.P.U. and engine started" through the intercom. The crew worked through the checklist, each voice sounding mechanical from years of repetition.

Hill and Arroyo checked out their guns, Hill glancing up occasionally to look across into the hangar where Rangers and D-boys were kitted up and ready to go, doing final checks of their own. Out the other side, Arroyo watched the rest of the helicopters of the 6/160th. All the rotors turning, feeling his own rotor wash, Arroyo looked out at the other crew chiefs in other helicopters looking back at him. He gave a thumbs-up to no one in particular and got half a dozen in return.

McCall put her hand to headset, and heard the call, "Steel Cable."

"Roger, Steel Cable," she replied. She could hear the other pilots calling in their understanding as well, the mission was a go. McCall flipped it to the intercom and repeated, "Steel Cable."

Hill heard it, and snapped his eyes over to the hangar once again. This time he saw hundreds of heavily armed soldiers sprinting toward him and the other aircraft. They ran, hunched over to avoid rotor blades. He began pulling the heavily burdened Rangers onto the helicopter, seating them where he wanted them, and these warriors, about to do battle, were completely compliant with his instructions. The pilots may fly these things, but it is the crew chief that will kick your ass if you don't pay attention. It would be better to mess with a mother bear's cubs than to not do exactly what a helicopter crew chief tells you to do on his aircraft. Arroyo never left his gun. All of the Rangers entered from Hill's side this time, and if Arroyo had tried to help, he would have been in the way. Even Arroyo didn't want to get in Hill's way.

"They're in," Hill said into the intercom and settled in behind his gun.

As if attached on some massive invisible plane, all of the helicopters rose as one, hovered a few feet off the concrete, and rotated ninety degrees. Then, moving as a single flock of death, they lifted up and forward. The SATCOM radios barked a bit with chatter that would soon end with prearranged and scheduled radio silence.

In each aircraft, cyclics were pushed forward, collectives were pulled, and throttles increased.

As darkness fell, the Night Stalkers flew with night-vision, and the anticollision lights off, barely one hundred feet off the ground, swerving through mountain passes, like a swarm of determined monsters. Hill and Arroyo strained to see outside their doors, although there would be no targets for almost two hours. Many of the Rangers were already sleeping. Arroyo never knew how anyone on their way to a fight could sleep, but except for the youngest and greenest of the soldiers, all would at least catnap. They slept whenever they could. "Why stay awake worrying?" they would say, "It wouldn't change a thing." On a field training exercise, Arroyo had once watched a platoon sergeant put an entire platoon of Rangers to sleep with three words—"Take a break." It had been as if the man had pulled the plug. The Rangers fell to the ground and immediately dozed off. They slept for fifteen minutes and woke with the words "On your feet!" as if they'd rested for four hours.

Hill looked out into the dark through his NVGs, green shadows racing by, the helicopter banking left and then right, rising over a terrain feature and then dropping over the other side. At times he was heavy with G-force and then he felt nearly weightless. Fresh mountain air poured into the aircraft from the cool summer night. He adjusted his flight gloves and watched outside again. Here he was, James Hill, cruising along at 150 miles per hour, moving through the mountain passes of Uzbekistan, on a mission to deprive terrorists of a terrible weapon. It was a long way from the Southside. Most of his old friends were dead or in jail. He had been on that path as well before he enlisted. A girl in the projects, just twelve years old, had been beaten up by a couple of local crackheads looking for money, in desperate need of cash and a rock. Hill and a few of his friends went out to make it right. They found the punks curled up in the boiler room of one of the buildings, sitting together, passing a crack pipe between them. Hill and his crew began to rough them up, give them a taste of what they had given the girl, when one of the crackheads pulled a knife and stabbed Hill's best friend, Brooks, in the chest. Brooks had turned, knife protruding from a growing dark spot on his T-shirt, and looked into Hill's face with eyes of shock and terror. The crackheads jumped up to run, and shots rang out. Hill fell to the floor as another of his friends shot the druggies dead on the stairs. An old janitor poked his head into the boiler room and saw the kid with the gun. He turned around quickly and ran. The shooter began to pursue the witness, until Hill stopped him, "Man, you can't kill old Lewis, man. Just calm down. They pulled a knife on us, and they killed Brooks, and you fought them off. That's it, I'll back you up."

The gun fell to the floor. And then Hill heard it. A loud snap. A cosmic lightbulb clicked on in his head. He had to get out of the projects or he was going to end up dead or killing someone.

He had drifted for a bit, trying out this job and that. He even had a roommate and a job as a bouncer. But he knew that long-term he needed something else. He came to visit his mom one day, and it was old man Lewis, the janitor, that suggested he enlist.

"Go be a soldier, son. They'll give you a place to be and some skills. They'll give you a sense of purpose. You can make a difference," Lewis had said. To Lewis's great surprise, Hill followed his advice.

Here, he was making a real difference. Not famous or rich, but making a contribution. His contribution. No one would ever be able to take that from him.

A Ranger to Hill's right seemed to want to stand, moving as if trying to get up. The Rangers did not have their NVGs turned on yet, they did not want to use up the batteries during a helicopter ride, and the dark gave the young soldier a feeling of invisibility. There was very little light inside the aircraft, limited mostly to instrument lights from the cockpit and radios. It also made it nearly impossible to see Hill coming. The Ranger got on his feet, pulling at the gear between his legs making him uncomfortable. Hill moved quickly through the Rangers and drove two stiff fingers into the young man's chest, yelling into his ear, "Sit down." The Ranger was badly startled, and sat down hard. Hill moved back to his gun and clipped himself back in.

Ahead of McCall's Pave Hawk, Sirois and O'Brien sat in their AH-6J, concentrating on keeping their position in the flight. They were surrounded on all sides by other helicopters. O'Brien watched as an MH-6, Delta operators riding on their benches, slid into view.

"They must get cold," O'Brien said into the intercom, "spending a couple hours out there. I mean it's summer, but this mountain air is pretty cool."

"They're probably so pumped they don't notice," Sirois said.

O'Brien grunted at this and then said, "Are you dating Mc-Call now?"

"Dating McCall? No, we just hang out. I don't think anyone actually dates McCall. I got a rule, 'Never date a girl who can kick your ass.'"

"Okay, I'll keep that one in mind," O'Brien smiled.

"See that you do," Sirois smiled back. "Still, she is pretty cool, and when she dressed up at the picnic . . ."

"Yeah, I know, she was pretty hot. I mean, if you aren't dating her or anything, maybe I'll ask her out when we get back. Think she'd want to catch a movie or something?" O'Brien teased.

"No, I don't think she'd want to catch a movie or something," Sirois snapped.

O'Brien chuckled. Sirois said, "Just stick to flying the helicopter."

MAJ Ryan, at the head of the flight, called out on the intercom, "Ten minutes to target. Let's go weapons hot, Coop."

"Roger that, sir," SGT Cooper replied, switching on the power to his minigun. Some of the more seasoned Rangers close to Cooper picked up on this, and they began tapping each other, bringing the entire chalk to a higher state of awareness.

Cooper was nervous on this one. He usually had some anxiety, but this time just felt different. MAJ Ryan was an amazing pilot, and Cooper knew they were in good hands, but this just felt off. As odd as it sounded, Cooper could feel Ryan's apprehension through the airframe. Like riding a nervous horse, as if the aircraft were a wire connecting Ryan to Cooper, transmitting the pilot's unease. Just a few years before, he was washing milkers on his family's dairy farm, complaining about being stuck with his work while his friends went off to hang out or see a movie. So many times they had gone up to the lake for a bonfire and he had been stuck pitching bales, pulling them off a conveyer belt, and stacking them in a loft where the temperature stayed above one hundred degrees. He had been so jealous of the experiences they were having and that he was not. But on this night, when many of them were at their desk jobs or working in factories, he was moving at nearly 150 miles per hour towards a camp full of people who would try to kill him because evil men had evil plans, and it was his job to help stop them. He was responsible for a helicopter, its pilots, and its cargo.

Cooper felt for his dog tags, and pulled them out. Through the NVGs he could make out the St. Christopher's medal attached to one of the little metal tags, held in place by an elastic band his girlfriend, Lara, had pulled from her hair long ago. Back in Kentucky, she was probably watching CNN again, hoping to hear something to give her some idea of where in the world he might be. Cooper could picture her sitting in flannel pajama pants, a baggy T-shirt of his, her blonde hair tied with a scrunchy, and biting her nails. He kissed the good luck charm, and put it carefully back into his T-shirt.

"Come on, St. Chris, one more time," Cooper whispered.

"Get them ready, Coop," Ryan's voice came through the intercom once more. Cooper was startled a bit by the call, and then turned to the rappel master, gave him a thumbs-up, and gritted his teeth over his gun. *Let's do it,* Cooper thought. The Rangers would not rappel out of the Pave Hawks, but once put down they would have to quickly rappel down the cliff into the fight. They were wearing their rappelling gear, cinched up and ready to go.

On McCall's helicopter, Hill had just done the same thing, wondering how close they actually were to the target, when two AH-6s peeled away. Hill saw them go and realized that those were the birds that would circle above the road. It was time.

"Here we go," McCall's voice came over the intercom again.

It was completely dark below. The IMU were there, but like well-trained soldiers, they were practicing excellent light discipline. Not even the glow of a cigarette smoked outside could be seen. The three MH-6 Little Birds carrying Delta operators swerved away and fell into the gorge. The Pave Hawks swooped down onto the lip of the cliff, flaring at the last possible moment to preserve airspeed until those last few precious feet. McCall flared so late, her tail very nearly struck the ground. Rangers poured out of the Pave Hawks onto the stone ledge. Rappel masters ran forward with immense, steel air guns and fired them into the solid rock. Titanium-steel shafts were driven all along the rock ledge, and ropes were immediately attached to these and thrown.

Hill scanned over his gun, not able to see directly down into the gorge. Then all at once, tracers whistled up and out of the dark space.

"They're awake," Hill said over the intercom. There was a flash below, and then another. McCall had barely climbed twenty feet when an RPG round struck the cliff's rock face, maybe five feet below the edge. The explosion, amplified in the NVGs, blinded Hill momentarily.

The Rangers hooked up to the ropes and ran straight off the cliff, rappelling down Australian-style, running forward down the cliff face. With weapons in one hand and the ropes in their braking hands, the Rangers swarmed down the cliff face. The dark was illuminated by enemy tracers stitching across the cliff, punctuated by the sickening hiss and whump of RPGs removing half a dozen Rangers off the face at a time.

On the ground, Ahmed Yuldash, even with his years of combat leadership experience, had no orders to give. Within thirty seconds, this battle had become nearly every man for himself. Seeing a huge number of soldiers running face first down the cliff behind the camp, something he had not seen since the Soviet Spetznaz in Afghanistan, he knew this was likely the end. He would serve the will of Allah for as long as he could. A small number of black-clad soldiers were inserted into the camp on the far side, and he guessed that the smaller force carried the more lethal men, pound for pound. He ran over to two of his fighters who were firing repeated RPGs against the cliff face.

"You two, concentrate your RPG fire on that smaller force. Do not fire twice from the same position. Get as many shots off as you can. *Inshallah*, you'll take many of them," Yuldash said.

"Yes, *inshallah*," they responded and began firing.

"And spread out!" Yuldash said, as he ran over to a small mud-brick building where three men knelt firing at the cliff face with AK-47s.

"You three, get the SA-7s, and fire them, use them all. Do not be careful with them, there are no friendly aircraft. The attackers will only be half as brave if they do not have their air support and no ride home. Do it," Yuldash said.

"Dammit!" MAJ Ryan yelled, and then into the radio, "I say again, any Bullet element, come in." The radio came back with nothing but static, the occasional garbled word. Jammed again.

Ryan thought for a moment, and then said into the intercom, "Hey Coop, from up here above the cliff, can you get a good angle on the bad guys?"

"No, sir, it's too far to really pick friend from foe, the only way I could is if you dropped us down in there," Cooper answered, praying to God that Ryan would not try it. To Cooper, it looked like sure suicide.

"I don't think we're quite that desperate yet," Ryan answered. Cooper closed his eyes and whispered, "Thank you."

They had planned for this contingency; he just hoped Sirois would locate the jamming tower, if one existed as it had in Lebanon, and take it out quickly.

"Why do I even bother coming along?" Hartman scowled to himself. The radios were dead, he was unable to direct the fight, and so he circled in the back of the C2 helicopter. For the moment, he was a furious spectator, nothing more.

"There are no comms, we've got to find the tower," Sirois said to O'Brien over the intercom.

"Intel had no read on a tower being up here," O'Brien said, swiveling his head. taking in the green horizon.

"It wouldn't have to be right here, but it would need line-of-sight," Sirois said. "Let's run some laps. We'll spiral out until we see something to shoot at."

The AH-6 Little Bird began running around the AO in ever-increasing circles.

"The Rangers are being torn up on that cliff; we still have guys waiting on top. They keep having to throw new ropes," McCall's voice came through in Hill's headset. They were running a low circle behind the Rangers. Hill turned back to Arroyo, who was already looking at him across the helicopter. Hill nodded at Arroyo. They both knew what was coming. The troops on the ground had very little air support; everyone was paralyzed by the loss of the radios. No one wanted to be responsible for accidentally killing Americans.

"The hell with it," came McCall's voice again. Arroyo set his teeth and McCall said, "We're going in and draw some fire. Hill and Arroyo, pick your targets carefully, but the more you shoot, the more of a distraction we'll be and the tougher time they'll have aiming at us."

"Yes, ma'am," said Arroyo. Hill said nothing. The Pave Hawk ceased its forward motion. It hovered a mere twelve feet above the earth, with in-ground effect. The air pushed down by the rotors did not have time to escape before more air was pushed down onto it. It created a cushion of air, requiring less power to hover.

"Hold on," McCall said as she looked at Willet once more, and then let the helicopter slide right toward the cliff's edge. The helicopter moved quickly as the in-ground effect made the aircraft feel like it was rolling over a ball of air. Rangers waiting to rappel hit the dirt and the big aircraft passed over them. When the ground fell away as the Pave Hawk passed over the cliff's edge, the helicopter plummeted, still sliding right but falling quickly, no longer having that cushion of air helping to hold it up. As soon as they had cleared that lip, everyone had gone weightless in the aircraft. The crew chiefs gripped their mounted guns, holding themselves in place. The Pave Hawk fell nearly to earth beneath the cliff. The rotor had missed Rangers on the cliff by only a dozen feet, but the space was so tight, it was do it this way or hover over the target and then descend. This way, while gut-wrenching and tricky, was better.

Hill held tight and as the aircraft stopped descending, he opened fire. Through his night-vision goggles, he watched as his minigun churned the earth. He would lose sight of his targets, wait for the dust to settle, and fire again. Off to the right were the D-boys, largely pinned down, but everyone to his front and left, he figured, was a bad guy. Just as he wondered why they were in essence standing still, the Pave Hawk pitched forward and began a short run. Hill never released the trigger again. His firing was scoring well, like a deadly wand of destruction dragged through an anthill. As hoped, the big helicopter sliding down into the faces of the enemy, guns blazing, drew the fire of nearly every member of the IMU forces. Sparks flew everywhere as rounds impacted and ricocheted around the aircraft. Arroyo, unable to have any role in his destiny at this point, was curled around his gun, eyes closed, screaming every prayer he knew in Spanish. The Pave Hawk suddenly soared skyward, Hill had to stop firing to hold on, and then it very nearly did a cartwheel. The aircraft came down for another pass. This time it was Arroyo's turn and the enemy was less surprised.

Hill watched as the number of Rangers coming down the cliff face doubled, the ground-pounders knowing that this insane pilot was creating an opportunity for them. On this run, RPG after RPG screamed in on the helicopter, most passing behind the aircraft and impacting on the ground, some hitting IMU positions. McCall had the Pave Hawk standing on its nose, flashing through the camp at the altitude of a man's hat, with Arroyo blasting away for all he was worth. The door gunner then saw an RPG in flight, and it looked like he would catch this one in the teeth. The enemy with the launcher had led the aircraft; someone with some real experience had fired this one. Everything at that moment slowed, and he actually felt as if he could shoot the rocket down with his minigun. It came in and he tried to shift his fire, but the gun was moving in slow-motion as well. He was never going to hit it. This one was going to strike the aircraft, without a doubt. Arroyo's prayers gave way to an ever-rising yell of rage. And then, inexplicably, the RPG suddenly dipped and passed beneath Arroyo's feet. He nearly fainted and stopped firing. Once again the Pave Hawk leapt skyward, but this time it banked right and over the cliff, out of the direct fire. Every remaining Ranger had made it to the base of the cliff, and the initial LZ on top of the cliff was clear.

McCall's voice came into their ears, "Is everyone alright back there?"

"Good to go," said Hill.

"Oh my God, ma'am, did you see that RPG?" Arroyo asked.

"Are you alright, Arroyo?" McCall asked.

"Yeah, ma'am, I'm okay, but I think I pissed myself," Arroyo answered, looked skyward, and made the sign of the cross while laughter ran through the intercom.

Willet and McCall grinned at each other, not really able to see the other's expression, but just knowing.

"Alright, I need to know what got off and what did not," McCall said into the intercom.

"Roger that, ma'am," Hill said. The crew chiefs began to do a physical check of the aircraft while Willet and McCall ran through a mental checklist of systems. McCall knew that they had no right to still be flying. The aircraft had been hit hundreds of times. They should be dead.

"Uh, ma'am, we're trailing some smoke it looks like," Arroyo said.

"I see it, too, not a ton, but something's smoking," Hill added.

"Understood," McCall said without looking at her copilot.

As long as everything felt okay, they'd hang in there. If things began to feel loose, they'd head for the FARP in Afghanistan. Willet looked at her for a moment, and then returned to checking systems.

MAJ Ryan had watched McCall's run through the gorge. "That's not a cowboy," said Ryan to himself, "that's heroic. There's a lot of her old man in her." He tried the radio again, still static. If they didn't get comms up pretty quick, this would remain a battle of attrition and the losses below would get very high. He was sure they would eventually capture the site; he just hoped there would still be soldiers to extract. Cooper had seen McCall's run, too, and felt ashamed that he had prayed they would not do what his friends had just done.

"There it is!" shouted Sirois into the intercom as he pointed south.

"Confirmed, I see it," O'Brien said. "Let's knock it down."

Sirois came around hard, lined up the tower in his sights, and made his run. As he got closer, he saw men running on the ground. He pulled the trigger.

"Firing rockets," he called out.

The nimble AH-6J was carrying two seven-tube 2.75-inch rocket launchers, one on either side, and plumes of smoke began streaking down toward the base of the tower. Men fell on either side of the small explosions, as the rockets "walked" their way into the metal tower. The structure shuddered, but stayed up. Small-arms fire rang off the helicopter as Sirois wheeled around.

"You've only got five rockets left, make them count," O'Brien said.

"Firing," Sirois said again. The five smoke trails led straight into the base of the tower. Once again it shuddered, but stayed erect. It seemed to lean just a bit, but then stopped.

"Dammit!" Sirois said.

Then all at once, bullet holes appeared in the windscreen.

Glass flew into Sirois's face and the helicopter's nose fell. He fought to see through the blood in his right eye and to pull the cyclic back.

"Mike, help me!" Sirois said. He heard nothing and glanced over. O'Brien was clearly dead, hit in the head, the dark color of his blood all around him in the aircraft. His body then slumped to the side of the cockpit, setting the cyclic free, and Sirois was finally able to pull it back. The helicopter's skids missed the ground by inches, and it lurched into the sky, still under withering fire. Sirois stood the helicopter on its tail, and let its nose fall left. He came back for another pass, not sure what to do without rockets, but knowing that knocking down this tower was his mission and if he had to ram the tower, he would. His guns blazed and he roared at the top of his lungs as he came swooping down like a crazed bird of prey. A dilapidated pickup truck came around the side of the small generator building, and a large machine gun in its bed opened up on Sirois as he dove.

It became personal, a game of chicken, and Sirois was not flinching. The rounds tore through his windscreen, through the rotor blades, into his engine. The helicopter was disintegrating around him, and still he came. Glass stuck in his face, blood in his eyes and mouth, the helicopter barely under control. The truck never stopped moving, firing at him as it drove surprisingly quickly across his path. Sirois's guns then tore right across the passenger compartment, tearing the head off the driver. With his body slumped forward and his foot pressed down on the gas, the truck lurched and ran into the base of the tower. There was an explosion and the screeching of tearing metal as structural load-bearing pieces surrendered and the whole thing came crashing to the ground.

Sirois pulled up and was able to level out, but his helicopter was on fire, and then began a slow spin as he lost tail rotor control. With the tower down, Sirois got on his radio.

"Mayday, mayday, this is Bullet 13, O'Brien KIA, aircraft is trashed, going in, south of AO." Sirois's voice suddenly announced to the entire 6/160th that he had both accomplished his mission and that he was going down.

"Say again location," LTC Hartman's voice came next. There was no response.

"Arrow 5, this is Arrow 6, get on the radio to SAR and get them looking south," Hartman said.

"Bullet 13, this is Arrow 42, where are you, Rick, we'll come and get you," said McCall's voice. No response.

"Bullet 13, this is Arrow 42," McCall called again.

"Arrow 42, this is Arrow 6," Hartman called. "Head south of the AO, see what you can see. Keep this channel clear though, if he could answer, he would have, over."

"This is Arrow 42, will comply, over," McCall answered. Her Pave Hawk was trailing smoke, and had holes all over it, but Rick was down somewhere in Tajikistan by himself. She was going to find him.

"Bullet 13 is down, we're going to go take a look," McCall said over the intercom. Hill turned to glance at Arroyo once again, who was shaking his head, but had not turned to meet Hill's look this time.

"This is Arrow 6, all Bullet elements, begin making runs on enemy positions. Our guys are pinned down against the wall of the gorge to the west, and the D-boys are pinned down among the enemy vehicles to the east. Hit the firing positions down the middle of the camp. Tune in to the ground net and adjust fire based on what they tell you. Just pour it in there. Otherwise, we'll be here until well after sunrise and the fuel runs out. Execute," Hartman called. Immediately, AH-6Js lined up and made run after run. The IMU fighters were blasted in all directions, cannon fire and rockets tearing large swaths through their positions. Much of the small-arms fire directed at the advancing Rangers turned skyward. The Rangers advanced rapidly and immediately, but then came a new threat.

Corkscrewing into the sky came three missiles, SA-7s. The AH-6s were so low, there was no time to avoid them. Almost as quickly as the missiles were launched, three AH-6s fell from the sky, crashing in spectacular fireballs into the buildings on the far side of the fight.

"Disengage! Disengage!" Hartman's voice bellowed through the radio, "Get out of there!"

Three more missiles raced skyward. Many of the attack helicopters leapt up and over the edges of the cliff and a couple dove deep into the gorge. The missiles impacted the rock wall. The air above the battle was clear once more, but the Rangers had been given renewed spirit, and the D-boys began clawing their way in. The Americans were more angry than scared at this point, after seeing their three aircraft shot down, and they wanted to put an end to this.

Ahmed Yuldash could not believe how lucky they had been. Three helicopters down in the first volley, truly Allah was with them, but the enemy's resolve had hardened. These were certainly Americans, or Israelis, or both, and it was just about the end of this fight. Yuldash hoped he had done his part well enough.

"Tighten the perimeter!" he was shouting, waving his men in. They would fight in an ever-tightening circle and take every one of the enemy with them that they possibly could.

A half-dozen of the IMU fighters decided they were going to try to live to fight another day. They jumped into a beat-up GAZ-69, the old Soviet equivalent of the trusty American Jeep, and grinding the gears in the deafening roar of the battle, pulled away. As they passed the Delta operators, shots rang out between the vehicle and the D-boys. An IMU terrorist promptly fell out of the back of the GAZ, dead. The five remaining in the vehicle sped off around an enormous boulder and down the winding road. They continued to pick up speed, hope rising that they might actually escape, when they came around a sharp corner on the treacherous path and the entire way was blocked by an AH-6J hovering inches off the ground. The aircraft's guns immediately opened up, tearing loose the road in front of the fleeing terrorists. The driver swerved left and they all plummeted out of sight into the gorge and the river far below. A small explosion marked the spot where the venerable GAZ met its end on the rocks. The Little Bird lifted away and resumed its figure-eight track, guarding the road.

Back in the midst of the fight, Yuldash shouted again, "Come on in, move this way!" He stood waving his men in. The bullet came in faster than the speed of sound, not that he would have heard the shot above the din anyway. Across the hood of a rusted Soviet-built truck, a Delta-force sniper had been waiting with his nightscope for someone to look like they were giving orders. Yuldash had obliged nicely, standing straight up, leaning against the sandbag wall, as if he didn't care if he died. It wasn't that Yuldash didn't care, he just expected to. The M107 .50-caliber Barrett sniper rifle put a devastating round through his body, catching him sideways, severing his spine. The huge round flattened to the size of a small circular-saw blade, moving faster than the speed of sound. When the ballistics were reasoned out, its effect was predictable, but on the battlefield no one is ever ready to see what happened next. Yuldash's body divided at the waist, the top half fell limply over the sandbags to the other side, while his lower half fell backwards into the dirt.

The men around Yuldash stopped firing and looked around in a panic, trying to decide from where such a fearsome injury had come. One fired blindly into another IMU position, and that position returned fire. It was falling apart for the terrorists. The D-boys began moving forward, covering each other with suppressive fire as they rushed ahead in teams. The Rangers were firing as they ran, so sporadic was the resistance on their side. Most of the IMU were still fighting and had not surrendered, but as MAJ Ryan made a quick pass over the fight to see what was happening, Rangers and Delta force were engaged in a fierce hand-to-hand fight with the IMU all the way to the center of the enemy perimeter. No missiles came after the aircraft this time, but the helicopters were now powerless to help. Friend and foe were completely mixed together, although not evenly. The Americans had a clear number advantage now, and the circle was pressing in. Still, the IMU fought on.

It was so chaotic that several Rangers struck shocked Delta operators before they realized that the two friendly forces had met in the middle. This led to scuffles between American forces before their leadership on the ground could stop it. The Americans had been immersed in a frenzy of violence, something tough to turn off. Only six members of the IMU were captured alive, all of them wounded. The others were dead. All over the camp Americans sat down where they were, many removing their helmets. They should have moved to set up a defensive perimeter around the terrain they had just won, but no one did so right away, and no one shouted any orders. Only the Delta operators were moving, fired up for their primary mission of locating and destroying the weapon of mass destruction. For the Rangers, they had already accomplished what they had come to Tajikistan to do.

"All Arrow and Bullet elements, this is Arrow 6," Hartman called, "the objective is taken. Take up your racetrack holding positions. I know we are cutting it close on fuel. Stand by, over."

"This is Arrow 42, we are at Bullet 13 crash site. SAR is on the ground, they are waving us off. Request instructions, over," McCall's voice called on the radio.

McCall circled above the ruined tower, the flames below still visible and the smoke billowing into the air. Men ran on the ground, but they were friendlies. A UH-60 Black Hawk Dust Off helicopter sat on the ground about five hundred meters from the site, its rotor still turning.

"Arrow 42, this is Arrow 6, roger, the SAR folks are saying they have recovered O'Brien, but there was no sign of Sirois or any resistance," Hartman replied.

"This is Arrow 42, let us take a look, we can't just split. There's a road here, we'll run it down, they can't be far," McCall said.

"Arrow 42, this is Arrow 6, negative. Return to the AO. We are out of here in minutes. How copy, over," said Hartman.

"We can't just leave him here, sir," McCall argued. "We can catch them. We never leave anyone behind. Night Stalkers Don't Quit."

"Listen to me McCall, your helicopter is shot up and low on fuel. We will depart for the FARP as soon as ground elements destroy the target here. We've lost enough people tonight and you have a crew to think about. We'll get him back," Hartman said. "But right now, get your asses back here. Immediately. That's an order, out."

"Dammit!" McCall shouted. Willet watched her for a moment and could almost see her weighing her options.

"Jeanie," Willet said into the intercom.

"Yeah, yeah," McCall hissed back.

Hill listened, and didn't quite know what was going on, but knew that McCall was pissed that they hadn't found Sirois. The helicopter banked hard and headed north.

Hartman froze. He turned up the volume on his radio and said, "This is Arrow 6, say again, Rattler 4, say again."

Below, a Delta operator stood outside amid the flames, the smoke, the bodies, and said, "I say again, this is Rattler 4. The targets are not here. The crates hold thirty-kilowatt generators. Nothing else. They are stamped with symbols for radioactivity, but there are no real targets here. We were tricked. Extract us and let's get out of here."

Hartman was immediately nauseated. As his helicopter passed over the narrow gorge and he looked down at the results of the butchery below, he couldn't believe it.

"All Arrow and Bullet elements, begin extraction as planned. Bullet elements take up covering positions, Arrow elements take turns going carefully into the gorge and getting a load out. Fill your aircraft, no half-loads. Wounded and dead first. Quick but orderly, out," Hartman ordered.

"Arrow 6, this is Arrow 5, are the targets already destroyed? I can see the flatbed truck back here, crates open but abandoned," Ryan's voice called.

"This is Arrow 6, bad intel, BOGINT," Hartman said. "We're out of here."

McCall keyed her mike, and then thought better of it. Sirois was lost, probably captured, and the whole mission was for nothing? Not to mention the pilots who had been killed, and the number of ground troops lost. Someone needed to pay for this. Somewhere there was an imagery specialist who needed to have his or her ass kicked, McCall thought.

"When I get home, I'm going squint hunting," McCall said into the intercom. Imagery specialists are referred to as squints, and there was one out there that McCall thought owed her an explanation.

"Hey, a flatbed truck brings large mysterious crates here?" Willet said, "Any reasonable person would have come to the same conclusion. We were baited up here."

"What, they don't think of that?" McCall demanded.

"Well, it's not up to a squint somewhere to decide what to do with the intel, he just reports what he sees. Coming here was a decision made by someone else," Willet said.

"I'd like to know who," McCall said, almost in a whisper.

McCall's Pave Hawk reached the AO, and she made a long, slow turn to get in line to extract the men below.

"Arrow 42, this is Arrow 5, your bird is smoking pretty good. Should you pick anyone up? Can you even make it back, over," Ryan said over the radio.

"This is Arrow 42, all systems nominal, we'll do our part," McCall said, her voice still angry.

"You've done quite a bit already. Pick up last, if there is anyone left to pick up by then, over," Ryan answered.

"Roger that," McCall said.

She could think of nothing else but Sirois. In her head she was trying to decide where they might take him, how far he might be. She had no idea where that other road went. Lost in her thoughts and worry, she came too close to another helicopter.

"Hey!" Willet said. "Want me to take it?"

"Was that you, McCall? You want to not cut it quite so close?" a voice came in over the radio.

"No, I've got it," McCall said to Willet. She refocused on the flying. She'd find Rick, but for the time being, she had to concentrate on getting them back.

McCall had two helicopters in front of her in line to pick up troops when Hartman called, "That's it, we've got them all, head to the FARP. No stragglers, we move together."

McCall was shocked. How could there be three empty birds? The MH-6s had no one riding on the outside benches on the return trip.

"If we picked up the dead, why is there so much more space than when we came out here?" McCall asked into the intercom.

Willet turned his head to McCall, "Because you can stack people when they are dead."

McCall was sorry she asked. So were Arroyo and Hill, who were also feeling a bit guilty that there were fellow crew chiefs flying out there in the night with a helicopter full of stacked bodies. Suddenly their helicopter felt oddly sterile.

McCall wasn't the only one worrying about Sirois. MAJ Ryan was thinking about him also, and about a night long ago when he learned what it meant to be shot down. He had been lucky. The SAR people had found him. There was no telling what Sirois was going through, if he was still alive. O'Brien may have been the lucky one on that helicopter. He rubbed the scar on his cheek.

"All elements, we're coming up on the FARP. I want Arrow elements down first, Bullets cover, over," Hartman said.

"This is Arrow 23, Arrow 42 is falling back, over," came a voice.

"We're good," responded McCall. "Just some vibration, we'll make the FARP."

"Arrow 42, put down just east of the FARP," Hartman said.

"The ass thinks we're going to crash into his gas station," McCall said to Willet.

"I think we might, too," Willet said, his voice shaking with the vibrations.

"Roger, putting down east of the FARP," her voice clearly stressed and vibrating. Hill and Arroyo were holding on in the back, trying their best to stay in one place.

"Arrow 42, sounds like you're in rough shape, how you doing back there?" Hartman called.

"I'm busy, sir," McCall said, working hard.

"Arrow 6, this is Arrow 23, she's looking like a nighttime skywriter now. She's got altitude, must be up near five hundred feet, and just pissing smoke," the voice said again.

"Arrow 42, this is Arrow 6, just put it down, we'll come get you," Hartman said.

"You mean like Sirois?" McCall said, shouting with the effort.

"Great, nice one, if we make it, you'll wish you hadn't," Willet shouted, trying to deliver the punch line as smoothly as possible through the intercom.

Hill tried, too. "And I only got to hear half the joke."

She had climbed higher on purpose. It would give her room to react if . . .

The first engine quit abruptly, as if a switch had been flipped. The second sputtered, Hill saw a flash of what might have been flame, and it died, too. The helicopter had no power.

McCall thrust the collective downward, flattening the rotors blades and keeping them from beating any more air. This kept the rotor RPM up. Without power, having the rotors grab air at this time would only slow their rotation to a point where the helicopter would fall like a stone. Once slowed, without an engine, there would be no way of speeding the rotor back up. She needed the rotor RPM to be as high as possible. The helicopter began to yaw left and McCall applied some right pedal. The helicopter began descending increasingly quickly, falling at two thousand feet per second. Arroyo and Hill were just hanging on for dear life. The blades whipped around above them, but still they fell. Autorotation, thought Hill, this is gonna suck.

Arroyo began a long howl as they fell out of the sky. Willet and McCall saw the ground rushing up at them. Willet shouted, "Now!"

McCall waited a couple seconds more, knowing Willet was too early, and seconds mattered here. She pulled the cyclic smoothly and firmly aft. The helicopter flared nose up. The long fuselage of the aircraft caught full the air, and much of their airspeed bled off. Hill and Arroyo felt as though they had fallen out a two-story window into the back of the helicopter. The nose fell again, making them level with the ground, about twenty feet in the air. McCall pulled the collective and the blades tilted, grabbing as much air as they could, producing a bit more lift, as the aircraft fell very nearly straight down. It hit the Afghan desert hard, and Arroyo was thrown against his gun. The wind was knocked out of Hill, but the helicopter stayed upright.

McCall shouted back, without the intercom in the deafening silence, "You guys alright?"

Arroyo and Hill were both moving, rolling from side to side slowly in the back. The blades slowed to a stop outside. McCall and Willet came back to the crew chiefs. Arroyo coughed and blood spattered his hand. Hill was lying still trying to breathe normally.

"Arroyo, we'll get you some help, you'll be fine," Willet told him, both pilot and crew chief looking at the blood.

"I can't breathe," Arroyo squeaked out.

"You'll be fine," Willet said as the SAR people landed and arrived with two litters.

They checked Arroyo over, announced, "Some broken ribs, punctured lung probably," and then to the patient, "You'll be okay." They loaded him up and ran with him to the other aircraft.

Another medic checked Hill out, who insisted he was okay. "I'm fine, get off me, I'm fine."

McCall, Willet, and Hill jumped down and ran to the other helicopter with the medic. Jumping in next to Arroyo, Hill held his hand, while the SAR folks worked to stabilize him.

Hill leaned his head back and blew out a lung full of air through pursed lips. That was a close one. He looked over at the pilots, and nodded his appreciation, and then turned back to Arroyo.

"Dude, hang in there, I'll need help fixing the aircraft after what McCall did to it," Hill said.

Arroyo squeezed Hill's hand, unable to see him, recognizing what Hill was doing, and grateful for it.

11

The old truck was an odd lime-green. At each side window was a hanging blind to spare the eyes of the occupants from the glaring sun; each with a row of tassels hanging beneath.

Two men sat in the front, each looked as ancient as the vehicle, faces expressionless and covered with white whiskers. They were exhausted, having driven in shifts for days to get this far, and they yet had far to go. Still, this was the last few moments of peril. On the other side of the Iraqi checkpoint lay the Iranian border, and Iranian troops.

The stared directly ahead. Low posts strung with razor wire framed a primitive gate, consisting mainly of a long cast iron pipe on a hinge. For the moment, the road was blocked by the gate, and half a dozen Iraqi men. They were members of the newly created Iraqi Frontier Guard, the border guard. Up until only a few months ago, the new government in Baghdad had allowed the Kurds to monitor this crossing point, as it was in their territory, but the Kurds had been replaced by men from southern Iraq. It was not because the Kurds were necessarily less trustworthy, but because the Turks to the north did not like the appearance of anything that made the Kurds look as if they had their own country.

Four of the Iraqis remained standing near the gate as two of them approached the lime-green truck.

"Papers," was all one said, placing one foot on the running

board beneath the driver's door. The driver immediately handed him a couple of documents and an identification card. His face was stony, and he did not look directly at the border guard.

"Cotton? Syrian cotton to Tehran. That seems odd. Iran grows a great deal of cotton, in every province. Why should Iran want to import Syrian cotton?" the guard asked.

The driver answered without hesitation. It had been an anticipated question and elicited a rehearsed response. "We are carrying cotton grown in Syria from American seed. Longer fibers than Iranian cotton."

The second guard walked around to the back and, looking in, saw bale upon bale of raw cotton.

The first handed the papers back to the driver, "I suppose we are all dealing with American imports these days. At least it was grown in Syria."

The driver smiled and said, "Freshly picked."

The guard froze and said, "Cotton is harvested in October."

The driver's smile fell. As the guard pulled the rifle from his shoulder, the second man in the front seat leaned over the driver and fired an antique revolver. The round struck the border guard in the forehead and he fell where he stood. The second guard jumped at the report, and took a few steps to come around from the rear of the vehicle. Bales of heavy cotton fell out of the truck suddenly and six heavily armed men jumped down. The second guard never had a chance. He was quickly dispatched with a burst of AK-47 fire to the chest.

The four guards at the gate came running, weapons at the ready. They had no idea what had gone wrong, but at least one of their number was dead, and there had been subsequent gunfire as well.

The six men from the truck, a team of Iranian Revolutionary Guard, broke into two groups, and came around each side of the vehicle. With three men on each side, one man fell prone, one took up a kneeling firing position, and the other stood with the truck for cover. All six immediately opened fire, and the four Iraqi border guards died without so much as an opportunity to aim their weapons.

The Iranian soldiers sprinted forward and checked the bodies of the Iraqis. One groaned and was hit with an additional burst of heavy 7.62mm rounds. They lifted the gate and the truck drove beneath it. Allowing the gate to fall behind the vehicle, the six Iranians jogged alongside the truck until it came to the Iranian guard post. The Iranian border guards had seen what had happened to their Iraqi counterparts, but they were unafraid. One of the men from the truck walked forward and said to the guard, "I am Second Brigadier General Mohammed Lashkagi of the Revolutionary Guard. Open your gate at once."

"Open the gate," a voice said from behind the guard shack. A slender man in civilian clothing with graying hair stepped out, his hands clasped in front of him. The general nodded to him, turned, and barked an order. The old men in the truck immediately climbed down and moved to the rear of the vehicle while the general and a much younger driver climbed up into the front. The remaining soldiers returned to the back and sat with the old men in the bales of cotton. On the floor, almost concealed by the cargo and surrounded by men's feet, was a large, metallic cylinder.

The truck pulled into Iran and continued on its journey to the capital. The Iranian border guards ran over into Iraq and carried the fallen bales into their guard shack. Then one guard knelt beside a fallen Iraqi and placed a scarf in the dead man's hand, the red-and-white-checkered scarf of a Kurd. There would be no mystery as to how these Iraqi border guards were killed and by whom. It would be blamed on separatist Kurds.

The Iranians returned to their posts and acted as if nothing had happened, while a light wind blew the clothing and the hair of the dead lying in the desert.

12

Juma Nagami walked through the ruins of what had been his organization's strongest redoubt. Bodies were strewn all around. The bodies of his men. No enemy bodies were left behind except those that had burned to cinders inside the wreckage of helicopters. There was evidence, however. The helicopters that had crashed were Little Birds, as they were called. A pilot had been captured near the ruined jamming tower they had just completed days before, and his helicopter had not burned. Nagami had not seen the pilot, but he had heard reports. There were rappelling ropes hanging from the far cliff, dangling from pins fired into the rock itself. Pins that cost more by the half dozen than all the AK-47s his men had armed themselves with combined. And poor Yuldash had been sliced in half by some terrible weapon. The few survivors claimed the attackers ran down the cliff face, rappelling and firing at the same time.

They were attacked by a wealthy opponent, full of resources. An opponent that thought any objective was not out of reach, and that it was only a matter of applying sufficient resources. In the world today, there was only one country with more resources than it could spend and a history sufficiently short to prevent shame at its own arrogance, thought Nagami. The Americans had come as they had hoped, but looking at the death and destruction, it felt like they had lured a bear into a goat pen. What had they really gained by following the Iranian's orders? He watched as two men dug a grave for his friend Yuldash. Is this really what the Consortium wanted? What end had this served? He lost hundreds of men and a great deal of matériel for what? To shoot down a few helicopters? There was no end to American helicopters. Had the punishment the IMU had taken been just a diversion for something else? For what had we paid so much?

He had never trusted the Iranian and decided he would not take orders through him again. From now on, he would only obey orders that came directly to him. Nagami picked up a shovel and helped bury his friend. He also decided that a large measure of revenge against the Americans was certainly in order.

13

MAJ Ryan had had no luck in tracking down the source of the faulty intel through his contact at INSCOM, so Hartman decided he had to talk to his own source. Enough members of his unit had been lost. He strode down the broad corridor, his shoes clicking on the impossibly glossy floor, buffed every night by an army of janitors. The hallway was twice as wide as it was high, the walls painted in an odd, angular pattern of royal-blue and white. Uniforms of varied colors and styles mixed with well-tailored suits, and the heart of the American defense system pulsed with life around him as he walked.

Hartman had been here before and was not awed by any of it today. He was livid, winding his way through a maze of hallways, rings, and floors, headed for one set of rooms in particular. He was just as angry with himself for not coming to see her sooner. He couldn't get past the idea that perhaps his pride and reticence had cost the lives of some of his people.

As he turned yet another corner, the office of the Assistant Secretary of Defense for Intelligence Oversight loomed ahead and he picked up his step. Coming into the outer office, Cat's administrative assistant Lucy Billings rose to meet Hartman. "Hello, Colonel Hartman, she's busy right now but . . ."

He ignored her and walked past, directly into the office of Cat Hartman, the ATSD-IO. Lucy was chasing after him, but only managed to enter the office a step behind. They both stopped and stared at Cat Hartman, who in a very smart navy-blue suit jacket and pants, stood on her chair with a ruler in her hand, jabbing at an air duct. When Cat Hartman saw them, she in turn froze, then smiled, embarrassed, and climbed down.

"A mouse?" asked Lucy hopefully, worried her boss might be cracking up.

Cat Hartman just straightened her suit and smiled again. "That's all, Lucy. I'll call you if I need you."

Lucy turned without smiling and exited the office, closing the door as she left. Cat Hartman said, "The duct, the vent, it vibrates and makes a buzzing sound sometimes." She smiled again, broad and cheerful. She had been caught showing the little kid in her, and while embarrassing, it was also a bit refreshing.

Jack Hartman did not smile back. He took another step toward Cat, menacingly. Her face turned to stone, "What is it?"

Jack Hartman said, "You know exactly what it is. How many pilots do I have to lose before you intel idiots get it right?"

"I don't collect it or analyze it, I just make sure they are not breaking the law in getting it," Cat snapped back, but then felt sorry for it. "Jack, I'm sorry for the pilots you've lost. There are mountains of information that come in and these people do their best with it. We've gotten so good at this, the tough part isn't gathering it. The tough part is processing it."

"Well, you processed it well enough to get us out to the Russian 'Stans. Rick Sirois is dead or worse because of bad intel. Six other pilots burned up. And then there are no W.M.D. Do you think it might be possible for the intel community to pull its collective head out of its collective ass before my entire unit is wiped out because of BOGINT?" Jack Hartman's voice had climbed to a shout for the last bit.

Cat Hartman had had enough, "Let me remind you to whom you are speaking, Lieutenant Colonel Hartman. You are not yelling across the dining room table this time. You cannot pound your fist and throw a tantrum in here. I am the Assistant Secretary of Defense for Intelligence Oversight."

"Don't hand me that . . ." Jack began.

"Don't interrupt me! Now I understand you feel that our familiarity gives you extra leeway, and maybe it has and that would be my fault, but you do not have that kind of freedom with this office. You will respect this office and maintain your bearing, is that clear?" Cat Hartman barked.

LTC Hartman's back went ramrod straight. His face darkened and Cat thought he might explode, but suddenly his features softened.

"Cat, I'm sorry. I've had to go to the families of these pilots. I've had to sit with small children who have no way of understanding what it means that their father is never coming home. I've held the hands of sobbing wives who had planned to spend the rest of their lives with men they had known since those men were boys, and I don't even have a body to give them. I can't even tell them what their husbands were doing, what they died for."

Jack Hartman was not a man given to emotion. He was a soldier's soldier, but he was struggling to keep it together. She felt for him. She went to her door and made sure it was closed and then locked it. Turning back to Jack she said, "The intel has been coming from CIA, it isn't coming from the DoD intel community. Department of Defense intel has controverted the CIA intel each time, Lebanon and Tajikistan, but the national-level consumers keep choosing to go with the CIA's analysis."

"Why?" Jack asked. "Why pick one over the other?"

"A lot of the folks running the show right now look at the civilian agencies as the true professionals. There's also some of the good-ol'-boy network at work," she said.

"Is Sirois alive?" Jack asked.

"Rick Sirois is right now being taken to Tehran, from what we can tell. It is also there, in Iran, that DoD intel suspects a low-yield nuclear weapon has been taken. Intercepts and chatter keep referring to something called the 'Hand of Allah,'" Cat replied.

"How low is low-yield anyway?" Hartman asked.

Cat deadpanned, "Fifteen kilotons."

Hartman blinked. "That's the size of the Hiroshima bomb."

"Almost," Cat replied.

"Cat, you've got to let me be a direct consumer of any intel having to do with Sirois. We don't leave people behind, we have to go get him, bring him back home," Jack asked. His eyes were pleading, he gripped her shoulders.

"Jack, if you don't have an official need to know, I . . . ," Cat began but then stopped, seeing the look on his face. "I'll see what I can do." She dropped her eyes, but then lifted them again, meeting his.

She was still breathtaking, Jack thought. He could feel the pull to kiss her. He was consciously resisting it, and then her head tilted invitingly, yet nervously. Her face came a bit closer, and Jack bent a bit, but then as if heeding the same command, they both straightened and Jack dropped his hands. They stepped back from each other, and Jack pulled his beret from his belt. "Thank you, Cat. Thanks."

She nodded and walked over to her desk, placing one hand on a three-ring binder lying on one corner. Jack turned, unlocked and opened the door, then walked out. Cat watched him go, and sighed. She missed him.

Lucy got halfway out of her chair, and Hartman waved her off. He stepped out into the hallway. Sirois was still alive and on his way to Tehran. But where in Tehran? Not that it mattered. Unless someone held an entire embassy of hostages in Tehran again, it was unlikely that they would be able to go get him. They'd likely lose several pilots in a rescue attempt like that anyway, and as fond as Hartman was of Sirois, he wasn't willing to trade half a dozen pilots for one. Maybe the Iranians would hold him at some remote outpost. That would be helpful. Hartman shook his head as he walked. He couldn't do anything until he got more intelligence, which was the real conundrum. Hartman felt it was the intel that created the dilemma that he needed more intel to solve.

14

July 1
In the air
Over the Afghanistan-Turkmenistan border

LT Rick Sirois sat on the floor in the middle of the helicopter, his hands chained to a floor tie-down, surrounded by armed men. Two seemed to be wearing uniforms of their own construction, but the rest of them were wearing issued gear. The inside of the aircraft was roomy, and the maintenance was nowhere near as meticulous as it was in American aviation units. Even loose scraps of rope lay around, along with a couple of empty cans that looked like they might have held drinks, and forms filled out—once important and now discarded. Recognizing the helicopter as a Russian-built Mi-171, a variant of the Mi-8 Hip built for export, and the uniforms as Iranian, Sirois knew things had gone from bad to worse.

He had not been conscious when placed in the helicopter, and had come to while already in flight. It had been hours, but he was not sure how many. His mouth was dry and his lips were cracked. The crash at the tower site had pinned his legs in his aircraft and when the IMU pulled him out, they had been less than gentle. While by some miracle his legs were not snapped in half, he was in a great deal of pain. Maybe some hairline fractures there, or just deep bone bruising. His left eye was swelling shut and he was missing three of his front teeth. Breathing was painful. When they yanked him out of his helicopter, they had taken considerable pleasure in kicking and stomping on him. He vaguely remembered looking once more into the ruined aircraft and seeing O'Brien's lifeless body, and then all went black. Now he sat, beaten up and surrounded by men who would just as soon throw him out as keep him alive, flying to God-knows-where. More than likely however, Sirois knew these soldiers were probably headed home. Iran.

One thing was certain, they had been up a long time. The helicopter must have external fuel tanks to have traveled this far, but even with them, Sirois knew that they would have to refuel if they were in fact headed to Iran. The target in Tajikistan was almost one thousand miles from the Iranian border. Even with the extra tanks, Sirois figured this helicopter could only make seven hundred miles or so. It is not that Sirois thought there might be a chance of escape during a refueling stop; he was just keeping his brain working. Guessing at the math of fuel consumption kept him from focusing on the fact that many people, even foreigners, had spent decades forgotten and lost in Iran's prisons. One incident kept flashing in his mind, and he kept pushing it away. An Israeli pilot had bailed out over Lebanon in 1986. He was handed over to terrorists in Lebanon who then sold him to Iran. There were stories of his legs being surgically injured to prevent him from ever walking, and thereby attempting to escape, again. Supposedly, he is still there, in Iran to this day.

"Maybe I'll get to meet him," Sirois said to himself in a whisper. He was immediately kicked in the back by an Iranian soldier seated behind him. Sirois rolled to his side in agony, and then began working on the fuel consumption numbers again.

15

SFC Joe Pettihorn came into the room with a bulging, size-able, brown cardboard box. The rugged West Virginian was straining under its weight. His soldiers sat around olive-green picnic-style tables, working on various radio repairs, and they looked up as he approached with his curious load. Pettihorn dropped the box on the table nearest the door and the weight of it threatened to flatten the homemade furniture.

The closest soldiers peered into the box and saw books. Technical and field manuals. From the most basic, *FM 24-1 Combat Communications*, to proposals written for future communications systems, Pettihorn had collected everything he could find.

"What is this, Sergeant?" a young corporal asked, pulling a worn manual from the box. "TM 11-282 Radio Set AN/FRC-15? What the hell is an FRC-15?"

"It's an old radio, from the 1950s, and we're going to look through all of these and when we finish, I have another couple of boxes like this one. I want some ideas on how we are going to provide comms to the chopper jockeys without using VHF or their current SATCOM radios," Pettihorn said. "They were jammed again, and it cost lives because the ground forces could not get the coordinated close-air support they needed. It isn't our fault, but we're going to fix it anyway. Everybody get it? The tough part isn't finding another radio, it is finding another radio that does not have frequencies in the jammed range, that can be easily mounted and powered in the aircraft, with sufficient range, an encryption solution, and a way to get the antenna to work without drilling too many holes into the helicopters. That's it, no tougher than that."

Pettihorn looked around the room as his soldiers rose from their seats and crowded around the box, each grabbing a book or two and then walking off to begin reading. It felt desperate, but he was out of answers. Radios that were supposed to be nearly jam-proof had been jammed successfully twice. They were going to have to think out of the box on this one. They needed to give the pilots yet another backup plan because the ones they had already were falling prey to a clever enemy. They needed to get that one-step advantage back and Pettihorn and his people would find it eventually, but it was a race. Find a way to beat it before the next mission or more people may die who might have otherwise lived. Pettihorn looked around at his soldiers, most of them not much more than kids, but they were talented kids. He reached into the box, grabbed a couple of manuals, and walked off to find a quiet corner.

16

July 1
In the air
Over the Turkmenistan-Iran border

Sirois felt the helicopter flare a bit and he sat up. It settled into a hover and then began to gyrate and bounce. Several of the soldiers grabbed handholds of helicopter, but Sirois just smiled with his broken teeth.

"Pit much?" he said aloud. PIT or Pilot-Induced-Turbulence occurs sometimes in a hover, especially when an anxious pilot hasn't had much time in a particular type of helicopter and is making irregular and needless control inputs. The soldier who previously kicked Sirois attempted to once again, but a strong shudder refocused his attention to holding on.

"Are you checked out on this bird or what?" Sirois yelled toward the cockpit, laughing. His seemingly maniacal shouting and laughing, with blood caked on his face and his eye swollen shut, was making the soldiers around him all the more nervous. They settled to earth hard; too hard to meet the standard at Fort Rucker's flight school thought Sirois. The impact made his cracked ribs throb and he grimaced in pain. The helicopter had no sooner stopped moving than the Iranian soldiers and the IMU terrorists pulled the large cargo door open and jumped down. One man stayed aboard with Sirois, staring at him impassively.

Sirois looked out at an air base, the rotors slowing above. The sunlight was bright and in the distance, the gray haze of smog over a city. A squat building sat off to one side. Three men rushed with a hose to refuel the aircraft. An Iranian flag flew in the summer breeze above the structure. Sirois wondered where exactly they might be. It had to be near the Iranian border, they could not have plunged very deeply into the country yet. An old Chinook helicopter with Iranian markings, built in America long ago during the reign of the shah, passed through the slice of blue sky.

"That's gotta be a sign," Sirois said to himself.

The soldier guarding him had not moved or made a sound, but at hearing Sirois speak again, he jumped up and moved quickly toward the American.

Sirois cringed and said, "Are we in Mashhad?"

The Iranian stopped and glared.

Sirois gestured toward the door and asked, "Mashhad?"

The soldier nodded, and Sirois smiled. "Mashhad."

"Mashhad," the soldier repeated, and then he savagely kicked Sirois in the chest. He fell over, gasping, the pain causing a flash and spots in his vision. He fought to stay conscious. The Iranian soldier walked back to his seat.

How far? Sirois struggled to think. *Four Hundred miles? Five hundred miles? How far to Tehran? Are we going to Tehran?* The Night Stalkers spent a lot of time in the simulator flying over Iran, training for the day when they would be flying here in a real-world mission. The training had intensified after the country had been labeled as a member of the axis of evil.

"Well, I'm in a helicopter in Iran," thought Sirois. He took a staggered breath, wincing in pain.

The men piled into the aircraft and there was a quick exchange in Farsi as an officer inquired as to what had happened to the American. At the response, everyone chuckled. Everyone except Sirois. The rotor began to spin up, the whine of the engine transforming into a steady hum.

17

Arroyo's bed was raised in such a manner that he was more sitting than reclining. He was slightly groggy, and moved and spoke more slowly than his guests. McCall and Hill sat on either side, trying not to make him laugh. Arroyo wasn't much in the mood to laugh anyway. His ribs were wrapped and an IV dripped painkiller into his arm. A tube ran from an incision in the side of his chest.

Flowers framed Arroyo's bed and a television hung across the room. The other bed was empty and Hill had his chair leaning back against it.

Things had gotten a bit dicey. Arroyo had hoped to be transferred to Blanchfield Army Community Hospital at Fort Campbell by now, but an infection had kept him at Walter Reed.

LTC Jack Hartman unexpectedly walked into the room and Hill nearly fell to the floor trying to get to his feet.

"As you were," Hartman waved him off. "How are you doing, Arroyo?"

"Just fine, sir, a little sore," Arroyo slurred slightly.

"I think he'd be a lot more sore, sir, if it weren't for the meds," Hill said.

"You need anything?" Hartman asked.

"No, sir, I'm fine, thanks though," Arroyo answered and then looking around slowly and asked, "Where the TV remote?"

Hill pulled at a cable until the television remote control

came free from within Arroyo's blankets. Arroyo turned on the TV and surfed until he found a game show. His hand fell and he sat watching intently.

McCall turned to Hartman. "Can I speak to you for a minute, sir?"

Hartman nodded, and McCall said to Arroyo and Hill, "We'll be right back." Hill sat down and Arroyo did not notice as the two left the room.

Walking down the hallway, McCall asked, "Do you know where Rick is?"

Hartman looked down to the distant nurses' station and said, "They think he is on his way to Iran."

"Are they drawing something up for us to go get him?" McCall immediately asked.

"Look, McCall, it's Iran. This isn't some band of malcontents, this is the region's natural superpower we're talking about," Hartman whispered, stopping to face her.

Her eyes were wet, but her face was stony. "Nobody gets left behind. Night Stalkers don't quit. How about all that? Is that just horseshit or what?"

"Watch your bearing, Ms. McCall," Hartman insisted. Her mouth closed and she straightened. Hartman then softened. "I want him back, too, and we'll figure it out, but we need to keep in control right now. Just trust me on this one. I won't quit."

She looked up at him, saw the sincerity in his face, and said, "Let me know what I can do, sir."

"Will do, McCall. Go take care of your soldier, and I'll see you in Kentucky in a day or two," Hartman said. He put his hand on her shoulder, a surprisingly familiar gesture from the commander, and then walked away without another word. She watched him go for a moment and then returned to Arroyo.

"Hi, ma'am! What's new?" Arroyo asked gleefully.

"Man, Arroyo, she was just here. She only stepped into the hall for a minute," Hill laughed.

"What the hell do they have him on?" McCall asked Hill.

"I don't know, but I want some," Hill grinned.

"Seems like he's getting too much of whatever it is," Mc-Call said.

Hill became more serious, "Do they know where Mr. Sirois is?"

"They have a guess," McCall said, not wanting to share too much yet.

Hill didn't press for the location. If she had wanted to share it, she would have.

"Are we going to go get him?" Hill asked. McCall knew the question was coming and she knew the truth.

"I doubt it," McCall said, "but they are considering all options."

Hill knew what "considering all options" meant just as well as McCall did. She had, in essence, just said, "No one has a plan yet so don't ask me for anymore details than I've given you."

Arroyo suddenly looked around and said, "Where's the remote?"

18

Sayyed Nasballah loved coming to Iran, to be walking among millions of Shia who were the majority in a land where they held a firm grip on power. It was considerably different than Lebanon, with Israeli fighter aircraft breaking the sound barrier above your head every day just to show that they still could. But this time he came with some apprehension. Someone had tried to kill him in Beirut. Maybe he was safer in Tehran, and perhaps maybe not. He walked down the stairs and out onto the tarmac. It was warm, but not unbearable, and the fresh air was welcomed after hours cooped up inside a smoke-filled passenger jet.

A young man in a suit walked directly to him and said, "Sayyed Nasballah, I am to drive you." He bowed slightly.

"But what of my bags?" Nasballah asked.

"They will be tended to," the young man replied. His Arabic was good, and was of the Egyptian dialect, but he had the broad, Asian face of someone from northeastern Iran, perhaps the Khorassan province. Nasballah nodded and followed his driver to a silver Chery A11.

"A Chinese car?" Nasballah asked. Nasballah could of course speak Farsi, but he continued in Arabic.

"A Chinese car built in an Iranian plant," smiled the driver as he opened the back door for Nasballah, who held his turban and ducked into the small sedan. The door closed and the driver quickly walked around the car, climbing into the driver's seat. He seemed proud, as if he had built the car with his own hands. The youth of Iran were so overconfident, thought Nasballah, and so willful. They made up the vast majority now in Iran and it was an issue that would soon have to be faced.

They drove into Tehran itself, modern buildings and ancient structures intermingled. Shades of American investment from the years before the revolution were still evident. The streets and highways were hopelessly crowded and in need of repair. Traffic signals added more confusion than clarification and the street lanes were not marked. The combination of car exhaust and dry air made breathing less than comfortable.

Nasballah sat back and asked, "How far is it?"

"Not far, not far," the driver said, turning on the radio. A singer named Googoosh filled the car with her melodious and soothing voice, singing "Kavir," a pop song, and Nasballah frowned.

"Is this Googoosh?" Nasballah asked.

"Yes, it is," the driver beamed. "She is very popular."

"I remember when she was not allowed to sing. She had childish songs of love and promiscuity, and now she is old and is allowed to howl once more, but now of politics and soldiers," he said. The driver quickly switched the radio off and stopped smiling, Nasballah grunted with satisfaction.

They turned onto Pasdaran Street in the northeastern corner of Tehran, passing a small Internet café where men outside stared as Nasballah passed. The car swerved to the sidewalk and stopped as suddenly as a bird striking a window. Nasballah was nearly thrown into the front seat. The staring men began to laugh. The driver ran around to the other side and opened the door, sheepishly announcing, "We have arrived."

"That is good news," Nasballah said, stepping out. When the men who had been staring, and then laughing, saw the black turban of a cleric and realized where it had stopped, in front of the Ministry of Intelligence and Security, they fell silent. The driver was focused on the street between his feet.

Sayyed Nasballah straightened, looked at the men who were unmoving and quiet, and walked around the back of the car toward the building's entrance. The driver rushed forward and opened the door, holding it as Nasballah entered the building, and then followed. They walked across the lobby, past a receptionist and guards without so much as a word, and went directly to the elevators. Getting off on the fifth floor, Nasballah and his driver made their way to an office, and with the door held for him once more, Nasballah entered.

"Sayyed Nasballah!" a man said. His hair was beginning to gray, but he was still in remarkable physical condition. His dress was very western in appearance, a charcoal suit finely tailored.

"Ah, Khalid Farmad, Allah protect you," Nasballah answered. The men embraced and exchanged a kiss on each cheek.

"That is all, Farouk, thank you," Farmad said to the driver, who immediately turned and left, glad to be free of his charge.

Nasballah and Farmad walked past a receptionist and into a well-appointed executive office. There were overstuffed leather chairs and a low mahogany table between them. The room smelled slightly of cigars and the upholstery. A massive wooden desk stood in a corner of glass, a view in two directions of Tehran. Farmad motioned for Nasballah to sit in one of the chairs as he went to the bar and poured himself a scotch. For Nasballah he poured an identical glass of apple juice.

"Here you are, my friend, some juice for you. Are you tired from the trip?" Farmad said, returning and handing the glass to Nasballah. Nasballah sniffed at the juice first, as a wary animal might, and then took a sip.

"The trip was terrible, so crowded these airplanes today, and the seats so small," said Nasballah.

"And we aren't all as small as we once were, eh?" said the trim Farmad, chuckling at his rotund guest. Nasballah snorted and took another swallow of juice.

"Khalid," Nasballah said, suddenly becoming serious and familiar all at once, "where is the Hand of Allah?"

Farmad's expression and composure remained unfazed; he had of course known Nasballah would ask.

"First, let me say how glad I am that we still have you among us. The unpleasantness, the car bombing, which nearly took your life, I think made us doubly sure how much we need you in our struggle," Farmad said sweetly.

"Well, I thank you. It was only Allah that spared me," Nasballah said. And then, testing, "We've yet to discover who made the attempt on my life."

Farmad's expression did not change. "The Israelis, wasn't it?" He took another sip of his scotch.

"No, my people do not think so. The Zionists would have used a far more sophisticated device, perhaps even remote control. If it had been the Jews, I would probably be dead. No, those behind this were far less skilled, less bright. They simply were not as capable, or as motivated," Nasballah said, again testing.

Farmad smiled. The testing had been obvious.

"Well, thanks be to Allah that you were spared," Farmad said.

"Ah, and speaking of Allah, what of the Hand of Allah? Where is it?" Nasballah asked, subtlety unnecessary at this point.

Farmad answered, "It should not concern you any longer, as your responsibility for it has ended. Besides, as you know, the hand of Allah is all around us."

"I am being serious," insisted Nasballah.

"As am I," Farmad said, his smile faded.

"It is here in the building?" Nasballah whispered, as if yelling might set off the weapon.

Farmad chuckled, "You needn't speak so softly."

Nasballah was quiet for a moment and then stood with Farmad, who had never taken his seat. "How do we get it back to Israel now?" Nasballah asked, "We cannot get it through Iraq to Syria. The Americans are everywhere."

Farmad only smiled at this, making Nasballah uncomfortable.

"Well, there is no other way, except to fly it, and you wouldn't make it very far against the Israeli air forces," Nasballah added.

Farmad shook his head and continued to smile.

"Well, what then? Stop grinning like a monkey. What good is a weapon we cannot deliver?" Nasballah scolded.

"My dear Sayyed, it is not that we cannot deliver it. The issue is to where we will deliver it. You need to think differently. What would the use be of detonating such a weapon to drive the Zionists from Palestine but then so pollute the land that it would be of no use to the Palestinians?" Farmad said.

"But where?" Nasballah puzzled.

"Well, who is the real enemy? Who keeps the Jews in Palestine with billions of dollars in aid and promises of protection?" Farmad asked.

"The Americans," Nasballah answered. "But, while we could probably get the weapon into the harbor of New York or Miami more easily than we could get it to Tel Aviv, there is still a risk we will be caught and the weapon will be lost. This is our one opportunity to change the course of history. Should we risk it this way?"

Farmad shook his head, "No, you are right the weapon is too valuable to risk it this way and the Americans are already hunting for it. The misinformation we have been feeding the CIA has been working, but with each effort we lose valuable assets involved in the deception."

"So, what then?" Nasballah asked, exasperated.

"We do not to go to America, it has already come to us," Farmad said, his voice intense for the first time since Nasballah's arrival. "There are thirty-five thousand American soldiers in the Baghdad area at this very moment. If the bomb were detonated in Baghdad, the American casualty count could exceed tenfold what Al Qaeda managed to accomplish on September eleventh."

Nasballah took a step backward, "But there are five million Iraqi inhabitants in Baghdad."

"This will show the Americans that anything they take

from us will ultimately be denied them. Most of the five million you worry about are Sunni, not Shia. This would clear the way for our Shia brothers to claim control and form an Islamic state of their own in the south. The wasteland that was once Baghdad will keep the Kurds, and even the Turks, at bay. In a country of twenty-five million, the killing of thirty-five thousand Americans is worth the death of five million Sunnis. The Americans and their allies would immediately lose all stomach for a fight. This would be the single bloodiest battle in the history of the American military since their civil war and it would be over in a flash of light! The American army has ten active divisions. This act would destroy one-fifth of that strength, and may even topple the current American administration. Think of it—thirty-five thousand American families mourning a loved one, and they do not even get a body to put in the ground," Farmad finished.

Nasballah sat back down. It was staggering. Could they really do such a thing? "What if the opposite is true? What if the Americans and their allies mobilize every ounce of their might against all that is Islamic? Including their nuclear capability. It could drive our great religion into being nothing more than a cult practiced in caves."

"You mean, as the Prophet once practiced?" Farmad said, sipping on his scotch. Western dress, forbidden alcohol, and using the prophet, Muhammad, as an example to further his argument, he stared at Nasballah. Would the old man go for it? He needed Nasballah to sell it afterward, to make the masses see it as the work and will of Allah. In the larger plan, the cleric leader of Hezbollah was a small piece, and surely expendable, but moving forward required less effort with his acquiescence. The Greater Islamic Consortium had asked his government to attempt to get Nasballah on board, and now Farmad had fulfilled their request.

"I'm not sure," Nasballah said softly.

Farmad's face froze for a moment, and then he smiled once more. "Well, I must go, but I've arranged for you to stay here, in this very building."

"I thought I might stay at the mosque in . . ." Nasballah began.

"Nonsense, you will be safest here," said Farmad opening the door and stepping into his outer office. A large man approached. "Rahim will show you to your quarters," Farmad said. Nasballah knew immediately that this was not open to discussion and that he ought to tread carefully. Rahim was clearly not employed as a bellhop.

"Very well," Nasballah said, "Perhaps I do need some rest." Nasballah even managed to smile. Farmad returned it and said, "I will see you soon, my friend."

An uneasy silence fell, and Farmad walked out. When he reached the elevators, he entered one, and inserted a small key into the panel. He turned it, and then punched in a floor selection and code number. The elevator descended, sinking below street level, and yet still downward it went. When the doors opened, a wholly different-looking hallway greeted Farmad. It was poorly lit and appeared ancient. The walls were gray brick, the floor was concrete. His footfalls echoed from every direction. A guard snapped to attention upon seeing him. Farmad waved him over to a particular cell door. The guard unlocked it and stepped back. Farmad entered.

LT Rick Sirois lay on a thin bed of straw in one corner of the cell, a cell he alone occupied.

"Are you awake, American?" Farmad asked in English.

Sirois did not move nor make a sound. Farmad walked over and stood on Sirois's ankle, pinning a steel chain between the bone and the hard floor. The pain was blinding and Sirois howled.

"Ah, I thought you might be," Farmad said, his voice friendly, sweet. Farmad lit a cigarette and exhaled slowly. "Do you know why the whole world hates America?" Farmad asked. "Do you think it is because of your foreign policy? You know, I will tell you truthfully that the world does not automatically object to an interventionist U.S. foreign policy. The world just wants that policy to be based on reality rather than slogans from mentally deficient leaders, such as 'With us or against us.' "

Farmad walked around to the wall and took another drag on his cigarette. "Your foreign policy should be based on America's true national interests rather than on the priorities of a few radical, Jewish lobby groups or American oil cartels. Iran was once a free democracy, we had an elected leader, Mossadegh. Then, because the British wanted our oil, they convinced the United States and its CIA to stage a coup d'état. We had free elections and a free press. Iranians loved Americans. And you put a savage dictator in place just because you could."

Sirois lay without moving. His head was pounding. He no longer knew if it were day or night. He had not eaten and had been given foul water to drink. He had been beaten repeatedly at random intervals, robbing him of the ability to sleep. He could feel himself breaking, and knew that soon he would answer whatever questions they asked of him. The truly frightening part of all this was that they had yet to ask him a single question since his arrival here. That is, until this man had come in and asked him rhetorical ones.

"It is exactly this type of American arrogance that led to the attacks on September eleventh," Farmad continued. "And the attacks will go on. The American administration will simply not be able to prevent every attempt indefinitely. Eventually, we will succeed again."

"And we'll come back to this part of the world and kick your asses again," Sirois said through missing teeth and cracked lips.

Farmad stepped closer and kicked the pilot in the knee. As Sirois rolled in pain, Farmad walked back to the wall and took another drag. Exhaling, he said, "Do you think that exchange can last forever?"

Sirois gasping said, "No. Eventually, we'll run out of assholes to kill."

"Ah, so you advocate genocide then. I see this in your supposed ally, in the Zionists. Why do you prop up the Israelis? Why do you support monsters? As you do the Israelis or as you did the shah until the revolution here in Iran."

Sirois croaked out, "Don't ask me, I was seven years old in 1979, you moron."

Farmad stepped forward and kicked Sirois again, and puffed once more, "I, too, was a young boy in the 1970s. I watched SAVAK, the shah's intelligence police, kill my parents."

Sirois tried to make a laughing sound, but it was a strange gurgle instead. He said, "It's ironic that SAVAK killed your parents and you grew up to work for its successor. VEVAK is just as bad, if not worse." He tried to sound amused once more, but instead began coughing.

Farmad walked over and knelt by Sirois's head. Gripping his hair, Farmad pulled his beaten face around, and looked into his one open eye. Sirois tried to raise his hands, but they were chained to his feet and the floor. They only came up to his chest.

"That is the problem with Americans. You always believe the good guy wins. What you do not realize is that every time you cross a border or an ocean, the identity of the good guy changes. Identifying the good guy is a matter of perspective. You should know, my friend, that in the Iranian story, you are the villain, and I am the good guy," Farmad said. Farmad slammed Sirois's head into the floor, and Sirois's body went limp.

Farmad rose and slowly walked out. He flicked his cigarette into one corner, and headed for the elevator.

19

Six members of the Islamic Movement of Uzbekistan waited for their prey. The newly elected president of Afghanistan, a true friend to America, as the last president had been, was visiting inside.

Each had an AK-47 and grenades as they sat on the next rooftop, eating their lunch. One among them peered over the edge of the building, watching for the president to emerge.

Outside the provincial governor's office stood four Americans. They had all served in the United States Army's Special Forces for more than twenty years, retired, and then had gone to work for DynCorp. DynCorp was contracted by the U.S. State Department to provide protection services for the previous and current presidents.

When the president finally appeared in the door, the members of the IMU scrambled to get ready. The president stepped out and was in plain view. He could be shot at any time. Still, the assassins waited. Three more American contractors came out after the president. As the president entered his armored car, they attacked. Grenades rained down on and around the car. The nearest American closed the door behind the president, and the car sped away. Grenades began going off below, and many of the Americans went down. The IMU soldiers, barely exposing themselves over the lip of the roof, opened fire on their trapped victims. Additional grenades were thrown. When the firing and the small explosions ceased, all seven of the Americans had been killed. They simply had not considered that assassins might have a target other than the president in mind.

One of the gunmen flipped open a satellite phone and placed a call. "Juma Nagami, we killed seven of them. We are coming home."

20

McCall downshifted and twisted the throttle hard. The 1300cc high-powered bike leapt forward, swerving left around the tractor-trailer. McCall shifted gears, let out some clutch, and the black-and-maroon Suzuki Hayabusa went faster still. The wind howled past her ears, clawing at her sunglasses, as her speed exceeded 110 miles per hour. Still she accelerated. She went right, crossing the path of a large truck and swooping down into the breakdown lane to get around two cars blocking both lanes. She swerved back into the fast lane in front of the honking sedans. She reached back with one hand and flipped them off. She continued to accelerate. Exceeding 140 miles per hour, she shifted into fourth gear. Aw shucks, she mused, only two more gears to go.

Even at this speed, McCall was not completely focused on the road. There was no feeling of elation, no feeling of freedom. She was angry. She was acting out. This was how a Night Stalker throws a tantrum. She was thinking of Sirois, and she was frustrated. She also hoped taking his bike out would help her connect with him, to help her know he was alive somewhere. She tried to feel him, tried to reach out to him, energetically. She wanted him to know that no matter what held them apart, she was there waiting for that day when they'd see each other again. So much left unsaid, and she was trying to say it now. But this was not a ride of sentimentality. It was an exercise in anger. She was furious that he was trapped, and worse, that she was helpless. At 160 miles per hour, the bike redlined again and she shifted into fifth, leaning low against the tank. A car pulled out into her path to pass a bus. McCall blasted between the two, exceeding the speed of the car by one hundred miles per hour. Then she heard it, a noise she had not noticed before, and realized it was her own scream of rage. She let up on the throttle, and her speed bled off. Coming down under one hundred miles per hour she felt she was creeping along. Braking gently, she slowed still to eighty miles per hour, and then sixty-five miles per hour. Up ahead, a sign, and she took the exit, turning onto Route 115 South. She knew where she was going, but she wasn't sure why she was headed there. In Hensleytown, she took a right onto Hugh Hunter Road. She headed up to Thompsonville Lane, and the motorcycle seemed to catch its breath and just purred. Up ahead, the Southgate Apartments waited. She pulled into the parking lot and coasted nearer to one particular apartment. As she approached, she saw a man and woman step out of a car, and she stopped. Her feet went to the asphalt, and she watched Jack and Cat Hartman walk into the apartment.

"What the hell?" McCall whispered. Sirois was probably dead, best-case scenario captured and tortured, and the CO was out dating? McCall gunned the engine, left a black, circular mark as she spun the bike around, and headed out for some more interstate therapy.

It had been no mean feat becoming a Night Stalker. It was not easy for a man, but at the time, it was impossible for a woman. She owed a lot to the Hartmans. When she applied to join the 160th SOAR, they were not accepting female applicants to the operational battalions. It was not the unit's fault. It was the law. She had sixteen hundred hours in a Black Hawk by then, a quarter of which was night flying, and was an instructor pilot. She had served with distinction, and even under fire, with the 10th Mountain Division. The law prohibited women from serving in combat arms positions, especially it seemed within Special Operations units. She could no more be a pilot in the 160th SOAR than she could try out for the Special Forces and become a Green Beret.

But Jack Hartman had seen her fly. He had been in the air with the Night Stalkers when she had inserted 101st troops under fire in Iraq. He had watched how, with men on her fast ropes, she had held her position when another aircraft very nearly flew head-on into her helicopter. Hartman was not sure he would have had the guts to not evade, which in turn would have surely killed some of the soldiers sliding down the ropes. She had further impressed him with her light touch. Under intense ground fire, she dropped beneath rooftop level, and from a distance and greater altitude Hartman watched as she worked her way down streets and alleyways, even flying sideways at times as if parallel parking. All this in the dark. Hartman, old-fashioned as he was, had been shocked to learn the pilot with the nerves of steel had been a woman, but then less so when he was told that she was the daughter of a near-legendary pilot named Seth McCall.

She had applied to become a Night Stalker knowing it was prohibited by law. She came to Fort Campbell and walked right into Lucas Hall on Night Stalker Way, marched into the recruiting office for the 160th SOAR, and was given a flat, "No." She was told there was nothing they could do and that her issue was with the U.S. Congress. That started things rolling. She contacted the U.S. senator from her home state of North Carolina. A tough, old broad, a Republican, and a member of the Armed Services Committee.

She called and asked for some of the senator's time. She mentioned that she was a combat veteran and the surviving daughter of a pilot killed in Desert Storm. The kind of résumé senators dare not shun. She flew to D.C. and met with the senator. The senator called the 160th SOAR. A staff officer, a major, took the call. The major actually rose to his feet while speaking to the senator.

"Yes, ma'am. Yes, Senator. No ma'am, we have nothing against women here. Yes, Senator, there are excellent female pilots. Well, ma'am, it's the law. No ma'am. Ma'am, I am not

the one to make that decision, you should talk to Colonel Al-
lan Albright. Yes, Senator, the commander of the 160th." The
major looked like he might throw up.

MAJ Jack Hartman sat in the room, waiting for his ap-
pointment, watching the staff officer sweat it out.

"No, Senator, I've never met Jeanie McCall. I'm sure she
is, ma'am." The staff major couldn't wait to meet McCall now,
though. He'd strangle her himself if given half the chance.

Hartman's ears perked up. McCall was behind this? A little
smirk came across his face. Well, if there was going to be a female Night Stalker some day, it might as well be her, he
thought. He flipped through an old magazine and the major
promised to transfer the senator to Colonel Albright's office.
He hung up the phone, exhaled loudly, and sat down. "I hate it
when the vote-chasers call." Hartman smiled sympathetically.

That night, on the phone with his wife, Cat, who had just
taken a position at the Pentagon, they discussed McCall.
"She's a terrific pilot, Cat. I think that she has the stuff to be a
Night Stalker."

"Why does the law prohibit her from joining the unit?" Cat
Hartman asked.

"Well, first of all, it's not like joining a club. We don't take
everyone who signs up, so it's not like it would be automatic,"
Jack replied.

"Okay, but why can't she apply?" Cat asked, getting impa-
tient.

"The American people simply are not ready for women to
be serving in combat roles. Combat is heavy work, it requires
physical strength that, generally, women do not have," Jack
answered.

Cat snapped back, "Oh, please. I could see if it were artillery or armor, or even infantry, but she is already doing the
hard work, as you call it. She is flying, even in combat already.
Besides, I don't necessarily buy the idea that men are physically more able than women."

"Come on, Cat. If you truly believe that, then you would

have to believe it would be fair to not have separate men's and women's events at the Olympics, just let everyone compete together. Or to have women and men try out for the same college sports teams. Even in the military, a woman gets more promotion points for doing twenty push-ups than a man gets for doing forty," Jack said.

"I don't want to solve the entire gender-equity issue with you, Jack. I just want to know; do you think she is capable enough to do what any other Night Stalker pilot does?" Cat asked.

Jack paused and then replied, "Yes, like I said, I think she has the stuff."

"Alright then," Cat said. "Will I see you this weekend? Are you still coming to Washington?"

"I'll try, hon," Jack answered. He hesitated and then, "Are you sure you want to live in D.C.?"

"Jack, how many times . . . ," Cat began.

"Okay, okay, just checking," Jack interrupted. "I'll do my best to get up there this weekend."

Little did Jack Hartman know that he had just pushed a little snowball off the top of a huge mountain. Cat Hartman, then a deputy to the Assistant SecDef for Intel Oversight, called the senator from North Carolina and they discussed CW2 Jeanie McCall's application to the 160th SOAR. Cat Hartman let the senator know that her husband was a field grade officer with the unit and he was all in favor of a female being admitted to the unit. Her husband had even said he thought McCall "had the stuff to be a Night Stalker."

The senator had her staff draw up a bill that would allow women to try out for duty as a pilot in the operational battalions of the 160th SOAR. As would be expected, MAJ Hartman received an invitation, one he really could not refuse, to testify before a hearing of the Senate Armed Services committee. He immediately called Cat.

"What did you do?" Jack asked.

"I talked to the senator. She is introducing a bill that

would allow women to apply for membership in your club," Cat answered.

"Why did you mention me? Don't you know that I have a whole lot of people looking at me sideways down here, not the least of which is the commander?" Jack demanded.

"Just tell the truth, Jack, the truth will set you free," Cat giggled.

"This isn't funny, Cat," Jack said.

"Aw, Jack, it's all just a conspiracy to get you to come to D.C. and visit your lonely wife," Cat said.

Jack shook his head and rubbed his eyes.

The bill simply would not pass through the committee as it was. Hartman went to the Capitol and testified that McCall was a fantastic pilot, but he pointed out that in every assessment phase fantastic pilots wash out. It seemed that McCall's chances at becoming a Night Stalker were dead before they even got off the ground. But then, the senator had a trick up her sleeve. She made the bill very focused and very personal. She went back to the drawing board, and her staff drafted a bill not to allow women into the 160th SOAR, but instead to create an experiment, an experiment around one woman. Jeanie McCall, and only Jeanie McCall, would be allowed to attempt to get through the assessment phase, and then four months in the Special Aviation Operations Training Company, followed by eighteen months as a copilot in an operational company. If she made it through all that, she would then be Fully Mission Qualified. At any point, she could be cut from the program. No special treatment.

The Armed Forces Committee bought it, and with the senator from North Carolina championing McCall's cause and sliding it into a relief bill for flood victims in the Midwest, it made it through the Senate, the House, and was signed by the president.

"No pressure or anything," McCall said when she heard the news. The senator was on the phone, filling in the details.

"There's plenty of pressure," the senator had replied, "and

you better kick ass. There are a lot of women who are count-ing on you."

"But these guys can wash me out and blame it on anything they want to," McCall protested.

"With an attitude like that, you are not going to get very far," the senator admonished. "The pilots and leaders of the 160th SOAR are the best. They won't let your gender get in their way. They will only insist that you are a pilot they'd trust to give the baby Jesus a ride. If you let your gender be a dis-traction, and worse yet, an excuse, then I will be sorely disap-pointed in you, missy."

"Yes, ma'am," McCall said. "Thank you for everything, Senator."

"'Bye now," the senator said. "I'll be watching."

With that, the phone call ended, and a new adventure be-gan. An adventure that had led to this. Sirois was being held and tortured, if he wasn't dead, and the people she most needed to talk to were probably tickling and giggling on a sofa.

Out on the main drag, her speed came up quickly, flashing through the gears, up to fourth and well over one hundred miles per hour. She didn't know where she was going, but she was going there fast.

21

Sirois awoke with his shirt missing and his hands tied behind his back. He pulled himself to a sitting position in the middle of a dark and dank room. He could not see anything save what illumination was seeping in beneath a door, but he could tell he was not in his cell.

The long, horizontal sliver of light was suddenly broken by what could only have been feet, and then there was the sound of a key working a lock. The door swung wide and light flooded the room. Two men walked in. One was very large with broad shoulders, a full head of black curly hair, and a moustache. The other was small, old, bent, with a receding hairline, and skin that was remarkably pale for an Iranian, or for a living human being for that matter.

The larger man walked over to a loop of chain hanging limp from the darkness above. Sirois squinted in an attempt to discern where the chain led, and the man began pulling. The chain rattled as the loose loop turned, half of the visible chain being pulled down, the other half rising into the unseen. There was a sudden tug at Sirois's hands. A searing pain ripped the remaining fog from his head as he was pulled to his feet by his bound wrists. As the large man continued to pull, Sirois was lifted to his toes. The agony in his hands, arms, and shoulders was overwhelming. Sirois could think only of that anticipated and terrible moment when his feet would be lifted

from the floor and he would swing free by the wrists tied behind his back.

The older man suddenly snarled a couple words, and the
man on the chains stopped pulling. Sirois gasped, breath he
had been holding in preparation of being picked up off the
floor. Only his toes remained in contact.

The older man had his back to Sirois, and when he turned
he was holding a ball peen hammer.

"Aw man, listen, there is no reason to use that. I don't know
anything. How about we just get a beer, huh?" Sirois said, seeing the tool in the man's crooked fingers.

The old man approached and said, *"Sayeh shoma sanguine
shoudeh."*

"What does that mean?" Sirois asked, afraid he would soon
find out. Kneeling in front of him, the old man tapped on
Sirois's right toes with the hammer, very lightly. His toes' grip
on the floor was the only thing keeping him from swinging,
and his breathing became shallow as fear welled up.

"What do you want? Do you speak English? Tell me what
you want from me?" Sirois said. The old man looked up and
Sirois met his dead gaze. Without lowering his eyes, the old
man swiftly brought the ball side of the hammer down on
Sirois's foot. His toes came off the floor and he twisted
slightly, howling in pain. He struggled to maintain his balance
and contact with the floor with his uninjured foot. Pain shot
through his shoulders as they took some of his weight in the
attempt to steady him. His left foot held fast to the stone, and
he gingerly brought his broken right toes back down. Sweat
ran down his face. He could taste the hatred. He looked down
again, and the old man was still there, looking up impassively.

"You son of a bitch, what do you want!?" Sirois screamed
at him.

The old man replied, *"Sar beh saram nagozar."*

The larger man chuckled.

"What? What does that mean?!" Sirois pleaded, but the
hammer fell again on the right foot, further smashing his broken toes. Sirois thought he might mercifully pass out, but the

blackness did not swallow him. He looked over at the large man near the chain, who stood arms folded, smiling. Sirois felt desperation washing over him. He knew that they wanted nothing from him, except some amusement. He decided they were going to kill him, and kill him slow. He resolved to speed up the process.

"Ayatollah Khomeini was a dog!" Sirois screamed, and tears ran down his face, "Islam sucks! Muhammad was a Jew!"

The larger man never stopped smiling, obviously not understanding, but the older man rose to his feet slowly and said, in English, "Ah, you have made a mistake. We were only to break your foot, but now you have said such vile things, we will have to teach you something of respect." The fact that the words were in English struck Sirois almost as hard as their meaning. The old man could have spoken to him in English all along. Instead, he had spoken only Farsi. Speaking that language once more, he turned to the smiling giant and said only a few words. The smile fell from the larger man's face and he walked over to Sirois.

The first blow robbed him of his ability to breathe. The next struck his already cracked ribs. Consciousness was fading fast. The large man lifted Sirois's head by his hair, drove a fist the size of a ham into his face, and all went black.

22

Jack Hartman watched what looked like Jeanie McCall do a doughnut in the parking lot of his apartment complex and speed away. It even looked like Sirois's bike. He made a mental note to talk to her about it, but he had no idea what he might say.

"You coming in?" Cat asked.

He followed Cat into his apartment. "Are you hungry?" Jack asked.

"Sure. Are you going to cook?" Cat asked.

"You bet, with the phone. You still like Chinese?"

"Yeah, whatever you'd like," said Cat.

Jack picked up the cordless phone and went to the kitchen. Cat turned and looked over the bookshelves. Military history. Political science. Cat smiled. "Same old Jack." She moved to the next set of shelves. There, standing without a frame, partially tucked between two books, was a photograph of the two of them in Germany. They were on the white stucco balcony of the military housing unit in Katterbach, the airfield behind them in the distance. Beyond that, rolling hills. Both were smiling, his arm around her waist, her head on his shoulder. Those were good times. She had no career then, and with her sense of ambition that had been difficult, but they were happy. It had been an exciting time to be in Europe, with the fall of the Berlin Wall and the Czechs' Velvet Revolution. They had been young and full of hope and potential. He had been less distant, warmer. Cat missed that Jack.

"I ordered General Tso's," Jack said, standing directly behind her. Cat jumped. "Sorry," he smiled.

"No, that's okay, that's sounds great," Cat replied, catching her breath.

Jack motioned for Cat to have a seat, and he joined her, but sat across the room.

"So, what's brought you all the way to Kentucky? And why such short notice? If I hadn't been home, you'd still be at the airport," Jack said.

"Well, I'm not quite that helpless," Cat said, and then shook it off. "I came to share what I can with you."

Jack shifted forward a bit in his seat.

"Lieutenant Sirois is being held in the basement prison of the VEVAK, underneath the Ministry of Information building in Tehran," Cat said, hesitating with each detail, as if carefully weighing each disclosure.

"Dammit," Jack said. "There's no way they'll let us go get him there."

"They may," Cat whispered, "because he may not be the only target in the building."

Jack looked at her for a moment, and tried to consider who else could be there that would convince the national-level players that a mission was worthwhile. Cat guessed what he was thinking and said, "It's not a person. It's the package you've been chasing around the region."

Jack was stunned. "They have that thing in the middle of the city?"

"DoD intel believes in the northeastern corner of the city, in the same building," Cat said. "CIA is pointing to a cave in the mountains between Afghanistan and Pakistan, but DoD says the intel ministry building."

Jack thought about this for a moment, and then asked, "How close are they to cutting an op order on the DoD intel?"

"Not close at all, I've heard they're leaning toward going with the CIA again," Cat sighed.

"No! Not again," Jack went to his feet. "I'm not taking my pilots on another one of their wild-goose chases. I've lost a lot of good people. I watched six of my pilots die in an instant in Tajikistan. Shot down with weapons our intel people weren't sure the IMU even had."

Cat looked at the floor. She had a card to play but wasn't convinced she should use it. "Jack, I am considering throwing the weight of my office behind making the collection and analysis of the CIA look suspect, and making the DoD intel look stronger. In fact, I might even have to throw a cloud of suspicion over the legality of the CIA's means of collection in order to make it have any weight." Jack listened intently, and Cat continued, "The problem is I have no such information. I would be misusing my office. And if I'm wrong, it could cost lives for nothing. Maybe even let a nuke slip away. I'm sure my judgment is clouded here because of Sirois, and because of you." Her eyes came up and met his. She looked vulnerable, and sad.

"Cat, we can't chase after the CIA's read on this anymore. Normally they either admit they are not sure, or they are right on. They often do magical things, and the people in the CIA work harder than anyone, but with this target, they are batting zero," Jack pleaded. "Just go with your gut on this one."

Cat stood, as well. "Jack, if I'm mistaken, I will have been a big part of why soldiers went into harm's way in the wrong place. And even if the DoD intel is correct, I will have to resign."

He stepped closer to her. "No one will come after you on this, no one would have to know you were doing anything more than your job."

"I would know, Jack. My job is all about integrity, it is the cornerstone of my mandate. I will not be able to continue in this position," Cat said.

A silence fell in the room. She had worked long and hard to get where she was. Jack had cheered, mostly from a distance, as she made her way up with sweat and elbow grease. No real political connections; just drive, effort, and talent.

"It's ironic," Cat said. "You were always Mr. By-the-book and I always competed with your job. Now you're asking me to choose you over my job and to break the rules." She smiled, but bitterly. His face fell. This hit him with much more force than she had intended. Jack felt a lot of guilt. Guilt for her feeling unfulfilled in the marriage, guilt for not being supportive or understanding enough, guilt for not realizing she was serious about leaving, and guilt for not fighting harder to get her back in the first days and weeks of separation. She was the only woman with whom he had ever truly been in love and he couldn't get out of his own way enough to make that clear to her.

"Cat," Jack said stepping closer still, "I won't pressure you. You're a big girl. Do what you have to. Thank you for sharing as much as you have." She had already crossed the line telling him what she had and Jack knew it.

"Are you trying to manipulate me, Jack?" Cat asked. "You don't think I can see right through that?"

"I'm not," Jack said. "I'm serious, I just . . ."

"Aw, that's crap, Jack, and you know it," Cat insisted. "I'm not a little girl, or even a big *girl* for that matter."

Jack grabbed her arms, "Catherine, listen to me, I am not manipulating you, I am dead serious. Thanks for what you've done already. You've already helped."

Cat stopped moving, gazed into his eyes, and the pull was physically powerful. Their faces drifted closer, lips parting slightly.

There was an incredibly loud knock at the door. They both started, their heads pulling back. Jack let her go and he walked over to the door. "Who is it?"

"Hong Kong Garden," a voice said through the door.

Cat stared at the brown, commercial-grade carpet. She felt like her parents had just caught her kissing a boy behind the garage. "How did I end up here?" she thought to herself. She hadn't even kissed him. She sat at the small table and moved an unlit scented candle to the floor to make room for the food. Jasmine. His candle was jasmine scented. She had always purchased that scent for them when they lived together, it was one of her favorites.

Jack closed the door and returned with a cardboard tray of white boxes. "Get it while it's hot," he said.

"General Tso's chicken, some rice, want some crab Rangoon?" Jack asked.

"Jack, I'll let you know what I decide when I get back to D.C., okay?" Cat said.

"Okay," said Jack. "Crab?" He smiled a sympathetic smile.

"Yes," Cat replied, "please."

He pushed a small wax-paper bag her way, and reached for a long-handled spoon to serve some of the chicken onto her plate. She did not need to be waited on. She could do it herself, wanted to at least feel in control of how large her portion was. She grabbed his hand. When her hand fell on his, he stopped and their eyes locked again. He released the spoon and pulled her to her feet. They grasped each other in a long-overdue passionate embrace, kissing deeply. He scooped her up and carried her toward his bedroom.

"What about my crab Rangoon?" she whispered.

"It'll keep," he kissed back, and the door closed behind them.

23

MAJ Ryan stood at the podium, and pilots filled the roomful of folding chairs, watching him intently.

"Night Stalkers," Ryan started, "we are going downtown."

A photo appeared on the screen behind him, an aerial shot of a major metropolitan area. There was an immediate buzz in the room.

"This is Tehran," Ryan said, and the noise ceased. The audience had been shocked silent.

"What?" one pilot asked, in spite of himself.

"The target is the Ministry of Intelligence building in Tehran," said Ryan, and he paused again to let it sink in. "We will bring D-boys and 5th Special Forces in, along with two teams of Israeli Mossad," he continued, "and the rules of engagement are liberal and broad."

"What the hell are we going after in downtown Tehran?" one pilot asked.

Ryan inhaled, about to respond, when Hartman slowly took the podium from his executive officer. "We have two objectives. The first is a low-yield nuclear weapon, the same W.M.D. we have been chasing from Lebanon to Tajikistan. Intel says it is in Tehran now," Hartman calmly said.

"They've been wrong before, sir," Arsten said, with as diplomatic a tone as he could muster.

"Well, I believe they are correct this time. And there is another objective," Hartman said. "We Night Stalkers have a second and almost equally important reason for going."

Before he could tell them, a voice spoke up from the back, "Sirois is there." A female voice. The pilots twisted in their chairs to look back and see McCall sitting, impassive.

Hartman nodded slowly. "Yes, Lieutenant Sirois is reportedly being held in a basement level. Fifth Group will seize the building and secure it while the Mossad and Delta teams sweep through it looking for the weapon and for Sirois."

The room was buzzing again.

"People, I want you to imagine Sirois in the basement of that building, almost certainly beaten and tortured. We know that he has not given up on us, he knows Night Stalkers don't quit. He is expecting us to come get him, he is convinced we will," Hartman said, scanning the faces, "and I for one am not going to let him down."

They all were intently focused on their commander. "If we do this one right, we save potentially millions of people and we get Rick back. There is no room for failure. I need you to be in this one completely, with total commitment, without apprehension. Clear?" Hartman continued.

"Clear, sir!" the room shouted back.

"Outstanding," Hartman said still stone-faced. "As we sit here, our aircraft are being packed up for the flight to Baghdad. There will be no iso this time, we leave immediately. We will set up a FARP in a desolate stretch of the Dashte Kavir desert, about two hundred miles southeast of Tehran. A place once known in April 1980 as Desert One. It was FARP for the less-than-successful attempt to free our hostages from Iranian militants. For obvious reasons, the D-boys would like to use that site again. I think they are looking for a little payback. Personally, I am, too. This will be the most dangerous mission any of you have ever flown. This will even make the Mog look tame, the difference being we should be in and out of Tehran in a fraction of the time." The Mog, or Mogadishu, was still a fresh memory for many of them, even though it was more than a decade ago. Some incredibly gifted pilots, and good people, were lost there. A comparison to that city and battle would not be made lightly.

"That's what they said about the Mog," one pilot said, a bit too loudly.

"If you don't want to go, don't go, dammit!" Hartman roared. "I don't give a damn. Stay here if you'd rather, but stay here and pack, because your days as a Night Stalker will be over. Night Stalkers don't quit and we do not leave our people behind. We will go get Sirois. I am going. Alone if I have to."

A cheer went up. Hartman lowered his voice.

"Frankly, our government and the American people are willing to lose every one of us and the ground-pounders in order to rid the world of that nuke, and I personally think it's worth it," Hartman went on. "But I'd rather get our guy back, blow the weapon, and bring as many of us home as we can. Better I die in Tehran than Sirois remains a captive one more day than absolutely necessary. They are holding a Night Stalker and I want him back."

Cheers went up from the crowd again, but McCall sat quiet. She was fuming. She just wanted to get going, get into the fight. For the first time, she was going into a mission angry.

"I'll see you in Iraq," Hartman said, and stepped down from the stage, exiting the briefing room as the pilots rose, many of them applauding.

McCall followed after him.

"Sir," McCall said. They were standing in a small office with no exterior windows.

"McCall," Hartman said turning to face her. "We'll get him back. We'll do our very . . ."

McCall snapped a forward punch at Hartman's head. He caught her fist mid-air, pulled it farther in the direction it had been traveling, and pulled the arm up behind her back. McCall sprawled across the desk.

"What the hell are you doing, McCall?" Hartman demanded.

"If you hadn't left him there in the first place, we wouldn't

have to go back now!" McCall howled, her arm pinned hard
between her shoulder blades. Normally, Hartman would never
have so much as blocked a slap from a woman, but McCall
was another matter. He had no illusions about her; she could
kick the asses of half the men in the battalion. Even now, she
fought to escape his grip, struggling on the desktop.

"Listen to me, if I had let you go after him in Tajikistan,
we'd be rescuing you and your crew, also. That is if you had
been lucky enough to survive this long. We were going to have
to go to Tehran anyway, it is where the nuke is. Now you get a
hold of yourself, McCall!" Hartman shouted. Her body went
limp. She felt tears welling up and then fought them away.

"Now, I'm willing to let this little outburst of yours go, because I know you are close to Sirois, but if you ever lose your
military bearing with me again, I will prosecute to the full ex-
tent of the UCMJ. Is that clear?" Hartman said.

McCall nodded, just barely perceptibly, and Hartman released her, backing off two steps. She popped up, turned, and
stomped out, without giving Hartman another look. She ran
right into MAJ Ryan. He stared at her, furious. She glared
back, and then her face softened. She stepped around him and
ran out.

Ryan came into Hartman's office. He was straightening
his desk.

"She's got that wild streak in her," Ryan said.

"Like her father," Hartman suggested.

"No, her father was brave and calculating. What you just
saw was what she inherited from Maggie McCall," Ryan said,
sitting down opposite the desk.

"Must have been a helluva couple," Hartman said as he
took his own seat.

"They really were, sir. You would've liked Seth McCall,"
Ryan said.

"Well, I like his daughter. If she sticks it out, she'll probably have my job someday. She'll need to cool that temper a
bit," Hartman said.

"Sir," Ryan rose, "If that were a prerequisite for the gig, you wouldn't be here either. With all due respect." Ryan smiled, and walked out.

Hartman watched him go, and grinned to himself.

24

"Hey, Sergeant, did you know the Air Force has air-conditioned tents on the other side of the airport?" PFC Rivera asked.

"Well, that's different, Rivera, you're in the military, not the Air Force," SFC Pettihorn answered. Everyone around chuckled, but they were exhausted. They were still trying to work out some way of ensuring comms would work. The latest efforts were based on an attempt to use SHF radios, hoping these frequencies would be out of reach of the jamming. The antennas, power, and reliability of signal were just a few of the issues they were facing, and in the wee hours of tomorrow morning, this mission was going to launch. With or without a solution.

"Sergeant," Specialist Stokes approached, "I still think we got to cut through the skin of the helicopter, attach the low-profile antenna. They would need line of sight and it would not reach far, but it would be better than nothing."

Pettihorn rubbed his eyes. "There's no way to get that done on every bird in time, and we're not sure it would work. Not to mention we might deadline a helicopter in the trying. I'm not telling Hartman that in trying to give him back-up comms, I broke a helicopter."

CW3 Glen Arsten strolled into the hangar then. "Who broke a helicopter?"

"No one, sir," Pettihorn said, "and I'd like to keep it that way."

"You figure something out, yet?" Arsten asked.

"I'm about ready to shoot myself," answered Rivera, who then added a quick, "sir."

"I'm starving," said Stokes, who hopped up and sat on the bench.

Arsten was carrying a flight bag and dropped it. next to Stokes, "I think I have an apple here." In the bag, there was a flight suit, gloves, a small radio, a vest, and a little, brown leather bag.

Pettihorn's face went slack. "Sir, what's that radio there?"

"That's my handheld, the Motorola, why?" Arsten said.

Pettihorn's eyes closed, as if falling into a trance. "Motorola Astro Saber III, sixteen-channel, five-watt, 480 to 530 MHz, encrypted . . ."

"Yeah," Arsten said, puzzled, "why?"

"You guys have the lapel mikes for those things?" Pettihorn persisted.

"Yeah, but I've never used it. They give us these in case we're shot down, we can talk to each other. They don't have much range. It's a cop's walkie-talkie. You mind telling me what's up?" Arsten asked.

The other commo soldiers already got it. "We'll use these. You wear the mike, sir, and use these radios as a back-up in case of jamming," Rivera said.

"If they are jamming VHF and SATCOMs, won't they jam these?" Arsten asked.

"We didn't think of them, maybe the bad guys haven't. When you were in Lebanon, the jamming only went as high as the highest frequency used by your SATCOMs, 410 MHz. These have a frequency range above that," Pettihorn said. "They don't put out a lot of juice, and you might have to relay information around, but it could give you a way to talk next time you're jammed. The battery is self-contained, the antenna is attached, capable of green comms. If they're charged up, they're ready to go."

"Alright, let's try it," Arsten said. "I'll let Lieutenant Colonel Hartman know. We'll make sure they get charged."

MAJ Ryan walked out onto the dark tarmac. A shape sat out there by itself.

"McCall, is that you?" Ryan asked.

"Yes, sir," the shape said. She was sitting on the concrete, holding her knees to her chest, watching aircraft take off in the distance.

"Hey, listen, make sure your portable Motorola is charged up. Pettihorn thinks it might work as a back-up in case of jamming," Ryan said.

McCall chuckled. "He's that desperate huh, sir?"

"I'm afraid so," Ryan sighed.

After a moment of dark quiet, McCall asked, "Sir, I'm sorry about what happened in Hartman's office back in the States. I was just frustrated."

"Any other commander, and you'd be on your way to Leavenworth right now," Ryan said, and then added, "Of course, your value as a pilot helps." He smiled.

McCall smirked, and then became serious. "Sir, do you think Sirois is alive? Do you think we'll get him back?"

"I think there's a chance," Ryan offered. "Sometimes that's all someone needs."

McCall thought for a moment and said, "It's hard talking about Sirois with the others, and no one wants to bring him up with me. They talk about him among themselves, and stop when I approach. I hate being treated like his girlfriend."

"Well, aren't you?" Ryan asked.

"That's not really the point," she said. "I spend a lot of time and effort showing these guys I am one of them, not a female Night Stalker, but a Night Stalker. I don't want someone to create a list of Night Stalkers someday and put an asterisk next to my name."

Ryan listened as McCall paused. "I'm in love with him, sir, and I'm sure I'm the only one in the unit who is, but that doesn't mean I need to be treated with kid gloves."

Ryan was suddenly uncomfortable; this was not his field of expertise, so he played the role most comfortable for him. "McCall, these men feel almost as strongly about Sirois as you do, stop trying to corner the market on worrying about him. Stop feeling sorry for yourself. It's not like you to use this as an excuse. If they are treating you differently, it must mean you are acting differently. Snap out of it." Ryan held his breath; the gamble was the only play he had.

"If you're trying to piss me off, sir, it's working," McCall said.

"Good," Ryan sighed with relief.

"I've been furious with Rick since that night," McCall went on. "He is reckless, taking unnecessary risks, just trying to be a hero, get attention. There was no reason for this. Now he's missing, has people worrying about him. We may never see him again and will always wonder what happened. I mean, people care about him, but he doesn't seem to think of those things. You can't go out there, let it all hang out, throw caution and sense to the wind when you have a wife and daughter waiting for you at home." She sobbed the last few words, and then realized she was no longer talking only about Sirois.

"McCall, listen to me," Ryan began slowly. "You know I knew your father, you know I was there that night and was in his flight. Your father was an incredibly skilled pilot. And he was always thinking about you. He carried your picture in the cockpit with him."

McCall's head was on her knees. She cried silently, and listened.

"Your father was not reckless. I have known pilots who were crazy and pilots who had guts. Your dad was all about courage, protecting his people and ground troops, and accomplishing the mission. Peterson's report said your father was out of control, and he was the sole survivor of that last run, but I knew Peterson. He was a coward, and to a coward in combat, everyone else is reckless and suicidal," Ryan said, going down on one knee beside McCall. "Your father was a brilliant pilot, careful and thoughtful, dedicated, and a hero. There are probably hundreds of little girls that would have grown up without dads if not for his sacrifice that night."

"But why my dad?" McCall sobbed. "Why did I have to trade my dad for theirs?"

"There's never an answer to that, Jeanie," Ryan said, putting his hand on her head. "But don't be hard on your dad for it. He did what he had to, and it was his time."

Ryan rose. "I know one thing, he would be very proud of you."

McCall's sobbing was quiet, controlled, but still steady. Ryan decided to let her cry, and headed back to the hangar. She lifted her head. "Sir?"

"Yeah?" he said softly.

"Thank you, sir," McCall said.

"Let's sit down over a whole bunch of beer sometime soon, and I'll tell you all about your old man," Ryan smiled. "Don't forget to charge up your Motorola." He walked off toward the hangar.

McCall wiped her eyes on her sleeve, watched another aircraft climb its way skyward, and felt the night breeze on her drying face. She looked south. Her dad had gone down somewhere out there, in that desert.

She got to her feet, spit, and said, "Talk to you later, Dad."

As she turned to follow where Ryan had gone, there was a bright flash. A crash and rumble followed, as a small fireball rolled into the sky right above the gate closest to McCall. A white van, packed with explosives and gasoline, had driven to the gate and then the explosives were detonated. The Iraqi guards at the gate were killed instantly by the blast, as was the driver of the truck.

Still, the gate had been left blown open, without guards, and with room to get around the white van. Three identical and rusting Datsun pickup trucks, white with a long red stripe running down each side, raced into the compound and onto the flight line. They spread out and each made a run at separate targets. One headed for a nearby radio tower, the next headed for the hangars, and the third went after an American gun emplacement. The third Datsun was the first one stopped. The gunner in the emplacement and his buddies, wrapped snug in a double cocoon of sandbags, had been brought to a heightened sense of urgency by the explosion and every weapon, the M240B 7.62mm machine gun as well as the two M-4 5.56mm carbines, opened fire. The first bursts went into the engine compartment, but when the truck did not so much as slow down, the three soldiers poured everything they had into the windshield. The truck turned right slightly, slowed a bit, and then lurched forward, picking up speed, and slammed into the steel fencing. The Datsun exploded. The blast ripped a long section of fence off the ground.

The men within the firing position watched open-mouthed, shocked that the small vehicle had carried so much punch. They quickly looked out to find the other two.

Other Americans had also seen the damage caused by the explosion and decided they would take no chances. As the first truck continued to accelerate toward the communications tower, a sergeant reached into the back of a nearby deuce-and-half truck and pulled a forty-inch-long cylinder from it. He tugged the transport safety pin free. Next, he snapped the shoulder stop down and, glancing behind him, threw the dark brown–green tube over his right shoulder. The Datsun was halfway to its target. He pulled the front sight cover back, and the front sight itself popped up. Pulling forward on the rear sight cover, it did the same. He set the range on the rear sight for 150 meters, his best estimate. McCall watched. With two speeding truck bombs racing across the tarmac, the sergeant stood in plain view, floodlights illuminating all of it, calmly going through steps he had trained many young soldiers to follow. He hooked his thumb under the cocking mechanism and pushed it forward, down, and then back. With his thumb once more, he pushed the trigger button. When it fired, the M136 AT-4 anti-tank weapon launched an 84mm HEAT cartridge. It blasted through the seal on one end of the launcher while its rocket propellant blew the seal off the back end. As the cartridge cleared the tube, six fins deployed to ensure it flew straight and it did just that. Functioning exactly as designed, the projectile whooshed across the space coming up to

950 feet per second and slammed into the vehicle just above the front right wheel well. A shaped-charge warhead designed to burn through fourteen inches of rolled homogenous armor detonated against the engine block in a series of events that passed in a fraction of a second. At impact, the tip of the projectile was crushed and the impact sensor activated a fuse. The piezoelectric fuse fired the electric detonator, which detonated the booster. This initiated the main charge that forced the warhead body liner into a directional gas jet that penetrated the engine block as if it were Styrofoam. Molten steel and hot gasses burned into the engine, melting and bending steel while the engine ran at nearly three thousand RPM. The kinetic energy of the engine's own parts did the rest of the job. The entire block was blown to fragments, the explosive forces blew down and lifted the front tires off the ground. The truck flipped onto its left side and slid to a stop. There was no major secondary explosion, but no one approached the vehicle. Not yet. Everyone had seen the other fireballs and no one was in a hurry to experience one firsthand.

The last remaining pickup sped directly at a hangar. Small arms fire was striking it from all sides, some rounds ricocheting, some finding purchase. Unfortunately, whether it was because no one else was quick enough or because there wasn't one readily available, nobody fired another AT-4. McCall watched the truck slam into the wall of a hangar only one building south of where Ryan had gone.

The blast lifted the hardened wall of the structure just a few inches, and then that weight fell. The hangar had been designed to prevent an outside force from flattening it, but the truck bomb had acted like a jack. The building was ratcheted up on one side a few inches and then violently dropped. The weight of the hangar and its mass, intended and designed to protect it and its contents, caused its destruction. The weight falling on a single side created an imbalance of forces and stress. The hangar fell over onto the charred remains of the truck and its driver.

Soldiers ran in every direction. Several to secure the

breaches in the gate and the fence, others to search the ruins of the hangar. The hunt was on to see if anyone had been in the building at the time it collapsed. McCall ran to the crushed hangar, the dust and debris strewn about and hanging in the air. She helped a young MP pull a twisted piece of concrete and rebar from the pile. As she moved forward to help with the next piece, she was spun around. It was Ryan.

"Are you okay?" Ryan shouted above the growing number of sirens and barked orders.

"I'm fine," McCall replied. "You, sir?"

"I'm alright," Ryan said, and released her. She turned back to the hangar wreckage and Ryan jogged over to the group approaching the truck that had not detonated.

"Sergeant! My name is Major Ryan," he shouted through the chaos. "Keep your people back! Let EOD take a look at it first! Set up a perimeter around it!"

"Yessir!" the MP sergeant shouted back, glad he did not have to clear the vehicle.

McCall pulled another piece of concrete free.

"Anybody know if anyone was in this one?" someone asked.

A flashlight suddenly came on, spotlighting a hand, not moving, but sticking up from the rubble.

"Yeah, people were in this one," another voice said. The flashlight switched off, and they went back to work. As McCall reached for the next piece, she heard a fresh wave of shouting behind her. She turned. The driver of the van, whom everyone assumed could not have survived the the AT-4 round, his face awash in blood, was out of the vehicle. He stood with his weight clearly on one foot, wobbly, with his hand raised above his head. In it, a black rectangular object, like a garage-door opener.

He was shouting in Arabic. The MPs all around had their 9mm handguns pointed at him, shouting at him to get on the ground and to drop the remote. The driver looked left and then right, showing everyone what he had in his hand and continued to yell in Arabic.

Suddenly, a man in jeans and a faded, red T-shirt with the words "Bottoms Up" written across the chest, sporting a long-handled moustache and hair just barely in regulations stepped through the line of military police and walked directly at the would-be bomber. There was a 9mm handgun in his hand leveled at the bloody man's head.

The driver blinked away blood and screamed with new intensity words that could only have been a threat in Arabic.

The man with the long-handled moustache answered in Arabic, in a calm voice, but never slowed his approach. It was a steady if not aggressive walk, closing the distance quickly. His legs moved, but his upper body seemed to float.

The driver waved the remote and shrieked one more shrill threat.

The man with the moustache said simply, *"Leh,"* and pulled the trigger. The 9mm round found its mark, striking the Arab directly beneath the nose, penetrating the lip, gums and teeth, the back of the throat, and finally severing the brain stem. The target did not have a chance to press the button, take another breath, or have his heart make one more beat. His brain had been instantly disconnected from the rest of him. He was dead on his feet, and crumpled to the ground.

MAJ David Gerlach, the man with the moustache and a member of Delta force, kicked the remote from the dead man's hand, holstered his weapon, and walked away. McCall watched him go and wondered what he felt at that moment.

Gerlach passed Ryan and said only, "Hey, did you eat? I'm hungry." Ryan didn't respond and Gerlach kept walking.

Ryan joined McCall and said, "I'm glad they're on our side."

McCall smiled a half-smile. "What makes you so sure?"

25

July 8
Launch minus 8 hours
Ministry of Intelligence and Security
Tehran, Iran

Farmad came to the cell door, slid the small peep slot open, and looked in. Into what had been total darkness shot a shaft of light, falling onto Rick Sirois, who was sitting on the floor mumbling with his eyes closed. Farmad thought the pilot might be going insane, but then he listened more closely.

"Game Five, May 24, 1986, Game Five," Sirois whispered. "Guy Carbonneau, Brian Skrudland, Mats Naslund, Claude Lemieux, Stephane Richer, Chris Chelios, Patrick Roy, Bobby Smith, what a roster . . . Naslund passes to Smith high in the slot, Smith shoots, scores!"

Farmad just stared, and Sirois went on, "Here come the Flames, about a minute left in the game, Roy sets up . . . the shot! Save! Shot! Another save! Puck comes out, shot! What an incredible save! An amazing, acrobatic save by the rookie goalie Patrick Roy to save the game and save the Stanley Cup for Montreal! And that'll do it, that's the game and the Canadiens have won the Cup!"

Sirois stopped, was silent, opened his eye slowly, and raised his broken face to squint back at Farmad. One eye was still swollen shut. His entire head was a mass of dried blood, his hair matted with it. Burns ran up and down both arms. His shirt was long gone and there were gigantic, hideous bruises across his chest. Four of the toes on his right foot were broken and blue. The Iranian returned the look and then slammed the peep hole shut, and Sirois was in the dark and alone once more.

Sirois lowered his head, "1993, Los Angeles has come to town, and Montreal is ready."

A loud clang echoed as Sirois's cell door opened. He froze as two large men walked purposefully in, grabbed him beneath the arms, and dragged him out into the hallway. He did not resist, except to hang as dead weight.

They passed Farmad, who turned and followed them into the elevator. Farmad used his key once more and they rose nearly to ground level. The door opened into an immense, underground parking garage. They pulled Sirois into the back of a tan military transport vehicle filled with armed soldiers wearing uniforms and bright green headbands. The truck, one of a small handful already lined up to drive up and out to the street, had a long bed with an arching canvas cover. The Iranian soldiers, sitting on wooden benches, stared without emotion at Sirois as he lay on the cool metal bed.

Farmad approached the back of the truck and said to Sirois, "Mumble your baseball scores now."

Sirois rolled to one elbow and said, "Hockey, asshole."

Farmad gestured to the soldier nearest Sirois, who viciously kicked Sirois in the thigh. Sirois fell back to a prone position, but did not make a sound. The kick had been pretty tame in comparison to what he'd been through.

26

In a meticulous choreography of war-birds, the 6/160th left the ground in stages, and soon the night sky was filled with aircraft. Every helicopter the unit had was up, and two additional Black Hawks joined them. The pair of Israeli helicopters, *Yanshuf* they called them, carried the two Mossad teams. On McCall's Pave Hawk, they had a team from 5th Special Forces Group. When Arroyo had asked Hill why there were no Rangers on this trip, and instead the American ground troops consisted of Delta and Special Forces, he was overheard by a weathered-looking Green Beret.

"Adults only on this ride," the Special Forces master sergeant had replied, spitting a toothpick to the dirt. Arroyo had looked at Hill and asked, "Then why do I have to go?"

It would be hours until sunrise, but they would need every minute. They would fly roughly 260 miles to the FARP, land and refuel, and then launch again for the final two hundred miles to Tehran.

McCall was just different today. She was not taking part in the normal nerve-soothing banter on the intercom. Willet was playing her role, provoking the others and then allowing himself to be their verbal punching bag, letting them loosen up.

"Hey, ma'am, why so quiet?" Arroyo asked. Hill winced.

McCall said only, "Let's do this thing."

"Hooah" replied Arroyo. "Yes, ma'am."

The swarm of helicopters flew so low that as they approached the foothills of the Zagros Mountains, which marked the Iranian border, Hill was sure they would skip off the surface at any moment.

"Coming up on Iran," Willet said through the intercom. Through the NVGs, McCall could see the fleet of airships on its way to flex some of America's muscle once more, and she swore to herself if the W.M.D. wasn't there this time, she'd go hunting for intelligence analysts when they got back.

Helicopters ahead of her began to rise, following the terrain. The Zagros Mountains loomed tall in front, and they would follow passes through them, hugging the earth.

As their helicopter crossed into Iran, and Willet pulled it into its careful climb, maintaining their position within the flock of death, McCall hit the play button on her portable CD player. Music poured into the intercom. She had never done that before. Other pilots did it all the time, but she never had. A heavy bass line kicked in as the song "Buena" by Morphine filled everyone's ears. Arroyo looked across the aircraft at Hill, who stayed focused on his gun.

Arroyo began to move with the music, and lost himself in the heavy beat. It came to a head when the music was suddenly replaced with Arroyo singing, "Buena buena buena buena, good good good!"

Hill leaned back and smacked Arroyo. The younger man fell silent.

Willet was chuckling, but McCall was not. She was a pilot possessed on this mission. It was deeply personal to her this time.

The roller coaster ride began. To Hill it felt as if the helicopter itself was riding on some fifty-foot-tall unicycle, jumping through mountain passes, plummeting into valleys, hopping over low ridges. The 5th Group guys were hooked in and many were seated back to back. They looked completely unaffected by the rising and falling of the aircraft.

The helicopter fell into a wide plane, and through his NVGs, Hill stared at the moon reflecting off some small unidentified body of water. The night rushed past once again, and Hill was soaking it up. He thought for a moment they had cleared the mountain range when the bird rose once more and they again gained altitude.

"Man, are we almost there yet?" Hill asked. It was a sign of how tense things were. For Hill, the steadfast crew chief whom everyone thought would calmly light a cigarette from the flames if his flight suit ever caught fire, the question was tantamount to panic.

As they dropped into another flat expanse, McCall's voice answered, "Yeah, FARP in sight. We are moving to the holding location to wait our turn." The helicopters would refuel without mixing aircraft types. The Little Birds would go first, and then the Pave Hawks and Black Hawks. As they moved off, Hill spotted the IR chemical lights, throwing off infrared light that could not be seen with the naked eye, from the two refueling points in the FARP.

"Switch off the HF," Willet's voice ordered. Arroyo moved to the HF radio and turned it off. The one thing no one wants at a FARP is a fire. The FARP personnel would use grounding straps and rods, a nozzle bonding wire to prevent static electricity from arcing and lighting fuel fumes, and anything else that might prevent an explosion. Especially at this site. This was the one FARP where they wanted to avoid another catastrophe, with real emphasis on not having two aircraft collide. Here at the former Desert One where, more than two decades before, a helicopter collided with a fixed-wing cargo plane. The crash was disastrous and cost the lives of D-boys and air crew who were on a mission to rescue the hostages being held at the U.S. embassy in Tehran.

This was a new rescue mission, armed with lessons learned from the previous one. This one had the added weight of a weapon that would cause destruction so massive as to render the quaint W.M.D. acronym too cute.

The Little Birds were clear and the Pave Hawks waited their turns, prearranged and oft-practiced. When it was time,

McCall flew and landed directly on her refueling point without hovering at all, trying to prevent "brownout," the primary culprit in 1980.

As soon as the helicopter touched down, like the most seasoned Indy 500 pit crew, the crew chiefs watched as the fuel specialists tanked up the aircraft. The fifty-foot hoses were detached, and the helicopter rose into the night sky, taking up another waiting position. The butterflies set in for everyone. Even the Special Forces guys were keyed up, alert, checking weapons. Hill and Arroyo double-checked their miniguns. Arroyo would have loved a test fire, but he couldn't think of a worse time or place than circling in the dark with a sky full of friendly aircraft and a giant gas station just south of the figure-eight track they were flying. After the last of the aircraft were fueled, the next stop would be Tehran. Hill contemplated this, remembering the briefing, knowing it would take barely more than an hour to get there, and then it would really hit the fan.

The last two helicopters to fuel up were the Israelis, and as the Americans cleared the refuel points, the Israeli birds came in. However, confused, they came in to the same refuel point. One slightly over the other. Hartman saw them, and jumped on his C2 radios. He was the only one that had a radio set to the Israeli frequency in addition to the American frequencies, but before he even had a chance to compromise radio silence, they collided.

"No! No!" Arroyo yelled into the intercom. Everyone watched stunned as the two helicopters fell together in a heap of twisted burning wreckage. Men on the ground were running away from the crash. Soldiers scrambled to shut down the pump, set in the middle of a triangle framed by three points. Two refueling points and a third with five fuel blivets, like giant bladders, which had been flown in by a CH-47 Chinook.

On the ground, it was every man for himself, and Hill watched them flee in the light of the flames. A bright line appeared and ran to the pump from the wreckage, and from there spread out to the other two points.

"Will the blivets go up?" Arroyo yelled to no one in particular.

A small explosion erupted from the connected blivet. They were puncture proof and self-sealing, but the fire had worked its way along the hose itself, and the flames had found a way into the blivet, which was mercifully nearly empty.

"Yup, the blivet will go up," yelled a Special Forces guy, putting a fresh wad of Copenhagen chewless tobacco in his lip.

"Dammit, this place is cursed," McCall said breathlessly over the intercom.

"Do we go to the emergency rally point?" Arroyo asked.

"Let's just head north and get this over with," Hill replied through gritted teeth.

Soldiers ran back into the light thrown by the flames below, looking for the injured and the dead. Hill watched them scrambling to pull bodies away from the fires.

Just then a Pave Hawk came through the FARP area, incredibly low, with its anti-collision lights flashing. It slowly passed over the FARP, where everyone's attention was focused, and then turned north, as if beckoning to follow. Its anti-collision lights went out as it left the firelight.

"Hartman's aircraft," guessed Willet.

"Or Ryan," said McCall. "Okay guys, hang on, we are reorienting ourselves and continuing with the mission. Let's go do this thing."

Despite McCall's attempt to fire them back up, it was gone. The momentum was gone. The crews in the other helicopters felt it, too. Watching two helicopters go down in flames before even engaging the enemy, they suddenly felt very mortal, very vulnerable. For the first time, words they so cavalierly tossed around on nearly every mission like "suicide mission," trying to sound like badasses, seemed suddenly too apt a description.

McCall sensed it. "Listen up, I need you all to reach down, grab hold, and give me everything you've got. We just need to look out for each other and do our jobs. Hooah?" McCall said.

"Hooah," they all returned. No one in the army was saying "hooah" much anymore since it started showing up in Hollywood, but nobody cared how cool or uncool they might sound at the moment.

Hill and Arroyo snugged in behind their guns and focused on what they were going to be required to do within a few minutes. There was a major street on either side of the Ministry of Intelligence building. The Night Stalkers would be inserting soldiers on those streets at the four corners of the building and the roof. It would still be nighttime, but there would be all the light of a major city. This would be about surprise and then execution.

With any luck, thought Hill, he wouldn't have to fire a shot. The Mossad teams they lost were supposed to be inserted in front of the main entrance. As soon as radio silence was broken, someone else would be instructed to insert their customers there in place of the Izzies. If the radios worked. If they didn't, this mission was going to be over quick.

"I see it," Willet's voice called over the intercom. He couldn't believe it. He was looking at sleeping Tehran. This wasn't some terror camp in the middle of the Bekaa or in some wasteland corner of the Sudan. This was Tehran, Iran's capital city.

"Roger that, Tehran dead ahead, we are on track, five minutes, get them ready, Hill," McCall ordered.

Hill nodded, although McCall couldn't see him, and he moved to the Special Forces captain. "Sir, five minutes."

The captain relayed this to the master sergeant, who held up five fingers and shouted, "Five minutes!"

LTC Hartman was in the lead bird as they entered Tehran's airspace. They were so low, he was sure his pilot would scrape satellite dishes off the roofs of the white concrete buildings below. It was time. He got on the radio. "This is Arrow 6. Arrow 33, you will insert you customers in front of the main entrance in place of the lost teams. Everyone else goes in as planned, how copy, over?" Hartman held his breath.

A blast of garbled sounds and static came back, broken snippets of voice. Jammed again. He picked up the small Mo-

torola handheld radio, switched it on, and spoke into the lapel
mike. He doubted anyone would hear him through this thing
from inside a noisy helicopter. "This is Arrow 6. Any Arrow
or Bullet elements. Please respond."

The responses were immediate. "This is Arrow 5, good
copy, over." "This is Arrow 21." "This is Arrow 42, good
copy." "This is Bullet 14."

Hartman cut them off, "Arrow 33, this is Arrow 6, you're
replacing the downed helicopters. Drop your team at the main
entrance. Please confirm, over."

"Uh, roger that, this is Arrow 33, confirmed, will comply,
over," a voice came back. It was weak, a bit choppy, but it was
there. They could communicate.

In his helicopter, MAJ Ryan grinned at Pettihorn's success.
When we get back, Ryan thought, I'm gonna kiss that commo
redneck full on the mouth.

"Target building sighted. One minute," McCall called back
to Hill, who relayed the message.

Willet pointed one block west of the target building. "You
see that? What do you think?" McCall followed his finger out
to a taller building, but instead of a satellite dish on the roof,
there was a small tower with many different types of antennas
attached to it.

"That might be something," McCall said on the intercom,
and then switching to her lapel mike, "Arrow 6, this is Arrow
42. We see an antenna that looks a lot like the one we saw in
the Bekaa. It's one block west of target building. Maybe a Little Bird could knock it down, over."

"This is Arrow 6, we didn't come here to make rocket runs
on neighboring buildings. Can you insert your customers on
that roof?" Hartman answered. She could understand what he
said, but just barely. The Motorolas were definitely just a
band-aid solution, they needed their SATCOMs. Besides, they
couldn't talk to anyone more than a mile away with the Motorolas. With SATCOMs, they could speak to anyone in the
world.

"This is Arrow 42, it'll be a tight fit. Should we proceed?" McCall asked.

There was a pause, and then Hartman: "Roger, insert customers and disable that antenna. Have them proceed on foot afterward to target building and continue with original mission. Confirm, over."

"This is Arrow 42, confirmed," McCall said. She switched back to the intercom. "Hill, there is an antenna tower on a building just west of the target building. Tell our customers that we will put them on the roof. They are to knock out that tower, and proceed to the target building from there on foot. Is that clear?"

"Clear," Hill said, and relayed the message. The captain nodded his comprehension of the new mission and passed it along. McCall's Pave Hawk broke off from the others; she slowed and descended. Turning broadside to the building, they crept in sideways slowly. The master sergeant began to gather up some of the fast rope in his arms in order to deploy it, but Hill grabbed his shirt and pointed. McCall was sliding in low enough that the Special Forces team would be able to jump out and down three feet to the roof. The tower was in the center of the roof, and there was not much room. Hill watched as the outer edge of the rotor disk inched closer to the steel tower.

"How close am I, Hill?" McCall asked calmly.

"Way close, you have maybe five feet between rotor tip and tower," said Hill.

"Can the guys jump to the roof now?" McCall asked.

Hill looked at the four-foot gap and said, "Maybe if they get a running start."

McCall inched the aircraft closer still. The distance closed another two feet, a mere yard between the spinning rotor blades and the steel that would ruin them. The gap between aircraft and building was only two feet across at this point. "Hold!" Hill called out, and the helicopter stopped.

"Go! Go! Go!" the Special Forces soldiers yelled to each other as they poured out of the Pave Hawk and onto the roof.

"They're clear!" Hill said as the last man left the helicopter, and the aircraft immediately pulled up and away from the tower and the building.

As they turned wide and 180 degrees, Arroyo saw the Special Forces team working at the base of the tower and then kicking their way through a roof door. As quickly as that, they were out of sight. As the helicopter gained altitude in a slow turn, charges at the base of the tower detonated and the structure fell over. It broke over the edge of the building, and the lion's share fell to the empty alley below.

"This is Arrow 6, radio check, over," Hartman's voice came in strong over the SATCOM.

"This is Arrow 5, good copy, five by five, over," Ryan said, more than a little relief in his voice.

Teams fast-roped down and streamed into every entrance of the Ministry of Intelligence building. One team was inserted onto the roof. The team McCall inserted could be seen sprinting from the first building, down the street, and into the other, joining the fight.

In the dark windows of the upper floors, there were occasional bursts of light from flash-bang grenades and muzzle flashes as the structure was being cleared. The building was heavily guarded and had alarm systems in place. They did not have much time. As the Special Forces team that McCall had inserted entered the immense marble lobby, they scattered in all directions joining two teams of Special Forces already engaged. Roused from their sleep, a company of Iranian Revolutionary Guards was attempting to repel the Americans. While some of their numbers had been scattered throughout the building in pairs on guard duty, the majority had been sound asleep on the ground floor. The idea that the building would be assaulted by any other than a lone crackpot with an AK-47 had frankly been unimaginable and yet here they faced three teams of Green Berets who were providing security for a team of Delta Force working on the steel door to the stairs. More than they bargained for, to be sure, but they were resisting. The Americans were taking casualties. These Iranians were not posted in the ministry building because they were inept or cowards. The Americans had run into the Iranian equivalent of U.S. embassy Marines.

From above, Ryan watched as two police cars screeched up to the front of the building. The four policemen jumped out, about to run to the ministry building, undoubtedly replying to a report of a break-in, when they all looked up. Two of the four simply sat down in the road. The air above, from what the city lights could reveal, was filled with circling helicopters. One of the police officers jumped back into his car, and the others quickly followed. Six 5th Group Special Forces men ran from the base of the building out to the police cars, rifles pointed at the Iranians. Ryan watched as the police were shoved face down and prone, their hands quickly secured with plastic zip-ties.

"This is Wolfpack, 16, Arrow 6, you there?" came a call from the ground.

Hartman answered, "This is Arrow 6, go ahead."

"This is Wolfpack, I've got a cop down here that got to his radio before we secured him. We're going have big company quick, over."

"This is Arrow 6, understood," Hartman answered and then made sure the Delta operators had heard it. "Black 6, did you copy Wolfpack?"

"Arrow, this is Black 6 actual, ah roger, I heard him and I can see him out the lobby windows," Delta Force MAJ Gerlach answered, clear sounds of a gun battle in the background.

A second team of D-boys ran down into the lobby where the three Special Forces teams were still in a pitched battle for control of the area. Just as they approached, the first Delta team hit the floor and someone yelled, "Fire in the hole!" Everyone instantly found cover. The breeching charges detonated and the immense steel door was blown off the wall, as if it had never been attached. A flash-bang grenade was tossed into the smoke caused by the explosive entry, disappearing through the doorway. At its report, both Delta teams rushed through the door and down a spiral iron staircase.

They skipped the first of the three floors beneath ground, as that was the parking garage and a Special Forces team was already clearing it. They descended farther, and blasted open the next door, locked but made of wood, with a Benelli 12-gauge shotgun brought along for exactly that purpose. They looked in to see a logistics storage area. Flash-bangs were tossed and the first team rushed in. This was where intel indicated the nuke was. The D-boys were met with a hail of gunfire. They dove for cover. The second team immediately left the first team fully engaged with the defenders of this underground warehouse. The first team fought their way inside in pairs, spreading out under covering fire among the various crates and drums. Not knowing what was stored where, none of them wanted to fire haphazardly, and they certainly did not want to use any fragmentation grenades. It would have been an easy solution normally, as the Iranian forces they faced were bunched together in a single spot. Instead, they threw six flash-bang grenades right in among the Iranians. As the grenades went off, the defenders were left staggering, holding their ears, unable to see. The Delta operators shot dead those who still held weapons, and zip-tied those who were unarmed.

The second Delta team ran down to the bottom of the stairs. The 12-gauge roared once more and they rushed in. A single guard fired a long burst and was dropped were he stood. The Delta operators fanned out and began yelling into cells.

"Lieutenant Rick Sirois, United States Army, we are here to rescue you!" the operators shouted up and down the hallways and into cells. The occupants of the cells began shouting in Farsi and Arabic. The sound was building to a roar of desperate men, the Delta operators scarcely able to hear each other.

MAJ Gerlach pulled his 9mm from his thigh and fired three rounds down the hallway. The prisoners fell silent, most cowering on their floors.

An English voice then spoke up, "Over here."

The Delta operators ran to the voice.

"Are you Lieutenant Rick Sirois?" they asked, sliding back the peep hole door. A face appeared, clearly not Sirois, an older man, gaunt.

"They took him away, maybe to Evin," the man said.

"Who are you, and who is Evin?" MAJ Gerlach demanded.

"I'm Bill McHendrick, I'm a Canadian journalist, Evin is the political prison," McHendrick gasped in a heavy Ontario accent. He was clearly not a well man.

"How do you know where they took him? How do you know who we're looking for?" Gerlach asked.

"How many six-foot-tall farm boys come through here? We passed each other in the hall one day. I heard Farmad talking to him once, also. Farmad took personal interest," McHendrick said.

"Who is Farmad?" asked another Delta op.

The old man rolled his eyes. "Aren't you guys on a tight schedule or what? Get me out of here and I'll tell you everything I know," McHendrick said. One operator pulled the key off the dead guard and three men covered him as he opened the door. It swung open and an emaciated skeleton of a man hopped into the light, on his only leg.

"Damn, he looks like Ben Gunn," the D-boy with the key said.

"No one else speaks English down here," an operator announced, approaching from the cells.

"Let's get going," Gerlach said. Two men snatched up McHendrick, carrying him as they might carry a surfboard, and the team ran up the stairs. As the approached the floor where they had left the first Delta team, those operators came out through the door.

"There's no W.M.D. here, we've been lied to again," the first man out the door said to Gerlach.

"Dammit, we're a bust, too. Sirois isn't here either," Gerlach said. "All we found was Hop-a-long."

"I am conscious, you know, I can hear you," McHendrick said, lying horizontal in the hands of the two Delta operators. His arms were folded across his chest. The Delta operators holding him couldn't believe a single person could smell so foul.

"Let's un-ass this place," Gerlach ordered, "Fight your way through the lobby and out into the street for extraction."

The men ran up the next two flights of stairs, past the garage floor, and up into the lobby area. The Special Forces teams had two or three Iranian soldiers pinned down. There was not much fighting to be done.

"Arrow 6, Arrow 6, this is Black 6 actual," Gerlach radioed Hartman. "We are coming out, no joy, I say again, no joy. Neither the target nor your man is here."

Another voice suddenly cut in, "Black 6, Arrow 6, this is Wolfpack 15, we've got a guy we bagged on the third floor." It was a captain from 5th Group. "He isn't a local. Says he is Hezbollah and wants to make a deal."

"Wolfpack 15, this is Black 6, bring him with. Arrow 6, pick us up, over," Gerlach said.

"Roger that, all understood," Hartman said.

"Sorry about your man Arrow 6, Black 6 out," Gerlach said, and then to everyone in the lobby, "Let's go! We need an extraction zone set up in the street out front! Set up security now, move!"

"All Arrow and Bullet elements, customers ready for extraction. There is no joy. No target and Bullet 13 was not here. Let's get these guys out of here. The sun is about to rise," Hartman called. The horizon was a thin line of red from the approaching dawn.

McCall could not believe what she had heard. Sirois wasn't here? Where the hell was he? She had set herself to either learn he was dead or to see him alive again, but to hear that he is still simply missing . . .

"This is Bullet 9, we've got company. I have two BMT-2's coming up the street, looks like the 30mm cannon on these, sure to be bad guys in the back," squawked the radio.

Hartman looked down and saw the Special Forces and

Delta guys forming a long oval perimeter in the street, and looked off toward where Bullet 9 was circling. "Bullet 9, this is Arrow 6, are you able to quickly engage the BMTs?"

"Roger that, want me to burn 'em?" Bullet 9 replied.

"Do it, execute, with haste," Hartman said.

"On the way," Bullet 9 replied and McCall watched as the helicopter seemed to stop in place as it pivoted and leaned into a high-speed run down the middle of the street. The BMTs saw him, too, and stopped. Their guns elevated and spewed great gouts of flame as two streams of lead flew up at the attacking helicopter. Bullet 9 opened up with the cannon and let his rockets fly. They churned up the street and asphalt flew into the air. Massive bullets came up all around and through the small helicopter as it dove, spitting rocket after rocket. Bullet 9 disappeared into the cloud of smoke created around the two vehicles.

Everyone who was watching held their breath until the AH-6J streaked up into the brightening sky on the other side of the smoke. As the cloud dissipated, the two ruined BMTs were revealed, punctuated by Bullet 9's rebel yell over the radio, "Woooooooyaaah!"

Hartman came over the radio, "Nice shooting, Reece. All Arrow elements, get those men out of there."

The Pave Hawks began swooping down, under small-arms fire from Revolutionary Guard and, two at a time, picking up full loads of Delta and Special Forces. McHendrick went on Ryan's aircraft. Cooper pulled the one-legged man onto the helicopter, staring at where the missing leg should be.

McHendrick snapped his fingers in front of Cooper's face, "Yeah, I noticed it was missing, too. Can we go now?"

"Sorry, you just look like . . . ," Cooper began.

"Ben Gunn?" McHendrick volunteered. "Well, if my memory of *Treasure Island* serves, he actually had two legs."

Cooper blinked and said, "I've never seen Treasure Island."

McHendrick sat stunned as Cooper returned to his gun. The old man turned to a Special Forces soldier coming into the helicopter. "The kid says he's never seen Treasure Island. What's the matter with American public education these days?" Bullets ricocheted off the cargo door of the aircraft, and the battle-tested Green Beret ducked instinctively but McHendrick continued, "I mean, why is it the average Canadian kid knows that George Washington was the first president of the United States, but the average American kid can't name the first prime minister of Canada?"

The Special Forces sergeant leaned forward and said, "I think it has something to do with the importance of the info there, pappy." More rounds impacted with the helicopter, throwing sparks. "Who really cares who the first governor of the fifty-first state was?"

McHendrick locked eyes with the Special Forces soldier for a moment and decided he wasn't really still sure if he was the craziest person on the aircraft, "Oh, okay, I was just wondering."

Nasballah went on Hartman's helicopter. McCall picked up MAJ Gerlach and the second Delta team.

"This is Arrow 6, we're headed southeast, they've set up a new FARP just this side of Qom, stay together, stay low, and stay fast, over."

The 6/160th raced across the ground, putting Tehran behind them. It was a foregone conclusion that the entire Iranian military, including its air force, would be looking for them. The only way they were getting home was some hard flying and a lot of luck.

As the sun broke daytime wide open, McHendrick abruptly began sobbing in Ryan's helicopter, sitting in the middle of a Special Forces team, choking down MRE crackers, with a blanket draped over his skinny frame.

Nasballah sat and rocked in Hartman's aircraft, praying or terrified or both. Hartman didn't really care. He knew who he had and, if not for his intel value, Hartman would have tossed him out at altitude and speed. The Hez cowards had killed Americans, including the Marines who went to try and bring peace to Lebanon, a country broken by war and a country Hez claimed they protected. More harm had befallen and surely would come to Lebanon as a result of Hezbollah's existence than for any other reason, including Zionism.

When the FARP was sighted, Hartman called Gerlach on the radio, "Black 6, Black 6, this is Arrow 6, I need an interrogator." And then switching to the air net, "Arrow 42, you will follow me and land east of the FARP. We're going to have a talk with the good Sayyed Nasballah."

"Roger that," Gerlach answered.

"On the way," said McCall.

Arsten landed Hartman's aircraft nearly a kilometer from the FARP. The sky was a mass of helicopters waiting their turns for fuel. McCall landed a hundred meters away. Gerlach jumped down and strode very purposefully toward Hartman, who yanked Nasballah off the Pave Hawk and down into the dirt. Hartman pulled Nasballah to his feet, and half-dragged him toward the approaching Delta operator. Nasballah stopped and fell backward.

Gerlach pulled his 9mm handgun from his thigh holster as Nasballah began to crab walk backwards, sure the black-clad commando was going to kill him. The Delta Force major walked right onto Nasballah, stomping on the man's chest, pinning him to the ground. Gerlach drove the 9mm into Nasballah's forehead, pressing the back of his black turban against the dirt. Nasballah whimpered.

"Where's the nuke?" Gerlach shouted.

Nasballah babbled in broken English, "No good understand you!" Then, the head of what the American State Department referred to as the A-team of terrorist groups, wet himself.

In Arabic, Gerlach shouted once more, *"Where is the nuclear weapon?"*

Nasballah froze. It was an interrogation, not an execution. They needed him. Nasballah was a survivor and had been in more than a few tight spots. *"Promise to release me and I will tell you."*

Gerlach stepped back, lifting his foot off Nasballah, who

rose to his elbows and said in Arabic, *"Now, that is better. I knew you could be reasonable, I . . . "*

Everyone recoiled from the sound of the gunshot, and Nasballah began screeching. Gerlach had put a round clean through the top of the fat sayyed's foot. Blood ran out onto the sand.

McHendrick, in Ryan's aircraft, looked down from the circling helicopter. It was clearly a violent interrogation. He fell over into a fetal position, closed his eyes, and lay silent.

McCall had not understood any of the Arabic, but it seemed that they were sure to make some progress with Gerlach leading the interrogation. At the very least, all the frustration had left McCall more than a little bloodthirsty and she almost hoped the Hezbollah leader would continue to resist the questioning.

Gerlach stepped back onto Nasballah's chest, pushed the handgun into his forehead once more, and asked in Arabic again, *"Where is the nuclear weapon?"*

"I will never tell you," Nasballah hissed.

Gerlach calmly stepped back again, aiming at the other foot, and Nasballah screamed, "Wait!" In English this time.

"Yes?" Gerlach asked.

"There is a convoy carrying the nuclear weapon to Baghdad, they left hours ago," Nasballah said, speaking in Arabic again.

"Why Baghdad?" Gerlach asked.

"What's he saying?" McCall shouted.

Hartman waved her down.

Nasballah tried to consider his options, and Gerlach reminded him of how few they were by aiming the handgun at Nasballah's knee.

"They plan to detonate the device in Baghdad to kill the occupiers," Nasballah said.

"He's says there's a convoy carrying the nuke to Baghdad where they are going to use it against the U.S. ground forces occupying the city," Gerlach said to Hartman, and then in Arabic to Nasballah, *"Do you think we are stupid? There are millions of good Iraqi Muslims in Baghdad."*

"Farmad thinks this is a fair exchange! I am not lying to you, look for the convoy!" Nasballah said.

That name again, Farmad, thought Gerlach. He set his jaw, stepped back and aimed at Nasballah's groin. The man folded into a ball, screaming, *"No, I am telling you the truth!"*

Gerlach holstered his weapon and turned to Hartman. "It may not be true, but I think this dumb-ass believes it." Gerlach nodded to couple of his men, who hauled Nasballah back to Hartman's helicopter and began treating his perforated foot.

Hartman jogged with Gerlach and McCall to the other side of his helicopter and pulled down a map board. "There are two major routes from Tehran to Baghdad," he said tracing roads on the map. "We'll break into two search teams. Team Alpha will take the more northerly route, through Hamadan, to Bahktaran to Baghdad. I'll go with them. Major Ryan will take Team Bravo and go to Qom, to Arak, through the Zagros pass we came through before, to Baghdad. There are other smaller routes, but we'll bet on these. Understood? We find it, we take out the convoy, and your Delta guys destroy the nuke. Split your guys between the two flights," Hartman said.

"You got it," and Gerlach was off at a sprint.

"McCall, Arsten, let's fuel up the aircraft and get going. McCall, go with Team Bravo," Hartman said.

"Yes, sir," McCall said. Arsten climbed aboard and started the engine. Hartman climbed into his seat and radioed MAJ Ryan to fill him in on what the plan was. McCall ran around to the other side of Hartman's Pave Hawk where the Delta medic was just finishing up wrapping Nasballah's foot. McCall pulled her helmet from her head, revealing her long hair tightly tied back, and approached Nasballah.

"Where is the American pilot?" McCall asked him in English.

"My English bad," he shrugged, wincing.

McCall pulled the medic's hands away from Nasballah's foot, and slammed her helmet down on the spot where she best-guessed the bullet hole would be. He shrieked in pain.

"What the hell?" the medic said.

She raised her helmet again, and Nasballah held a hand outstretched. "Wait! I not know where is your pilot! Maybe convoy. Not know." McCall turned and walked away, pulling her helmet back on. Nasballah fell backward, lying on the Pave Hawk's floor.

"Hold on, Rick," McCall whispered as she broke into a run to her aircraft.

27

"This is not a drill. All American military personnel are to proceed with all possible speed out of Baghdad. Possible W.M.D. on the way," the orders came over the radio at 1st Armored Division's headquarters.

COL Ken Aksander was the 1st Armored Division's G-2 or chief intelligence officer and it was 1st AD that held the Baghdad Area of Operations. COL Aksander couldn't believe what he was hearing. It had to be a nuke. If it were a chemical strike, they would don their protective gear, wait it out, and then decontaminate. In a chemical strike there would be more casualties from trying to get away rather than hunkering down and riding it out. A nuke was on the way, but how? What was the method of delivery? If in the air, it might be shot down, but if it was in the air already, why evacuate? It must be coming on the ground. If on the ground, should they send 1/1 Cav out to meet it? Even if it meant the weapon would be detonated, wouldn't it be better to stop it out in the border mountains than to let it reach Baghdad? They must be betting it will be destroyed before it gets here, but they are trying to get as many Americans out of Baghdad as possible, just in case.

Aksander stood up and walked outside. Soldiers and vehicles were moving in every direction. Aircraft of all types were lifting off. He looked out at the chaos and decided that most of them would not make it out of the city anytime soon. The few highways leading out of the capital were almost sure to be clogged already. He looked off to his left, through the tall chain-link fence. The "fans," as the men called them, were there. Dozens of Iraqi children who sat out there and watched the American military at work. They particularly liked the Chinook helicopters, with their dual rotors. Now with the flurry of excitement, many of them were on their feet. One young girl with a baby sitting on her out-thrust hip bit on one fingernail, not sure what to do. The road she would have walked home on was filled with military trucks, driving away as if madmen were behind the wheels. Aksander walked that way, and passed through the gate, dodging a couple of the trucks himself as they honked at him. He coolly strolled over to the middle of the pack of children, the oldest perhaps twelve years old, and sat down. The children could not tell his rank, or what his position was, but he was older than many of the soldiers, and was so calm that they gravitated to him. They sat all around Aksander, pressing in on him from every side.

There was no way everyone could get out of Baghdad, and although the division's G-2 could certainly have hopped on any of the 4th brigade's helicopters, he was not going to abandon seventeen thousand American soldiers, or even these kids for that matter, in the face of what may well be the end of Baghdad.

No, Aksander thought, come what may I'll stay right here. He smiled at the kids, who had been waiting for some sort of sign that everything would be okay and then returned his smile. The colonel removed his hat in the Iraqi heat and dropped it on the head of the girl holding the baby. With any luck, in a few hours, he'd be putting it back on and these kids would be walking home.

28

The sun was beginning to warm the canvas and the soldiers sitting beneath it in the back of the five-ton truck. Sirois sat on the steel bed still in serious pain. He was also confused. He had been sure they were taking him out to shoot him, but they had driven through the night. Where were they going? He could tell by the morning sun and shadows cast that they were headed roughly west. Where to?

He saw it as it passed through his view out the back. Sirois was shocked. He leaned forward to see if he might catch another glimpse, and a second one passed. HINDs. Mi-25D HIND-D helicopters. With Iranian markings. The Iranians aren't supposed to have HINDs. At best, they were thought to have old, American-built AH-1 Cobras, shot up and repaired by Iranian engineers. The Mi-25D HIND-D was a serious helicopter: nearly seventy feet long, heavily armored, and a top speed of over two hundred miles per hour. It carried a 12.7mm Gatling gun mounted under its nose, rocket pods, and 23mm gun pods. It had all the firepower of an American Apache and yet could carry a contingent of troops like a Pave Hawk. In some corners the fearsome helicopters are referred to as "flying tanks." To American soldiers fighting the Cold War in Europe and elsewhere, the distinct silhouette of a HIND-D made them shudder. The aircraft would have won the war in Afghanistan for the Soviets if the CIA had not supplied the mujahideen with countless Stinger missile systems. It, in short, was the most feared helicopter flying, as it had been for twenty-five years.

Sirois saw the pair fly by again. They were flying air cover for the convoy. Why and where would the Iranians send him in a truck, guarded by HIND-Ds? They would amount to an Iranian secret weapon. Why risk our satellites spotting them? What was going on?

The truck slowed, almost stopped, and then picked up speed again. They passed another truck, of the same size and type, pulled over on the side of the road. A driver was just climbing in. Driver fatigue, a fresh driver probably, thought Sirois, but not only do we have air protection, I am in a convoy.

It's not all for me, Sirois decided. Someone or something in this convoy is more important than I am . . . I'm just along for the ride.

29

"All elements, stay low," Hartman called. "I know it's tempting to climb and take a look over the next ridge, but be patient, we will fly the entire road back to Baghdad. We'll find them."

"Arrow 6, this is Bullet 9, we are coming up on Hamadan," Reece said. The Bullet elements were leading the way, and they were approaching a city of 400,000.

"This is Arrow 6, follow the main road right through the city, stay at rooftop level. By the time the citizens decide to be worried, we'll be gone," Hartman replied.

As they approached, the skyline ahead was that of a city the size of Tucson, Arizona. "This is insane," said Hartman to himself, and then over the radio, "Keep your speed up and keep searching the highway beneath. They have considerable anti-aircraft capability here, and I'm sure Tehran has everyone on their toes by now. We want to zip through before they figure out we're the ones they should shoot at. Whatever happens, do not hang around and engage anything. We're blasting through Hamadan."

A series of "rogers" came back to Hartman.

Below, in the city streets, the residents all looked up at once as air-raid sirens began wailing and rooftop anti-aircraft guns began firing. They had not heard anything like this since the war with Iraq in the 1980s, and many of the young people had no memory of that dark time. The populace scattered as

waves of black American helicopters dashed by over their
heads.

"Holy . . . hang on, sir!" Arsten said into the intercom as
rounds crisscrossed through the sky. Bullets pinged off the
open cargo door; Hartman flinched and leaned forward, as if
ducking.

"Get us out of here, Glen," Hartman said into the intercom.

"Yessir, doing my best," Arsten replied.

"All Arrow elements, push through the city, push through,
do not engage," Hartman called. Then, as if punched in a bar
fight, his head whipped around, and a cloud of blood sprayed
into the rushing air. He growled in pain, clutching his face
with both hands. A Delta medic, one of four operators riding
with Hartman and Nasballah in the back of the Pave Hawk,
came over to Hartman and pulled his hands down. The large
anti-aircraft round had come through, grazing Hartman's right
cheek, carving a deep gash from the corner of his nose back to
near his ear. Blood rushed down his face. The radio was alive
with pilots screaming that they were shot, or that a crew member was wounded or dead, or that their helicopter was taking
dozens of hits. It seemed Team Alpha would never make it out
the other side of the city.

Another round popped by Hartman's head as the medic
bandaged the wound. "This will need a lot of stitches, you
want something for the pain?" the medic asked.

Hartman waved him off. "I need to be able to function."

"When you start really feeling that, come find me," the
medic shouted. He looked over his shoulder, and turned back
to Hartman. When he inhaled as if to speak again, yet another
round came in, whizzed past Hartman's face, and removed
most of the medic's head, spraying Nasballah with blood and
brain matter.

Nasballah sat stunned and Hartman cursed and bellowed,
"Dammit! Get us out of here!" Another Delta operator moved
to check his teammate, but knew he was dead.

• • •

"This is Bullet 9, I am clear of Hamadan!" Reece called, indicating a light at the end of the tunnel.

Hartman replied, "As we leave the city, stay low, follow the road, let's find the bastards in that convoy."

"Arrow 6, this is Bullet 11, I'm shot, sir, and my copilot is dead. My aircraft is all shot up," a voice came back, sounding more confused than scared.

"Bullet 11, we're all shot, can you make it?" Hartman replied.

"This is Bullet 11, I don't know if I can make it, I think so," the voice said.

"Bullet 11, just focus on the mission; put it down if you have to, but work through the pain if you can. Remember, Night Stalkers don't quit." Hartman said. They put a mile between them and Hamadan, and Hartman watched as Bullet 11 caught up with his bird, passing it on the left. Hartman managed a smile through the building pain and gave the pilot a thumbs-up. The Little Bird then suddenly tumbled to earth and exploded beneath them.

"Arrow 6, we've lost Bullet 11!"

"This is Arrow 6 . . . continue with the mission. The next thing I want to hear is, 'We found them' or 'I see Bakhtaran.' Arrow 6, out," Hartman said.

30

July 9
Team Bravo
Led by MAJ Ryan
Searching southerly route

"Coming up on Arak," called McCall.

"Roger, Arrow 42, stay on course, don't lose sight of the highway. All elements, follow Arrow 42 across the city, I want all possible speed. We'll pass nowhere near the petrochemical plant and that is where they have most of their AAA. Bullet elements, keep up as best you can, see you on the other side of Arak," Ryan said.

McCall saw a normal-looking city at rush hour, and then she saw something more. Anti-aircraft guns opened up from buildings up ahead.

"ZSU-23s on those two towers, south side of the highway," McCall radioed.

Ryan saw them and answered, "All elements, fly beneath the level of those two rooftops. I say again, we're going to fly down this road so low, those guns won't get an angle on us. It's a straight shot. Let's open them up, fly fast and straight, and don't hit anything."

The Pave Hawks and Little Birds dove for the deck. They flew down the main street of Arak at barely twenty feet and at 150 miles per hour. One AH-6 picked up a bit of altitude to avoid hitting a large lorry. Cars collided beneath them as they passed; terrified drivers panicking. One of the ZSU-23 guns fired a long burst in desperation, trying to get the barrel down low enough, but could not. The large rounds tore across a distant office building.

"High cable!" McCall warned.

The helicopters, like an insane tide, rose and fell over the streetlight power line and continued on. The shocked residents of Arak looked down on the helicopters from as low as the fifth floor in some buildings. They stood hands and faces pressed against glass, open-mouthed.

31

July 9
Team Alpha
Led by LTC Hartman
Searching northerly route

"Coming up on Bakhtaran," Bullet 9 called, dread in his voice.

"I don't know if my bird can stand up to that again," called a voice.

"Mine either," called another pilot.

Hartman heard MAJ Ryan's voice come in on the other frequency, "Arrow 6, this is Arrow 5, we've got them! We've found the convoy! Fifty miles west of Arak!"

"Arrow 5, this is Arrow 6, understood, take them out, we're on our way," Hartman answered.

"This is Arrow 5, will comply. We . . . what the hell?"

Silence.

"Arrow 5, this is 6, come in," Hartman said, focusing on the floor.

"This is 5, we're being engaged by HIND-Ds! Absolute confirmation, Mike-India-Two-Five, HIND-Ds, over!" Ryan exclaimed.

"This is 6, understood, do what you can, we are best speed to your location," Hartman said, and then to Team Alpha, "Team Bravo has located the convoy, fifty miles west of Arak. They are engaged with multiple HIND-Deltas. We are turning south to support them. All elements, make best possible speed. Bullet elements, stay together. Team Bravo needs our help. Let's do it," Hartman said.

Bullet 9 peeled off to the left and called, "That's okay, I didn't want to see Bakhtaran anyway."

No one laughed, but everyone felt the same relief. Still, Hartman thought as he pressed his hand against the pressure bandage on his face saturating with blood, this might be a case of flying out of the frying pan and into the fire. If they have HINDs, what other surprises might they have?

32

"This is 5, we're being engaged by HIND-Ds! Absolute confirmation, Mike-India-Two-Five, HIND-Ds, over!" Ryan shouted into the radio.

"This is 6, understood, do what you can, we are best speed to your location," Hartman replied. He was promising Team Alpha was on their way, but would it be soon enough?

"Arrow 5, this is Arrow 42, be advised we have a ZSU-23-4 in the convoy," McCall radioed.

"This is Arrow 5, roger that, I see it, all elements be advised there is a ZSU in the convoy," Ryan emphasized.

The ZSU-23-4 was a lightly armored vehicle whose only purpose in life is to shoot down aircraft with a four-barreled 23mm cannon. The convoy pulled off the road on alternating sides. The ZSU's deadly gun came alive, burping huge bursts of deadly lead into the bright sky, trying to tear one of the Night Stalker helicopters to shreds. Men jumped down from the backs of two of the trucks, fanning out. Each group carried AK-47s and RPGs. The latter streaked skyward. And, of course, the HINDs were hunting the Night Stalkers, as well. The radios, so often recently jammed and ineffective, were jammed with overlapping intense calls from pilots fighting for their lives. This was a fight to the death. Having caught the convoy, they could not let it go at any cost. Here they would have to make a stand. Ten helicopters, five AH-6s and five

Pave Hawks, of the 6/160th SOAR against two HIND-Ds, a ZSU, and two squads of infantry guarding a nuke.

"Breaking left!"

"Breaking right!"

The sky was filling with rockets leaving smoke trails and their exploding proximity charges. Ryan slalomed through the unguided explosive projectiles, flying for everything he was worth. The ZSU was blasting away at the target-rich environment. The Pave Hawks and Little Birds flashed around in every direction trying to avoid the fire from the ground, get a good angle of attack on the HINDs, and not hit any of the mountains or aircraft around them.

"This is Arrow 33, I've got a HIND on me, someone get him off!" a Pave Hawk pilot's voice came on the radio.

"I'm coming around, John, hold on," was the answer.

As the HIND-D raced after the Pave Hawk, both helicopters at full throttle, it was clear that the HIND was closing the gap. The Little Bird attempting to help would never catch the two faster aircraft. "Arrow 33, this is Bullet 40, John, come due south, one-eight-zero, and give me a chance to cut this guy off."

"On the way! Breaking left!" Arrow 33 answered. The radio was an incessant source of forceful voices, fearful and intense; adrenaline-charged chatter filled their ears.

Arrow 33's aircraft made an incredibly sharp turn for a Pave Hawk at that speed. McCall wasn't sure the rotor blades would stay on the helicopter as she watched it pull itself around and upright. She cut off the angle also, intent on helping Arrow 33 escape.

"Hey, Hill, feel like shooting at a HIND today? Going to be big and ripe off your side in a few seconds, be ready," McCall said into the intercom.

"I'm ready now, ma'am," Hill replied.

The HIND, more powerful but much heavier, turned wide and followed. Bullet 40 came down on the HIND, ambushing it perfectly. His guns blazed, he raked the aircraft from left to right, passing overhead. The rounds threw up sparks and small pieces of debris, but the HIND was still flying. It peeled off from pursuing Arrow 33, however, and banked hard left. It was higher than McCall, but her aircraft was going to cross its path at point-blank range.

"Shit!" McCall spat, and banked hard right to avoid passing directly in front of its turret cannon. The two helicopters passed within forty feet of each other, on Arroyo's side instead of Hill's.

"Arroyo!" McCall shouted.

More out of being startled than ready, Arroyo's minigun sprayed the enemy helicopter, the rounds impacting all along the bottom of the HIND's left side.

"Damn!" was all Arroyo gasped.

Both aircraft straightened their courses. McCall then executed a climbing right turn, pulling the cyclic right, pulling up on the collective, increasing throttle, and giving it just a bit of right pedal. The HIND floated right into Hill's sights. Hill not only aimed at the big bird of prey, he was so close he aimed at the HIND's door gunner. His opposite must have sensed this, because the HIND's door gun erupted with muzzle flash. It was a duel of door gunners, and the tough street kid from the Southside of Chicago was determined to win. Rounds pinged off the metal all around him, and were passing through the Pave Hawk's two open cargo doors. They popped past his ears. Everyone in the back of the helicopter went down praying or cursing or both. Arroyo was screaming into the intercom, "Get him! Get him! Get him!"

Hill was so focused, he felt like he was flying with his gun through open space. Just him and his gun, and the other guy and his gun. He released the trigger, and looked across at the black glass bubble covering the face of his opposite. Hill squinted and fired a very short burst, and the HIND's door gunner was blown off his position. Body parts flew. McCall dove suddenly to avoid an RPG and Hill snapped back, gripping a handhold to stay in the helicopter.

"Did you get him?" Arroyo breathed.

"Yeah, I got him," Hill replied.

The HIND had lost its door gunner, but was still incredibly lethal. It wheeled right. A Little Bird was making a run on the ZSU, and the HIND fell in behind.

"Bullet 40, break off, the HIND is right on your tail!"

The AH-6 pilot fired a stream of rockets at the ZSU, and it in turn ferociously shot at the small aircraft with its guns. The rockets missed their mark and Bullet 40 climbed, but rose right into the turret-gun sights of the HIND. There was a loud report, and the AH-6 folded where the tail met the fuselage. Tumbling in flames, Bullet 40 slammed into a granite cliff face.

"Dammit! All Bullet elements, concentrate all rockets on the HINDs," Ryan yelled into the radio. If only they had mounted Stinger anti-aircraft missiles on a few of the Little Birds, this might have been over by now.

"This is Bullet 23, roger that," a call came back. There were only four Little Birds still in the air with Team Bravo, "Bullet 19, Bullet 31, take the southern HIND. Bullet 22, you're with me. Let's knock these things down," Bullet 23 said.

"Bullet 22, I've got your HIND right here, he's putting holes in my helicopter," Arrow 23 called. Smoke began trailing from the Pave Hawk.

"Arrow 23, this is Arrow 42, you're the one who looks like a skywriter this time, you're smoking. You holding together?" McCall radioed.

"I'd be a lot better if someone got this guy off me," replied Arrow 23.

"Arrow 23, come right to two-seven-zero, Bullet 22, get on my wing, let's make this count!" Bullet 23 said.

"Roger!" Arrow 23 called back. "I've just lost a crew chief!" The Pave Hawk turned and dropped its nose, running hard on the requested heading. The HIND pursued. The Little Birds cut off the angle, one flying just ahead and to the right of the other. All four aircraft seemed to be on a collision course.

"Arrow 23, on my command, you flare that aircraft. I want you to stop dead in the air, copy?" Bullet 23 said.

"Roger that. I've got pretty strong vibration in my pedals, she won't hold together for much longer," Arrow 23 said.

The two pairs of aircraft converged, each set moving over one hundred miles per hour. With the eye of an NFL-Hall-of-Fame receiver, Bullet 23 lined up the catch, and yelled into his radio, "Arrow 23, now, flare!"

The Pave Hawk's nose rose nearly straight up, and the aircraft lost all forward airspeed. The heavy HIND tried to pull the same maneuver, nearly colliding with Arrow 23, but slid past. Arrow 23 reversed course, 180 degrees, and as the HIND turned, it was, for all intents and purposes, a big, fat, stationary target. Both AH-6s let loose their salvos and it rained 2.75-inch rockets. The HIND was buried in high explosives, nearly all of which struck the rotor disk and rotor head. The entire rotor system tore itself apart, and the once proud aircraft became nothing more than eighteen thousand pounds of falling debris.

"Awright!" shouted Bullet 22.

"Splash one!" answered Bullet 23.

"Excellent, well done, well done!" MAJ Ryan shouted.

McCall made a low and fast run across the deck, allowing Hill to blast away at the RPG-toting infantry. The ZSU couldn't track her helicopter quickly enough, and two of the men went down. The remaining infantry ran to their trucks, climbing in. The vehicles scrambled back onto the road and sped off.

"Arrow 42, Arrow 23, the convoy is going to disappear through that mountain pass. Disable the vehicles immediately, over," Ryan ordered.

"This is Arrow 42, roger, over," McCall replied.

The two Pave Hawks swooped down to catch the three vehicles, Arrow 23 trailing smoke badly. The Iranians released the canvas from two of the trucks and began firing their assault weapons at the approaching Pave Hawks. McCall dove headlong on the last truck. Rounds ricocheted off the metal around her. A round cracked the windscreen. "Truck's going to be on your side Arroyo, take it out," McCall said on the intercom.

"Hooah," Arroyo said.

They came alongside the truck, and McCall looked into the

back. Among the Iranians, she saw him. Rick Sirois. Sirois had looked up, and then realizing what was coming, had thrown himself against the bed.

"I see Sirois in the back of the last truck!" McCall shouted over the radio.

"Disable the vehicle," Ryan said flatly. He knew Sirois could be killed, but the convoy could not be allowed to escape.

"Roger," McCall replied, and then on the intercom, "Arroyo, Lieutenant Sirois is in the back of that truck. Think you can take it out without strafing the entire vehicle?"

"Just get me to the engine block, ma'am," Arroyo said through gritted teeth. Rounds were sparking off his door as they came alongside. In the truck, Sirois rolled and stomped his feet into the backs of the knees of the nearest rifleman. His legs buckled and he fell. The other Iranians turned to see what had happened and one butt-stroked Sirois with his weapon. Sirois clutched his head with both hands and rolled onto his side, but his act bought Arroyo a second, maybe two, just the time he needed to carefully aim. The young doorgunner fired a six-round burst. The hood on the truck blew open, covering the windshield. Fuel sprayed the engine and caught fire. The truck swerved hard left and rolled in a cloud of sand, smoke, wreckage, and people.

"Shit," McCall hissed.

"Sorry, ma'am, I just hit the engine," Arroyo said.

"It was a perfect shot, Arroyo, don't worry about it," Willet replied.

Perfect might not have been good enough this time, thought McCall. She wanted to circle back to look for Rick, but the other two vehicles needed to be stopped. Arrow 23 opened fire on the next vehicle, the one with the canvas cover still on the back. It, too, swerved and rolled.

McCall hopped over Arrow 23 and chased the lead vehicle. It abruptly stopped. Men jumped out and ran for cover.

"Hill?" McCall called back.

"I got it, just make a turn around it, my side," Hill said. As

McCall complied, Hill nearly tore the engine block out of the truck with his minigun. McCall then pushed the nose down and raced back to look for Sirois.

"There he is!" Willet said, pointing. The Pave Hawk immediately descended, and out of the dust and smoke, Sirois ran, limping badly, to McCall's aircraft. Hill fired past Sirois to cover his extraction, while Gerlach and his Delta operators pulled Sirois aboard.

"We've got him!" Hill yelled.

McCall grinned from ear to ear as she climbed away. Sirois lay back as the Delta medic examined his injuries and started an IV. Sirois looked at the ceiling of the Pave Hawk and simply could not believe he was alive and being rescued.

"Arrow 42, insert your customers and have them destroy the target," Ryan called.

"Roger that," McCall answered, and to Hill, "Get them ready, I'm going to put them down near the vehicle that seemed to have no infantry in the back of it."

Hill leaned into Gerlach. "She's going to put you down near the vehicle she thinks has the nuke in it." Gerlach nodded his understanding, and told his men. They did a quick commo and weapons check.

McCall came in near the second truck, and Arroyo lay down suppressive fire on the infantry. They got off one RPG, but it was a panicked shot and went wild. Gerlach and his team jumped off, and ran to the truck.

She began to lift away when Ryan came into her ears like thunder, "McCall, the HIND!"

The HIND had seen what was happening and was making a diving run on the Pave Hawk. McCall was climbing and turning, barely twenty feet off the ground. She had no airspeed to speak of, and she was caught. There was no getting out of its way. The two aircraft were nose to nose. The HIND opened fire with its 12.7mm 4-barrel Gatling gun. The huge rounds came slicing through the windscreen and Willet's arm was torn off just below the shoulder. He screamed as blood sprayed in greats gouts. Huge pieces of the Pave Hawk were

blown away and suddenly McCall couldn't control the aircraft. She stomped pedals and yanked the cyclic and collective, trying to have some effect. In the windscreen, there was
sky and then dirt and then sky and then dirt.

"Lost hydraulics!" was all McCall managed to say before
the aircraft slammed into the ground. The blades snapped at
the rotor head and drug to a stop on all sides of the helicopter.

The HIND leveled out and opened fire on Gerlach and his
men. Half went down in the first pass. The Iranian soldiers on
the ground were emboldened by this and rushed the Delta operators still in the fight. Two Pave Hawks swooped low, making a pass on the Iranians. The miniguns blasted away and cut
them to shreds. The HIND swung around, returning for another pass, the Little Birds still in pursuit. The D-boys simply
had nothing to counter the HIND's attack and nowhere to
hide. The ground was churned up around them and when the
dust cleared, every one of them was down. The HIND
climbed out and turned. The Little Birds fired a volley of
rockets, and a few hit their mark. The HIND trailed smoke
and gained altitude.

In McCall's Pave Hawk, the Kevlar seat had crumpled, as
designed, to absorb much of the energy of the crash. She
climbed up and over to Willet. She searched for a pulse. He
was dead. She gently closed his eyes, and placed her head on
his shoulder, as if drawing strength from him. She scampered
back to Hill, Arroyo, and Gerlach. She found Hill first.

"Hill. James, are you okay?" she asked.

"No, ma'am, I'm not," he wheezed. "My back."

Sirois and Arroyo appeared in the door. They had been
thrown clear and out of the aircraft. Sirois fell to his knees and
hugged McCall. "Oh my God, it's so good to see you."

"Oh, Rick, I thought you were all done. Are you hurt?"
McCall said. She saw blood on his arm.

They pulled apart and Sirois said, "No, nothing new. My
IV got ripped out of arm, that's all. How many times can a guy
get shot down?"

Arroyo moved past them both. "Hill, you okay?"

"Naw man, my back, I think it's broke," Hill said.

"Listen, Luis, stay here with Hill, we're going to go set those charges," McCall said.

Arroyo looked up at McCall. He took Hill's hand. "Listen man, you'll be okay. I'll need your help to fix this thing after what McCall did to it."

Hill looked around at the ruined aircraft and answered, "Can't we just start over and build one from scratch? I think it'll be easier." Both men laughed, and Hill winced in pain.

Sirois, puzzled, looked at McCall. His entire head was a scabbed-over bruise, his right foot was a fleshy bag of broken bones, and he couldn't move any muscle on his body without feeling pain. "What charges?"

She looked at him. "I need your help. There's a nuke out there on that truck."

Sirois looked even more shocked. "A nuke? The nuke we were chasing all over the region? How did it end up in Iran?"

"Can we figure that out later?" McCall asked impatiently.

Arroyo asked, "What about Willet?"

"Willet's dead. Stay here with Hill," McCall replied.

McCall pulled Sirois by the sleeve over to the door. The ZSU could be heard in the background firing into the sky, the rockets and gunfire of the circling helicopters answering. The smoking HIND was still hunting, a deadly ballet continued above their heads. It was unable to corner any of the more maneuverable prey, and the Little Birds were still attempting to knock it down. "We're going to sprint to the second truck. We have to find the charges the D-boys brought. We'll set them and destroy the nuke," McCall said.

"Won't that detonate the nuke?" Sirois asked.

"They were going to do it!" McCall yelled, exasperated, pointing at the Delta operators strewn about on the ground. "Come on!"

McCall and Sirois ran across the open space with Sirois's limp slowing them terribly. They made it to the second truck and fell against it.

"We have to find the explosives," McCall said.

The two pilots split up and began searching the bodies of the D-boys. As they did, Bullet 31 was hit hard by the ZSU. Smoke billowed out the back of the helicopter as it streaked close over their heads, bursting into flames directly above them and slamming into the ground just beyond the truck.

Sirois felt desperation welling up as he watched another pair of Night Stalkers killed. He searched even more frantically for the explosives.

McCall was going through Gerlach's pack as he lay unmoving, a stripe of blood from his ear crossed his face. Her hands closed around a satchel. "Sirois, I've got it!"

"McCall," Gerlach suddenly said, eyes still closed.

"Oh my God! Rick, Gerlach's alive!" McCall shouted, and then to Gerlach, "Don't move, we'll get you out of here. You'll be okay."

"I'll be dead in a couple minutes, I'm bleeding out," Gerlach said.

McCall started looking for a wound to treat and instead found large parts of his torso were simply torn away.

"Don't bother, McCall," Gerlach said.

"Will you knock off the macho Delta shit for a minute? We'll get you on a bird. You'll be in a hospital in no time," she said.

"I don't have much time, and you . . ." Gerlach paused, gasping for air, and then, "and you don't know what you're doing. Listen to me." Gerlach was right about McCall not knowing how to employ the explosives. They were soldiers, but they were pilots, and did not have extensive training in explosives. The little they did have was throwing a few training grenades and setting up a dummy claymore in basic training.

Sirois limped over and knelt beside McCall and Gerlach.

"Set the charges, and blow the weapon. You place the satchel charge on top of it. It looks like it's out of the truck and lying in the dirt. You won't be able to move it, it probably weighs half a ton. Don't try to dig and put the charge underneath it." Gerlach swallowed hard. "You'll launch its contents into the air when you blow it. Make no mistake, this AO is go-

ing to be no good for ten thousand years, but you'll make
things worse if you put the charges underneath."

Gerlach's eyes finally opened. The white of one was completely blood-red. "You see that on the charge? That's the fuse
igniter," Gerlach said as McCall held up a metal, cylindrical
object. It was attached to the satchel by the fuse. "When you
place the charge, pull the pin out of that thing, hold the barrel
in one hand," Gerlach said, his eyes closed again, "pull on that
ring slowly to take up the slack, and then make one final hard
pull. You should see it light up." Gerlach began gasping again,
like a fish might when first pulled into a boat.

"Go do it," Gerlach said.

The HIND made a pass at the three on the ground, rounds
tearing up the ground. MAJ Ryan dove with his Pave Hawk
and passed within feet of the nose of the HIND. They came so
close that as Cooper blazed away with his minigun, scoring
many hits, he turned his head, closed his eyes, and clenched
his teeth bracing for impact. McHendrick was howling a
strange coyote sound, and the Special Forces soldiers hung on
for dear life.

The huge HIND-D helicopter had to make a quick turn to
avoid colliding with Ryan's helicopter, causing it to break off
its attack before the strafing reached McCall, Sirois, and
Gerlach.

"Still with me, Coop?" Ryan asked in the intercom.

Cooper opened his eyes and said, "Me and St. Chris."

"That's good, son, you hang in there," Ryan answered.

McCall said, "Stay here with Gerlach. I'll do it."

"I'm coming with you," Sirois said.

"Don't stay here with me, you can't help me and you only
draw fire out in the middle of the . . ." Gerlach didn't finish his
sentence, but instead started choking. Blood spattered over his
teeth and lips, and his skin turned gray. His eyes opened again,
this time with fear in them, and then they closed forever.

They stared at the Delta major, not moving until McCall
put her hand on Sirois's shoulder. They turned and ran low to
the truck.

A large, wooden crate had fallen into the dirt when the truck had rolled. McCall and Sirois moved to it. The crate had cracked open, and a large, stainless steel bomb case was revealed. Like an elongated egg, it was bigger than McCall had expected.

Sirois was just as surprised, "It's the size of a Volkswagen." He was exaggerating, but it was large enough that the pilot could have lain down inside of it. "Will that satchel charge be enough?"

"I guess we don't have to vaporize the thing, just break it, right?" McCall answered. They pulled a larger piece of the crate out of the way and were able to place the satchel charge on top of the nuke.

"This thing is still cooking," Sirois said. On his end of the steel sarcophagus-looking device, red digital numbers ticked down. "You better hurry, we only have three hours until this thing goes off," Sirois tried to joke.

"Oh good," McCall attempted to play along. "We're early. Normally, in a movie or something, we would have arrived with ten seconds to go." She concentrated on the charges.

Rounds impacted in a stripe of potential death four feet behind them, throwing dirt over them and their work. They both hit the ground, and then slowly rose.

"I don't know about you," Sirois said, as McCall picked up the fuse igniter, "but I'd just as soon hurry anyway."

She pulled the pin, and then hooking her finger through the steel ring at one end, pulled up the slack as Gerlach had instructed. Then, she pulled the ring hard, and dropped the igniter. They both sprinted away.

She stopped, and walked back.

"What are you doing?" Sirois yelled, in so much pain now, he held his right foot off the ground.

The igniter had not done anything. "Gerlach said we'd see it light up," McCall said. Sirois did not move.

"Is it a dud or something?" asked Sirois.

"I think it just didn't work on the first try. I'll do it again," McCall said. The HIND turned in the distance, once more toward Sirois and McCall. She pushed the ring all the way back into the igniter, and pulled it out forcefully once more. This time smoke and flame whooshed out of it. She dropped it, and turned toward Sirois, "Run!"

Just then, Hartman and Team Alpha arrived. McCall and Sirois saw a fresh pack of Little Birds and Pave Hawks come racing through the sky.

"Holy shit," Arsten said, looking down at the death strewn about on the ground. The ZSU was blasting away at the AH-6s still up and tormenting it. Like hawks after a cobra. They would dive on it, and be beaten off by the hail of fire, circle and try again.

Hartman immediately began giving orders. "All Bullet elements, break into split formation. East half take that ZSU out, west half, knock down that damn HIND."

Half of the Little Birds instantly dove at the ZSU, making a run at it from behind, its attention focused on the aircraft it had been battling since the engagement began. They swooped down, racing at it, closing the distance before it could detect their presence, and blasted it with rockets. It appeared the aircraft were balloons on smoke-trail strings, all connected to the lightly armored vehicle. The ZSU was shredded and burst into flames.

The other half of the nimble newcomers let everything they had loose on the HIND. It turned to run, to disengage, and took a heading that would have taken it directly over Sirois and McCall, but it did not get far. It suddenly spun. As it pivoted to perpendicular with its previous course, Sirois looked up. The tail rotor and the tail itself were in absolute shambles. The HIND, which had been nose down, could not pull up. The spinning armored giant missed McCall and Sirois by fifty feet and crashed into the ground, rolling across the surface like a broken toy.

McCall pulled Sirois's arm across her shoulders. They ran together, Sirois grunting loudly with every step, in vicious pain and effort. The satchel charge detonated, and the explosion threw the two pilots to the ground. The blast was much more powerful than they had expected. The satchel had set off the conventional charges within the nuke. They were not detonated as precisely as they needed to be to create a nuclear event, but the area was still hazardous, with the radioactive material spread out over a large area. Destroying the nuke had in essence created a dirty bomb, and it was time to get out of there.

McCall and Sirois rose and ran to the wreckage of McCall's aircraft. Arroyo had pulled Willet's body free of his seat and laid it out. Ryan's Pave Hawk came down to extract them. Medics put Hill on a litter, and McCall and Arroyo carried Willet's body to Ryan's bird. Sirois limped after them. Cooper was scanning for something or someone at which to fire, but there was no one. When they were all aboard, the crowded Pave Hawk lifted off and McCall looked out at the carnage: smoldering wrecks of trucks, the ZSU, downed helicopters, and bodies. While normally nobody gets left behind, in this case the bodies of the Delta operators were likely radioactive. They were not leaving the bodies to the Iranians in any event. Now that it was confirmed that the nuke had been rendered useless, they could be less surgical. McHendrick sat beside McCall, giggling. McCall and Sirois looked at the wizened, old man. McHendrick waved happily at Sirois, who held up a hand to return the wave. McHendrick then fell abruptly silent, and McCall couldn't help but wonder what Sirois had really been through.

Hartman's aircraft circled until the survivors were airborne. The commander of the 6/160th waited and watched until all his people were up, and called, "All elements, let's head for home." Switching radios, he called, "Eagle, Eagle, this is Arrow 6. We are clear, mission accomplished, we need a cleanup mission, to include downed aircraft, over."

"Uh, roger that, Arrow, this is Eagle, just give us the grid that you want us to make go away, over," a voice came back.

Hartman gave the grid coordinates of the nuke and the wrecked aircraft. As the Night Stalkers flew back to Iraq, somewhere high above them, a strike package went in. Eleven

F-15E Strike Eagles from the 332nd Tactical Fighter Squadron each carrying four CBU-72 cluster bombs. The 550-pound bombs contained three separate, 100-pound fuel-air mixture bomblets, which fall separately covering a large area.

The F-15Es, in a formation to maximize the distribution of the bombs, passed over the target. As the cluster bombs fell, the outer shells opened, and the bomblets were released. At thirty feet, the bomblets air-burst, each creating an aerosol cloud of ethylene oxide that was fifty feet across and ten feet deep. Together, the 132 bomblets formed a cloud nearly a mile in diameter. As it descended, the embedded detonators ignited the gas. The explosion was so immense the likes of it had only been surpassed in the region by Pakistan's nuclear weapons testing. There was a rolling cloud, looking more like a fiery head of cauliflower than a mushroom, as dozens of fireballs came together. The overpressure created a rapidly expanding wavefront that flattened and incinerated McCall's ruined Pave Hawk, the wreckage of the HINDs and other helicopters, the trucks, the ZSU, the nuke, and the bodies of Gerlach and his men. The F-15Es headed for home.

33

"How long were you held there?" she asked. She was pretty enough, average everything, but she was the first woman McHendrick had seen in years who was not a prisoner. He fought a persistent urge: not an urge to do anything lewd but instead just to be held, to just fall into her arms and cry. To be mothered. He was a broken man.

"In the ministry building? I don't know. Evin before that," McHendrick answered.

Two men sat stoically, saying nothing, not taking notes, just watching. A tape recorder whirred quietly. The office was not brightly lit, but everyone was clearly visible. The colors were soft. There were curtains on the windows. They all sat in comfortable office chairs.

"We have you listed as disappearing in 1997. Do you have any idea what year it is?" she asked. He just blinked at her, waiting to be told. She moved on.

"Did they take your leg?" she asked.

McHendrick put both hands on his head, in an almost simian manner, and suddenly shouted, "No! I hopped into Iran!" The two watching men tensed slightly waiting to see if the old man would lunge at the woman. He did not, and brought his arms back down, folding his hands in his lap. The woman glanced over at the two men and continued, "Of course, sorry. Who is Farmad?"

McHendrick grimaced and then his face relaxed. He squinted at the woman and said, "He is a member of VEVAK, a senior officer in VEVAK. And he is an evil man. Second only to Lajevardi in his hate of mankind."

"Who is Lavejardi?" she asked.

McHendrick burst out in a loud shrieking laugh. Abruptly, he became serious and said, "Lavejardi ran Evin prison. Used to order torture. Used to come watch. The wardrobe, the dog box, the coffin."

She shook her head. "Wait, slow down, what is all that?"

"The wardrobe was a box, they lock you in, but you can only stand. For days, weeks, months. Open the door only for food and such," McHendrick wheezed. "The dog box is thirty inches by forty-five inches, they make you sit cross-legged in it, after a few days your legs don't work at all. Completely numb."

"And the coffin?" she asked.

"What do you think?" McHendrick replied.

"It was an actual coffin?"

"Well, I didn't see anything like a stamp on it that read 'Genuine Coffin' but that's just what it looked like and they closed it and when it was closed I couldn't even bring my hand up to touch my face," McHendrick said, demonstrating the limited movements he could make while in the coffin. His hands jerked in turn half a dozen times, his facing twisting in frustration. Finally he stopped and said, "A person could go loony in there you know."

"I'm sure," she said. glancing at the two men once more, "You were a journalist. What were you covering?"

"Am."

"I beg your pardon?" she asked.

"You said 'were,' I am a journalist."

"Of course," she said. "What were you covering when you were taken prisoner?"

"Iran."

"Yes, but what about Iran? The politics, the lack of democracy?" she persisted.

"The connection between Iran and terrorism and how that squared with the teachings of Islam," McHendrick said flatly.

"All that?" she asked.

"Initially yes, but I cut it down to just Evin prison, political prisoners. I've certainly got a scoop now," McHendrick smiled.

She looked over at the two men again. They shrugged in tandem.

Meanwhile, not far away, Sayyed Sahim Hussein Nasballah knelt on a wooden pallet inside an empty hangar, his hands secured to a metal bolt sticking out of the concrete floor. His foot was wrapped in a ridiculously large bandage. His face was fatigue-worn, his turban was long gone, and a pair of spray-painted goggles covered his eyes. He was not completely sure if the sun was still up.

"May I have some water?" Nasballah asked in Arabic.

"If you don't start answering my questions, there will be no water. You will be rendered. Do you know what that means?" asked a man Nasballah could not see. He spoke Arabic well, but was not a native speaker.

"Leh. I do not know what that means," Nasballah said, but he could guess.

"It means you will be rendered out of American custody into the custody of some government that might be far less patient," the voice spoke again.

"Like the Zionists," Nasballah said, resigned to the idea that he had guessed right. It would be better to die than to be handed over to the Israelis.

"The Israelis would love to spend some time with you," the voice echoed in the vacant building, making Nasballah unsure of its exact origin. *"You will tell us who is Farmad."*

"Go ahead and kill me," Nasballah said in his best attempt to sound brave.

A man Nasballah could not see swiftly moved from behind him and kicked his wounded foot. Nasballah, who had not seen anything for more than twenty-four hours, saw a flash of colors and pain as his foot settled into a steady throb. He fell forward and was yanked back to his knees.

"Do you know that the Israelis are already aware we have you in custody? Tel Aviv calls Washington hourly demanding we turn you over," the voice said. *"So tell us who Farmad is. Does he work for the Iranian Ministry of Intelligence?"*

"Nam, he works for the ministry," Nasballah hissed.

"In what capacity?" the voice asked.

"He is a civilian contractor," Nasballah said.

"McHendrick says he is a senior officer in the VEVAK," said the voice. *"Don't lie to me."*

"Yes, yes, he is VEVAK, I remember now," Nasballah said.

"Where is he now?" asked the voice.

Nasballah hesitated, straining to see through opaque goggles.

"You know," the voice said, *"we believe it was you and Hezbollah who were behind the nuclear weapon. We have been in touch with Iran and they say they have no knowledge of a weapon, of a man named Farmad, and they have promised to help bring him to justice."*

"That is not true, Farmad was the man who ran it all. We only hid the weapon briefly," Nasballah said, panicking.

"The Israelis support Iran's position, saying it was you who masterminded the attempted murder of five million Iraqis and tens of thousands of Americans. Perhaps we should just turn you over to the Sunnis in the slums of Baghdad," the voice said.

"You can't do that! You must not! I am only a simple cleric," Nasballah whined.

"Tell us where Farmad is," the voice asked again. This time Nasballah felt the man's breath in his face.

"I do not know, but if you allow me to contact my people, I can find out," Nasballah said, his voice breaking.

This was followed by whispering between several people Nasballah had not known were there. *"We will allow you to make a phone call,"* the voice said. *"If this does not work perfectly, we will drop you off in the middle of Baghdad minutes after announcing what evil you were conspiring."*

"Sirois, Lieutenant Colonel Hartman wants to see you.

He's in the administration building," MAJ Ryan said as he entered the hangar.

"On the way," Sirois said, and then to SFC Pettihorn, "Alright, Sergeant, thanks a lot. I'll get back to you." Sirois turned, nodded to Ryan as he passed, and limped out into the scorching Iraqi summer day. His foot was in a small cast, and he was clean now. His eye, swollen shut for days, had begun to open and his sight was returning. His ribs were sore, but he had refused to stay in the hospital or to be flown to Ramstein in Germany for treatment. The physical injuries were the least of his problems, and he felt like he had unfinished business here.

Ryan walked straight at Pettihorn. The other communications technicians watched, some of them even coming to their feet. Pettihorn squared his shoulders and clasped his hands in front of him. Ryan could not hold back any longer and broke into a broad grin for the last couple steps. He offered his hand, and the sergeant took it.

"It wasn't pretty, Sergeant, but it worked. We were able to coordinate our efforts in those key minutes at the beginning of the engagement. I just wanted to come down here and thank you and your people personally, and to let you know what a terrific job the CO and I think you did. We know in the end the solution was simple, but that does not diminish the effort you and your people made," Ryan said. He paused and then continued, "I also want to say that I apologize for going off as I did after the Bekaa mission."

Pettihorn smiled back. "Well, thank you, sir. Apology accepted. I bet that was tough for a college boy to say."

"You have no idea. How mission ready are we right now?" Ryan asked, looking to move on.

"As far as communications go, we're ready. Y'all still have the Motorola's as backup, so you're good to go. We've got the replacement helicopters all set," Pettihorn replied.

Ryan's good humor waned suddenly and he said, "It will be a lot tougher to find replacements for the pilots we lost."

"Yes, sir," Pettihorn said.

"Okay, I'm outta here, but thanks again," Ryan said, and turning to the others, "Thanks to all of you."

Ryan spun and walked out the way Sirois had gone.

"What a weenie," Pettihorn said and his soldiers roared with laughter.

Sirois walked into the administration building, the air conditioning blasting him with cold as he entered. He found SGT Derek Cooper making coffee.

"Hey, Coop, what's up?" Sirois asked.

"Orderly room duty, Lieutenant Colonel Hartman is in there, sir," Cooper said.

Sirois watched the crew chief fumbling with a packet of coffee and said, "I bet you can't wait to get back up in the air."

Cooper turned away and focused on his coffee. Sirois's smile fell, and he didn't press Cooper further. He walked into the next office. Hartman was sitting behind a gray metal desk and didn't look up. Sirois stepped in front of the desk, snapped to attention, saluted, and said, "Lieutenant Sirois reporting as ordered, sir."

Hartman looked up, gave a quick salute. "Sit down, Rick." Hartman had black stitches running like a stripe across his face.

"How's the wound, sir?" Sirois asked.

"Fine, fine. They suggested I go to Germany, but I told them to just stitch it. I've seen worse cuts from a fall in the bathroom," Hartman said.

"Yes, sir, they offered me Germany as well. How many stitches?" asked Sirois.

"What? Oh, sixty-eight, sixty-eight stitches. Listen Rick, I understand that you want to be on flight status, but you've been through a rough time," Hartman said.

"No, sir, I'm fine, I can fly, really," Sirois said.

"Sirois," Hartman sighed, "you have joined a very exclusive club. You are one of the few people alive today who has survived being tortured. That screws a person up. You need to talk to someone. In fact, a lot of someones. I'm afraid I can't put you in a gunship and then worry if you're hearing voices." Hartman was being his usual less-than-delicate self.

"Sir, I need to go on this one," Sirois said.

"What one?" Hartman asked.

"The next mission. The hunt for the Iranian. I know we've got to be going after him. A snatch or a termination. I have to go," Sirois said.

Hartman's eyes narrowed, and then he answered simply, "Forget it, Rick."

Sirois came out of his seat and pounded the desk. Hartman neither flinched nor backed up.

"Sir, I need to go on this one. After we get him, I'll wear a jacket with extra-long sleeves and sleep in a round rubber room, but if you don't let me in on this . . . I need to go," Sirois said.

Hartman stared into Sirois's face. "Your loss of military bearing is not helping in your effort to convince me of your sanity. I'll tell you what, I'll think about it. Now get off my desk and get the hell out of here."

Sirois straightened, threw another salute, and Hartman returned it. He turned and left the office. As he passed through the makeshift orderly room, he saw Cooper sitting at the desk, stirring his coffee slowly, almost in a trance.

"Coop, you okay?" Sirois asked.

"Yeah, yes sir, I'm fine," Cooper answered, unconvincingly.

"You need to talk about it?" Sirois offered.

Cooper stopped, looked up, and said, "Sir, just leave me alone. Please?"

Sirois was taken aback, but said, "Sure. Sure thing, Coop. Catch you later," and limped back out into the heat. He looked down at his left hand. It was trembling. He gripped his hands together, and returned to the hangar.

Cooper stood and walked to the window. A Chinook was taking off from the flight line. All he had wanted to do in the army was work as a crew chief. Now he was beginning to wonder how much longer he could do it. He knew that if he was not one hundred percent committed, he would not be able to continue. He would take himself out of the game. He wasn't a coward, but even people with courage to spare can have second thoughts about being a crew chief in the 160th SOAR. It takes a special edge, a special combination of guts and caring. Cooper was beginning to question if he still had it.

Sirois's eyes took a moment to adjust to the dark hangar once he stepped in from the bright Iraqi sun.

"Where have you been?" McCall said. Sirois blinked twice. He could make out her silhouette, and slowly features became distinct on her face.

"I was talking to Hartman. He was wondering if I should sit the next one out, go talk to Dr. Phil or something," Sirois mocked.

"Maybe you should," McCall replied.

"Not you, too? I'm fine, and even if I'm not, I'm going on this one. I'll get my head shrunk after, but I am not missing the opportunity to go get this guy," Sirois said.

"Revenge, huh? How's that working for ya?" McCall teased.

Sirois glared at her for a moment, and then softened. "It's important to me. It will help in me getting over it. Call it revenge or closure or whatever other psychobabble crap you want to. I need this," Sirois said.

McCall felt sorry for him, could tell he was hurting. She tried to think of something soothing to say, but instead said, "Hey, you don't need my permission, I'm not your mommy."

Sirois's eyes showed hurt, but he laughed, a little too much, and then a quiet fell. McCall broke it. "The replacements have arrived. We've got a couple of green copilots in the next hangar. Want to go make them feel welcome?"

"What fun would that be?" Sirois said.

McCall laughed, but then said, "It's going to be very strange not having Willet in the next seat. He was such a dependable guy. No flash, no ego, just rock steady."

Sirois thought of O'Brien and the times they had gone out drinking. He pushed it out of his head. The one thing Sirois did not want was to start trying to sort out his feelings.

Sirois said, "Listen, Jeanie, you have to think about how hard it is for the new copilot. He'll never measure up, he's flying with you, and you're a bit of a legend. Give the guy a break."

McCall looked into Sirois's face, and allowed a small smile. "A legend?"

"Yeah, you break more aircraft than anyone. Single-handedly proving the woman-driver thing to be true," grinned Sirois.

McCall's face darkened. Sexist jokes were never funny. "I'm twice the pilot you are. And trying to cheer me up about the death of my friend by telling me I lost the helicopter because I am a woman, does not help."

"I was just kidding!" Sirois cried.

"It wasn't the least bit funny, you jerk," McCall said.

Sirois stopped, not knowing what else to say except, "I'm sorry. I was just trying to change the subject."

McCall saw he was hurting, and hiding it even from himself.

"Let's go meet the copilots," McCall said.

"Are we okay?" Sirois asked.

"No, we're not okay," McCall said, and then a smile broke from one corner of her mouth. As they walked out into the heat and bright sunlight, she said, "Rick, this last mission was too real, too intense. When you were missing, and then to see you in the back of that truck, the way it rolled. I thought for sure I had lost you."

"Jeanie—" Sirois started, but she raised a hand, cutting him off.

"Don't give me the lecture. You never say the right thing anyway." They laughed at this, and she continued, "I love flying. But something is different now. All this time, I've been flying to prove something to others, to you, and maybe even to my father. I understand now why he flew, fought, and died the way he did. I love him all the more for it."

Sirois just stood silent, looking into her gentle eyes. Her features were surprisingly delicate sometimes, Sirois thought.

"From now on, I'm not flying for anyone except myself,

my unit, and my country, as corny as that sounds. The whole game is fundamentally different for me now. It's more real. Does that make sense?" she asked.

He put his arms around her, and even in the heat she felt warm to him. She took his face in her hands, and they kissed deeply and passionately. The kiss ended, and their foreheads came together.

"It's about time," she whispered.

"I would've earlier, McCall, but you're too damn scary," Sirois said.

She pulled away, laughing, "Don't you forget it."

"Let's go meet the new guys," Sirois said, and took her hand, pulling her toward the administration building. "By the way, how is Hill doing?"

"They say he'll walk again, but he's going to spend quite a bit of time in hospitals. He's going to be evacuated back to Walter Reed eventually," McCall said. "I'm going to see him in a bit. He's out on the *Comfort*, going to hitch a ride with Dust Off. You want to go?" Dust Off was what the medivac helicopters had been called for decades, and the *Comfort* was a hospital ship.

"Sure, it's a date," Sirois said.

"Dream on," McCall chuckled.

Nasballah was on the phone, having been moved from the hangar and into a comfortable office. Seated at a large metal desk, he was flanked by two men in civilian clothes, dressed much as combat photographers might be. They were members of the CIA's paramilitary forces. LTC Hartman was present, as was COL Ken Aksander, the 1st Armored Division's G-2. First AD held this Area of Operations, and so it was COL Aksander who had arranged the phone call.

"Hello, Hamed Druha, it is me. Yes, I am fine. I am in Iraq at the moment and will be home soon," Nasballah said in Arabic, when the call finally went through. *"Yes, the Akhbar al-Mustafa mosque."* A large reel-to-reel tape recorder ran on the desk.

The CIA officer beside him placed a hand on his shoulder.

Nasballah looked up and was visibly shaken by this simple gesture. *"Hamed, have you heard from our friend?"* Nasballah looked up at the others in the room and nodded. This was the first bit that Hartman understood. He wished that he had taken Arabic at the Defense Language Institute in Monterey instead of Polish. In the 1980s, the Warsaw Pact had been where it was at. Now the Poles were members of NATO and Hartman was stuck in this office waiting for someone to be nice enough to translate. Nasballah's face then twisted into what could only be described as shock.

"Yes, I understand. I will be there by week's end. Yes, to you, too," Nasballah said, and hung up. He looked up again and said a word Hartman understood, "Syria."

The CIA officers pulled Nasballah to his feet, and helped him into the next room. COL Aksander looked at Hartman and walked past him, following the others out of the room. When Hartman attempted to follow as well, Aksander stopped and turned. "Sorry Hartman, you have no need-to-know. We've bent the rules already, haven't we? We'll let you in on it soon enough. You and your folks hang loose."

Hartman half-expected it, but he was dying to get planning, get the details. He also didn't know why the local division G-2 had anymore "need-to-know" than he did. Instead he gave a curt, "Yessir," reversed his direction and stepped outside. Syria, Hartman thought, Syria was good. It was close.

34

July 11
USNS *Comfort*
Hospital ship
Persian Gulf

It was strange to be on a helicopter and not be at the controls. McCall and Sirois sat in the back, with the crew chiefs, and watched out the cargo doors as they descended to a large, white ship out in the Persian Gulf. Huge, red crosses adorned her sides and a large flat area above her bow. This ship had been in the Gulf when her dad had died here, and it was the USNS *Comfort* that MAJ Ryan had been evacuated to that night.

The Black Hawk alighted gingerly on the moving deck, and one of the crew chiefs gave Sirois and McCall a thumbs-up. A medical team ran out to the aircraft and pulled a litter with a badly burned soldier down. Running low, carrying the litter and an IV bag, they moved as a single unit to a nearby door. McCall and Sirois jumped down and, bending low, jogged over to a waiting officer. Sirois still limped badly, but he kept up.

"How are you doing?" the young ensign greeted them, her whites standing out in the late afternoon sun. She was very tan, and with her auburn hair and bright green eyes, Sirois was paying attention.

"Good, I'm McCall and this is Sirois," she yelled over the renewed rotor wash as the Black Hawk lifted away.

Speaking in a normal voice, the ensign said, "I know. We don't get many unannounced visitors here." She smiled a warm smile at Sirois, who returned it. "Are you hurt?" she asked.

"I was, but I'm much better now," Sirois grinned.

McCall rolled her eyes and said, "Come on, toothless, let's find Hill."

"I'll take you to him," the ensign said and she stepped through the nearest door.

"I'll take you to him," McCall mocked and Sirois laughed.

She led them into what looked very much like a cabin from a rerun of *The Love Boat*. It was small, and not private, but it was more comfortable than McCall had expected. Arroyo was there, and he rose as they entered. "Hey, Hill, look who's here."

Hill turned his head and saw McCall and Sirois. He didn't smile but instead only stared.

There was some sort of large, metal contraption around him.

"Hi, how are you, Hill?" McCall said in a soft voice.

"I'm fine, ma'am, they say I'll walk, just need to heal up first," Hill said, still stonefaced.

"Well, that's good news," Sirois said.

Hill looked at him and asked, "You're going back out, aren't you?"

Sirois and McCall looked at each other.

Hill's face filled with recognition. "Yeah, uh-huh, I knew it. I don't want to be in here eating Jell-O while you three are up there."

"Just think of it as a much-needed rest," McCall said.

"Yeah, bro, just a vacation," Arroyo added.

"A vacation that probably will never end," Hill said. "They're saying I'll walk and all, but they also doubt I'll return to flight status. It's all I know how to do. What else can I do? After being a Night Stalker, what am I going to go pump gas? That's a bit of a letdown, ya know?"

All three of Hill's visitors looked at the floor. They all felt the same way and knew that if they were in Hill's shoes, they would be reacting as he was.

McCall thought of suggesting college or some other endeavor, but she understood Hill wasn't looking for options. He was just venting. No one knew how to break the silence that fell next, so Hill did it.

"What do you think of my boat?" Hill asked.

Relief swept through the room.

"They don't give boats to people from Chicago, too far from the water," Arroyo said, grinning.

Hill snapped a look at McCall and Sirois. They looked back at him and shrugged.

"You ever heard of these things called the Great Lakes, Arroyo?" Hill asked.

"Yeah, I heard of them, they're in Michigan not Chicago," Arroyo laughed. "Damn, you don't even know where you come from?"

Everyone laughed at this, and the mood was thankfully lighter. They pulled chairs up to his bedside and talked about dozens of meaningless things until it was time to go.

Hill grew serious again. "Be careful."

"We will," McCall answered.

"You stay on your guns and don't fall out," Hill grinned at Arroyo.

"No problem," Arroyo said. "We'll come back. I'll smuggle in some rum next time."

"Gin," said Hill, and then they all saw the fatigue wash through him. They had stayed too long.

Arroyo and Sirois stepped out, and McCall lingered. She looked down at Hill, who smiled wearily back. She quickly and awkwardly hugged the massive Chicagoan.

"I'll be alright, ma'am," Hill said. "You take care of Arroyo."

"I will," she whispered. She stood, turned, and left without looking back.

Hill was alone again with a snoring cabin-mate. He worked his jaw in frustration. He should be going with them.

35

July 12
Baghdad International Airport
Baghdad, Iraq

"Good morning," Hartman said.

"Good morning, sir," the room of pilots responded, in unison.

"With intel gleaned from our mission, a one-legged guest, and a prisoner we took on that mission," Hartman began, "combined with other information and after much analysis . . ." Hartman paused and smiled, his stitches crinkling his face, pulling against his expression of sarcasm. Intel had led them astray several times, and he was asking them to believe it again, so he had to let them know he was on their side, one of them, and not an automatic true believer. There were snickers and catcalls from the audience until Hartman raised a hand. "Our target is in Syria, in an eastern town called Salhiya. His name is Khalid Farmad, an officer with the Iranian Ministry of Intel, and recently Lieutenant Sirois's less-than-hospitable host. Iran now disavows any knowledge of Farmad's operation or even the nuclear weapon he so recently possessed."

The pilots jeered again, knowing that this of course was a lie on the part of the Iranian government.

"He is due a bit of misery, and the Night Stalkers will deliver it," Hartman said.

A cheer roared from the assembled pilots. Again Hartman raised a hand. "It gets better. He will be moving across

Syria, to the Bekaa Valley tomorrow . . . with a large flight of helicopters."

There was a roar of laughter.

"We will intercept those aircraft, but this time we will bring ATAS with us," Hartman said, his voice lowering a bit.

A muted cheer. ATAS were air-to-air Stinger missiles. The losses in the battle with the two HIND-Ds still stung badly. It would be different this time, thought McCall.

"The objective is to capture or terminate Farmad. The intelligence he might provide could potentially be worth a great deal, but if we cannot get the Syrians to turn him over, we cannot allow him to escape and try again. He tried to kill millions of people, and was almost successful in wiping out a couple of American divisions. Tonight we will move to a FARP set up just this side of the border from the Syrian town of At Tanf. We will intercept from there. AWACs will try to guide us in, although we expect them to fly low, making them hard to track," Hartman said.

Some chuckled at the obvious bit of information, preached to a very devout choir.

"Also, the U.S. Air Force will be looking for them, as well. I cannot stress how happy it would make me if we could beat them to this man," Hartman said.

Another loud cheer.

"We'll mount up in a few hours. Get some sleep. Fall out," Hartman barked, punctuating the last words. The pilots rose, their voices buzzing. Hartman shot Ryan a glance, his face grave. Two HINDs and a ZSU had been damn tough to beat. If the Syrian mission turned out to be against HINDs, Hartman prayed the ATAS would not let them down. Ryan nodded slowly and left.

Hartman looked out at the dispersing pilots and barked, "Sirois, come here."

Sirois, who had been trying to leave with the other Night Stalkers as nonchalantly as possible, turned and strode back to Hartman. "Sir?"

Hartman lowered his voice. "I don't think you're ready. I

think any reasonable person would leave you behind, but I understand you might need closure, and like my grandfather used to say, the best thing to do with a shot hunting dog is to take him hunting."

Sirois couldn't help but grin. He was going after his tormentor. How often do people get that chance?

"You better wipe the smile off you face. You make one mistake, you act reckless or lose your bearings even for a second, you're done flying for me and Uncle Sam. You read me?" Hartman asked.

"Yessir," Sirois said.

Then Hartman softened a bit. "Listen, Rick. If you feel at any time that you aren't ready or that you need to return, no one will think anything of it. We need you to be a professional about this one, put the revenge away."

"Yessir," Sirois said again.

Hartman stared at him for a moment, trying to read into him. "Are you sure you can face this?"

"Yes, sir, I can," Sirois said flatly.

Hartman nodded. "Alright then, see you up there. Get some rest."

Sirois did not nod, did not salute. He simply turned and left Hartman there.

Hartman gently ran his finger over the stitches. They felt like a row of stiff bristles sticking out of his face. He pulled a picture from a zippered pocket on his sleeve. It was Cat, wearing dark Vuarnet sunglasses. Her face was rosy from the cold, her hair was windblown. They had gone skiing at Heavenly in Lake Tahoe. It had been a simple time, a fun time. God, how he missed her.

36

Khalid Farmad looked out as a band of light just cracked over the horizon, the dark orange-red made a silhouette of the ruins of Doura Europos, an ancient city and once an Assyrian stronghold. Farmad heard the approaching helicopters and looked north past the citadel overlooking the Euphrates valley.

The aircraft appeared, coming up from the valley, one after another, like wasps rising from a nest. There were six HIND-Ds and four Mi-28 HAVOC helicopters. The HAVOCs were smaller, and much newer. The Russians first deployed them in 2001, ten years after watching American Apache AH-64 helicopters tear Russian-built tanks to pieces in Desert Storm. In fact, the HAVOCs looked like a Russian copy of the Apache. While not as tough to knock down as the HINDs, they were just as deadly, almost as fast, and were substantially more maneuverable.

Farmad smiled. It was an armada. These new weapons would change the face of the conflict. They had been wrong to acquire the nuclear weapon so early. It had attracted too much attention without suitable defenses yet in place to protect it. This would have to be a long-term effort. They should first acquire the matériel and skills necessary to ensure that they could keep what was still theirs, and then strive to become powerful enough to take on the Jews and the Americans. Perhaps, Farmad thought, the struggle may yet last longer than my part in it, but our victory over the Zionists and their supporters was assured.

The aircraft circled above, save one. It landed a short distance from Farmad. He ran to the HIND-D as its side door opened in two pieces. He grabbed outstretched hands and was pulled inside. The door closed, and the flying tank was airborne again. The formation turned west.

The E-3C AWACS aircraft from the 562nd Air Control Wing was flying a circular route along the Iraqi-Syrian border. Four crew members flew the large aircraft, with a thirty-foot rotating radar dome mounted on top of the fuselage, as fifteen mission specialists worked diligently to locate the flight of the target helicopters. A young 2LT, Jim Haley, an Air Weapons Controller aboard the AWACS, spotted something. Blips flashed on the ochre-tinted screen, and then were gone. He focused his eyes on that area of the screen, and the blips returned. Appearing and disappearing. He struggled to get a count and a real idea of heading. There, thought Haley, six abreast. Slow and low. Probably the helicopters.

Haley radioed, "Hunter 33, Lighthouse, traffic one-eight-five, one-hundred-twenty miles, heading two-four-zero, six ship, line abreast, on the deck."

Hunter 33 was a flight of two F-16Cs, fixed-wing fighters patrolling the Syrian-Turkish border. They turned south.

"Thirty-three copies, we're supersonic, be there in five minutes," Hunter 33 called back.

"Roger," Haley acknowledged.

Haley watched the six blips, rarely all on the screen at once. These bandits must be skimming on the ground, flying between the mountains and cliffs, thought Haley.

"What the hell?" Haley muttered, and then on the radio, "Thirty-three, Lighthouse, make that seven ships, I say again seven ship at one-eight-zero."

"This is 33, roger, copies seven ships."

"Roger," Haley said.

He was straining his eyes, focusing as if the small blips might take shape and reveal all their secrets. He felt the adrenaline kick in. He could picture the whole thing in three dimensions, his flight coming in from the north at fifteen hundred miles per hour. Helicopters hop-scotching their way across his screen from right to left. All on a collision course.

"Hunter 33, Lighthouse, traffic one-eight-zero, fifty miles on the nose, heading still two-four-zero," Haley called.

"This is 33, I have contact at one-eight-zero for forty-five."

"Hunter 33, this is Lighthouse, contact bandit."

"Uh, roger that, Hunter 33 has Judy." Haley straightened in his chair and relaxed his eyes a bit. When a pilot says he has "Judy" it means he doesn't want any more air traffic control, he's taken responsibility himself. If something weird happens, or if he asks for assistance, Haley would be back in it, but from this point on, he was an observer.

Haley watched as the two F-16s dove for the deck. The distance between them was gone in seconds and his flight seemed to fly right through the bandits.

"Lighthouse, this is 33, tally. I count six ships abreast, HIND-Ds, running through a canyon, fast," Hunter 33 called.

"This is Hunter 34, confirmed, six ships," Hunter 34, the wingman radioed.

"Hunter 33, Lighthouse, I don't have constant contact, I show between three and six at any given time, but I did see a seventh bandit. Heads up," Haley called. He watched as his flight, the two blips, turned hard from a southerly heading, to east, to north, to west. They were lined up behind the bandits, and going in fast.

Hunter 33 saw them again, up ahead, flying in the canyon just below the lip. Six HIND-Ds, flying in two sets of three abreast. Hunter 33 took his nimble fighter down into the canyon. It was straight enough, and he lined up a shot with his M-61A1 20mm multi-barrel cannon. He had never tangled with HIND-Ds before and thought the cannon would quickly bring them down. No sense wasting his missiles on these slow movers. His wingman flew higher, to his left, above the canyon wall.

Just as Hunter 33 was about to fire, Haley screamed in their ears, "Break off! Break off! Traffic zero-six-zero, heading two-forty, they're right on top of you, four ship abreast!"

Both F-16C pilots broke off, and separated, climbing and turning, afterburners engaged. Missile lock tones wailed in their ears. The HAVOC helicopters had hidden after the first pass the fighters made and waited in ambush. As the F-16Cs had blasted past them, without detecting them, the sleek attack helicopters had jumped up, unmasking, and fired a total of eight air-to-air missiles.

The Russian-made AA-11 Archer air-to-air missiles were locked on and coming fast. Haley could hear his pilots grunting as they pushed their aircraft to the limits of the pilots' ability to cope. The F-16Cs could make 9-G turns. At that rate, a man weighing 180 pounds feels like he weighs over 1,600 pounds. Breathing is terribly difficult, he can hardly raise a hand, and begins to black out as the force drains the blood from his head into his feet. The G-suit tries to counteract this, by inflating and compressing around the legs, preventing much of the blood from going below the waist, but it isn't enough. In any event, the Archer missiles could make 12-G turns. The F-16Cs could not outrun the missiles either. The only thing that would save them would be luck and countermeasures. The heat-seeking missiles were closing fast and the fighters threw showers of flares out, hoping to fool death. Three pursued Hunter 33, and five had locked onto the wingman. While two were fooled, three slammed into the engine of Hunter 34's aircraft. Each missile delivered a 7.4kg high-explosive expanding rod warhead into the engine and fuselage of the doomed fighter. The aircraft came apart from tail to nose and fiery debris rained down. There had been no time to eject.

"Lighthouse, 33, I'm punching out!" Hunter 33 called. He pulled the ejection handle just as two missiles collided with his engine. As his canopy ripped away, and the ejection seat's rocket motors ignited, his cockpit became a fireball. Flames rose all around him. He was sure he would die. He could see nothing but bright orange-red and feel the searing heat of his impending death, but then suddenly all was wind and cool air. His chute opened wide above him. He looked down just in time to see the remnants of his once proud fighter fall to earth.

From the AWACS plane, LT Haley had watched the whole thing. When the second of his two blips disappeared, he stood, ripping his headset off, and cursing. Ten ships, he thought, ten. He sat back down.

"Okay, assholes, what else do I have to throw at you?" Haley said, and began scanning his scope.

37

"Arrow 6, Lighthouse, traffic three-five-oh, ten ships, multiple HIND-Deltas, seventy-five miles, heading two-four-zero, nap of the earth," Haley called.

"Roger, Lighthouse, this is Arrow 6, vector us in," Hartman replied. Ten. Hartman suddenly worried. Ten HINDs? He didn't say that, he said multiple HINDs. He was leading twelve helicopters, four Pave Hawks and eight AH-6Js. The imbalance in the makeup of the force was a testament to the true nature of the mission. They were not ferrying customers this time. This time the Night Stalkers were hunting. If not for needing Pave Hawks for C2 and potentially for extraction or medivac, not to mention the unlikely event of a capture, Hartman might have gone pure Little Bird. They were going hunting, but the prey was exceedingly dangerous. It was not unlike twelve men in kayaks hunting a pod of killer whales. More than likely, there would be no halfway to tragedy on this day. Either you came through it virtually unscathed, or you did not come through it. Hartman looked out at the sky filled with his people, and shook it off. Where is this poetic, philosophical crap coming from? "My advice to you," Hartman said to himself, "is start drinking heavily."

"Arrow, Lighthouse, take heading three-three-oh, best possible speed," Haley said.

"Roger," Hartman replied, and then he radioed the Night Stalkers, "Okay, listen up, all elements, we are taking heading three-three-oh. We are being vectored into the target, a flight of ten helicopters, multiple HIND-Ds. We are about seventy miles out. We should catch up with them in about thirty minutes. Keep low, we don't want to have to fight off the entire Syrian Air Force along the way."

"Arrow 6, this is Bullet 13, you think they could get both their jets in the air at once?" Sirois asked.

McCall laughed. She looked over at her new copilot. He wasn't even smiling.

"Lighten up, Morrison, we're going to be just fine," McCall said as an AH-6J slid into place in front of them. On either side of the Little Bird were the ATAS, the air-to-air Stinger missiles everyone hoped would make this encounter a little more one-sided.

"I know we'll come through," Morrison answered, "but I've heard you never bring a helicopter back in one piece."

"Hey, sir, think about why you're in that seat, here with us. That is nothing to joke about," Arroyo broke in.

"It's alright, Arroyo, it's no big deal," McCall said, but she was stewing. "Mr. Morrison, anytime you feel like getting off, feel free."

Arroyo looked out his door as the ground flew past at 150 miles per hour a mere thirty feet beneath him. "I'd be glad to help him, ma'am."

Arroyo and McCall laughed.

"Better watch your mouth, Sergeant," Morrison snapped.

"Sir, yes sir," Arroyo answered.

"How we doing, Coop?" Ryan asked into his intercom.

"Just fine, sir," Cooper answered.

Ryan worried about Cooper. He hadn't been quite the same since returning from Iran. Everyone goes off the deep end now and then, but he wasn't even doing that. It was as if he was just treading water, minute by minute.

• • •

"Arrow, this is Lighthouse, traffic three-five-oh, ten ships, multiple HIND-Deltas, ten miles, heading two-three-zero, maintain current heading," Haley radioed Hartman.

"Roger, Lighthouse, we'll take it from here," Hartman said, and then, "All elements, we are ten miles from intercept. Fan out into your pairs. Wingmen do not leave your leaders. Do it."

The helicopters spread out over a mile-long line, paired up, wingmen slightly behind, above, and to the left. McCall pulled in behind Arrow 5, MAJ Ryan was her lead. Arsten, flying Hartman's helicopter, was backed up by Arrow 33.

Sirois and Reece, Bullets 13 and 9, paired up. It was Bullet 9 who spotted them first. "Tally bandits, two o'clock, running right down the valley."

"This is Arrow 6, Bullet 13 and 14, take your flights in, knock as many down in your first pass as you can, over," Hartman called.

"Bullet 13, roger," Sirois called back.

"Bullet 14, roger."

The four AH-6Js began their run. As they lined up, Sirois called back, "I only count six."

Sirois's words were like a punch in the gut to Hartman, "Break off! Break off! Stay low and reverse course!"

Without so much as a moment to consider the order, all four helicopters broke in different directions and turned 180 degrees, dropping right to the deck. And then, there they were.

The four HAVOC helicopters emerged from behind the last turn in the valley, trailing the HINDs at some distance, providing guard. The HAVOCs were as surprised to see the small American aircraft as the Americans were to see them.

"HAVOCs! Four of them!" Sirois shouted, "Firing Stinger!"

The HAVOCs broke in four directions without firing a shot. The Stinger missile was an aging design, but it had one of the most feared reputations in the world. Especially for those flying Russian-made helicopters. Its corkscrew smoke trail suggested the missile was not quite under control. Nothing could be further from the truth. It banked left and climbed, locked on to one of the HAVOCs. The helicopter dove and banked incredibly hard, and the missile, as merciless as a shark, followed. It seemed to eat halfway through the helicopter before actually detonating, its high explosive warhead blowing the HAVOC in two.

"Splash one!" Sirois roared. The Iranians had HINDs, and the Syrians, who should have at best HINDs, also have HAVOCs, thought Sirois. Damn. This was going to be even tougher than they thought. His ruined foot was swollen, black, and throbbing on the pedals, and both he and his copilot could feel that his hand was not as steady on the cyclic as it should have been. For a split second, even Sirois wondered what the hell he was doing flying. Reading his mind, the copilot quietly spoke into the intercom, "I've got your back. Let's do this."

Hartman looked out and saw the six HIND-Ds turning around to get into the fight. "Bullet 13 and 14, you are on your own with the HAVOCs, we'll try to keep the HINDs off you for a bit."

Farmad was aboard one of the HINDs, callsign Rah-ed Four, and he could not believe they had turned around. "Why are we engaging? We can outrun them!"

"Sir, our brothers are engaged and we will fight," the pilot answered curtly.

"This is madness!" Farmad was apoplectic. "Turn around at once and make best speed for Lebanon!"

Silence.

Farmad pulled a handgun from his pack. He racked the action back on the CZ85 9mm and pointed it at the pilot's head. "We're going to Lebanon." Other crew members began to move. "Sit down or I will kill the pilot," Farmad ordered.

"Sir," the pilot began slowly, "first, let me point out that we have a second pilot, so if you shoot me, they will survive, and surely you will not. Second, even if we did run for the border, those helicopters are American and they are carrying Stinger missiles. While our missiles are more advanced than theirs, their missiles would still be able to reach us for some time, and there is nothing Stinger missiles enjoy more than to bring down the very type of helicopter in which you are riding. Now if you do not mind, lower your weapon, and go sit down. Trust our fates to Allah."

Farmad looked around at the crew members; they had hate in their eyes. He backed away from the pilot, handgun still raised, and moved to the last seat in the HIND. He slowly sat down and turned to the window. The crew members who could still see him wanted nothing more than to pitch him out of their helicopter. Farmad could feel it. Looking back at them, he returned their stares for a minute, and then turned once more to the window. "We are going the wrong way," he hissed to himself.

"Arrow, this is Lighthouse, I have two fast-movers on their way to give you cover. That's the good news. The bad news is I have two bogeys, at one-nine-zero at one hundred, heading zero-one-zero. They're coming after you. They'll be there in four minutes. My guys won't be there for six."

That's going to be a long two minutes, Hartman thought.

As if hearing his thoughts, Haley added, "Good luck, Arrow."

"All elements, we have four minutes to end this thing before help arrives for the bad guys," Hartman said. "Make every missile count."

Sirios was racing so close to the ground, he kept waiting to feel the front tips of the skids impact the ground. His wingman was right there with him.

"Bullet 9, Bullet 13, let's run back down the valley, away from the HINDs, and see if we can keep their party broken in two groups," Sirois said.

"Roger," Reece replied. "What do we do when we have them all to ourselves? We can't outrun them."

"I know. Let's pull them away, pull them apart, and then let the Stingers do the rest," Sirois said. He knew it would be nowhere near so easy.

The lone HAVOC, the one that lost his wingman to Sirois's missile chased the two AH-6Js down the valley, as Sirois had hoped. However, the other two HAVOCs engaged Bullet 14 and 23 at the point of first contact. Hartman listened to the voices of his people, nearly helpless at this point.

"Bullet 23, this is Bullet 14, they're coming around again. Tighten your circle."

"Fourteen, this is 23, every time we tighten up and it looks like we have a shot, they hit that speed. If all we do is run in circles like a dog chasing his tail, this will become a contest of who has the most fuel."

"Well, depending on where they came from, I think we'd win that one."

"Bullet 14 and 23, this is Arrow 6, we have fast-movers on the way. If we can't knock these guys down quick, things will only get worse," Hartman called.

"Open to suggestions," said Bullet 14.

"This is Arrow 5, I'll set them up for you, and you take them," Ryan's voice said.

"Arrow 5, this is Bullet 14, what does that mean?"

MAJ Ryan banked hard right, saying only, "Hang on" into the intercom. He gave the Pave Hawk full throttle, and dropped the nose. Cooper gripped his gun in an effort to stay in place more than in an effort to aim it.

Hartman watched MAJ Ryan's run. Without any sign of hesitation, his Pave Hawk rocketed directly at the two Little Birds engaged in a tumbling dogfight with the HAVOCs. Each of the four combatants was intent on getting a good lock on the other, flying circular laps around an imaginary track, waiting for an opponent to make a mistake. They were so intent they did not notice the large black helicopter racing at them at nearly two hundred miles per hour.

"What are we doing, sir?" Cooper asked.

"When two dogs are fighting, best thing to do is throw a bucket of cold water on them," Ryan answered.

"Are we the cold water, sir?" Cooper asked.

"Yup, hang on," Ryan said again.

"Will comply, sir," Cooper's voice low.

The Pave Hawk screamed into what would have been the infield of their unseen racetrack, burning through the melee.

"Look out!" Bullet 14's voice came over the radio. Hartman winced, as if watching a dog run out in traffic.

Aboard the first HAVOC, the pilot was straining to catch a glimpse of the Little Bird he was pursuing when suddenly his windscreen was filled with the fuselage of Ryan's Pave Hawk. Cooper flashed by through the Syrian's sights, but both were too startled to get a shot off. The Syrian pilot screamed and went into a steep climb pulling the cyclic back and the collective up, bounding over the passing Pave Hawk, but as he cleared Ryan's helicopter he saw the other HAVOC coming right at him. As the other HAVOC instinctively climbed, he pushed the cyclic forward and his aircraft dove.

The HAVOC was falling to earth faster than gravity's pull could have dragged it alone. The helicopter entered a low-G condition, and this robbed the main rotor of all lift.

Within that split second it got worse for the HAVOC. The main rotor not producing any lift allowed the blades to flap uncontrollably. The pilot moved the cyclic frantically in every direction but it had no effect. The tail rotor continued to produce thrust and the aircraft began to roll to the right. The Syrian pilot panicked and slammed the cyclic to the left, causing the blades and the rotor head, to which the blades are attached, to flap to their limits. This caused the rotor head to jump and fall. The rotor head repeatedly struck the rotor mast violently. The rotor mast is the rotating shaft that connects the rotor head to the helicopter's transmission. The shock of the rotor head slamming down into the immovable rotor mast tore the blades off the helicopter and the HAVOC fell like a stone. All this happened so quickly that the experienced Syrian pilot never had time to figure out what was going to kill him before he died in a fireball on the valley floor.

"Splash two!" called Bullet 14.

The remaining HAVOC climbed and banked left, looking to at least reestablish the stalemate they had been in before Ryan's run, but it was too late.

"Firing Stinger!" Bullet 23 called. The missile raced the short distance, striking the helicopter just above the armament wing, penetrating the side of the left exhaust. The HAVOC exploded in two large pieces, the entire rotor coming apart and free.

"Splash three!" Bullet 23 announced.

"Only one more HAVOC, and Sirois and Reece have him running down the valley," Bullet 14 answered.

"Bullet 13, Bullet 9, this is Arrow 6, SITREP," Hartman requested, wanting a situation report.

Nothing until, "Bullet 13, this is Bullet 9, let's split up, one of us will get the drop on him that way," Reece called.

"No, stay together!" Sirois answered.

"He's right on top of us," Reece replied. "Sooner or later, we'll run out of these mountain passes and he will have a shot."

"Stay together, Reece, trust me," Sirois replied.

Silence.

"Screw this," Reece said and broke left and climbed.

"No! Get back down here! Reece!" Sirois shouted.

The HAVOC pilot, nearly driven insane at trying to catch the nimble Little Birds in the winding passes, almost chuckled when he saw one climb free. He put his nose on the one headed skyward. It spun suddenly in space, coming back at him, and both aircraft fired. Both aircraft broke right in opposite directions, and dove for cover. The Stinger tried to follow, but the HAVOC wheeled around an immense outcropping of granite. The missile tried to cut the corner and slammed into the stone. The HAVOC immediately resumed its hunt for Sirois.

Reece ran into the pass once more and turned corner after corner, left and then right, and still the missile came.

If not for the slaloming action, the missile swinging wide in each turn, Reece would have been downed already. He threw out flares. The missile was not fooled.

"Doesn't look good, man," Reece called.

The AA-11 Archer missile closed the distance, its laser proximity detector signaling to the warhead that it was time for Bullet 9 to come down. The missile never made contact with Reece's Little Bird. It wasn't designed to and it was not necessary. At a distance of three inches from the fuselage, between the spinning rotor blades and the tail boom, it detonated. The blades were blown upward, the tail was blown down, and Bullet 9 was ripped open as one might open a car's hood. The ruined aircraft fell to the ground, killing both Night Stalkers.

"Bullet 9, Bullet 9, this is Bullet 13, Reece, you still with me?"

"Bullet 9, this is Arrow 6, come in," Hartman called.

"Arrow 6, this is Bullet 13, I've picked up the HAVOC again, right on my ass," Sirois called.

"Bullet 13, this is Arrow 6, make your way back to us," Hartman said.

Sirois looked for a place to reverse his heading without climbing into the open, but then he had an idea. "Maybe aft cyclic is what we need, but just a whole lot more of it."

Sirois waited. A long open stretch of valley appeared. It was what he had dreaded, but at this point, it was exactly what he needed. He put the Little Bird into a run at maximum speed.

The HAVOC turned into the valley and also increased speed. The HAVOC pilot was confident the chase was over, and his quarry was finished. He took his time, making sure he had a perfect tone, perfect missile lock.

Sirois let the HAVOC close the distance. Closer and closer. At any second an Archer missile with his name on it would be racing at him. He eased back on the cyclic, pulling it firmly but not jerking it. The Little Bird streaked skyward.

"Foolish," thought the HAVOC pilot. He copied Sirois's move.

Sirois held full collective and full throttle and the AH-6 was soon in a vertical climb. The HAVOC moved to a vertical climb as well. The HAVOC pilot focused on Sirois's aircraft, following and seeing the skids and belly.

Sirois broke into a sweat. He needed to be very focused, but his confidence was fading. "This won't work," he muttered, nausea rising. His copilot, however, did not let up at all: full collective, full throttle, cyclic held frozen and back. The Little Bird went inverted, rotor blades to the ground. Sirois's teeth were clenched, hands trembling. He heard his new copilot in the intercom. "Get back on the stick, come on, help me!" Images of Farmad were flashing through his head, "It's no good, we won't go around, Jon."

"Come on, Rick, stay with me!" his copilot said.

The HAVOC, although theoretically capable of doing a loop, could not follow. The pilot had not known, had not set up for the maneuver. The Syrian aircraft flipped to its left, and came back to level flight.

Sirois saw the HAVOC fail in its attempt. He blinked the haunting memories away, and reduced collective slowly. The aircraft went into a vertical dive. He very gently pulled the cyclic further back, and lifted up on the collective. The Little Bird resumed level flight.

"Now we're talking!" his copilot grinned, letting Sirois have the aircraft. Sirois banked hard left, and there, about five hundred meters out, was the HAVOC.

"Firing Stinger!" Sirois announced. The missile seemed personally angry with the Syrian aircraft, not considering any other option, not allowing it to make a single evasive move. The HAVOC was struck directly in the exhaust and was blown to barely recognizable fragments.

"Splash four," Sirois said in a low voice.

McCall heard his call and grinned. The HAVOCs were gone, but more important, Sirois was still alive. She looked out at the HINDs. They were six abreast running on the Night Stalkers.

"This is Arrow 6, all Bullet elements, engage HINDs with your Stingers," came Hartman's voice.

"I don't think I can get there in time, boss," answered Sirois's voice.

Hartman grinned in spite of himself. "Bullet 13, Arrow 6, just get back here as soon as you can, we can use the extra hands."

"Arrow 6, this is Lighthouse, those bandits are two minutes from your location, bandits one-nine-zero, fifty miles, heading zero-one-zero," Haley's voice came in, reminding Hartman that the AWACS was still out there.

"Lighthouse, Arrow, ETA on our friends?" Hartman asked.

"This is Lighthouse, still looks like almost four minutes," Haley replied.

The six Little Birds still with Hartman came online and made a headlong run at the HINDs. Six on six. Except this looked like six Ferraris playing chicken with six cement trucks. Their combined closing speed was nearly 350 miles per hour. They drew closer and closer, missiles locked on to every aircraft on both sides, and no one fired. The two lines passed through each other.

"What the hell are you guys doing?" roared Hartman.

Aboard the HIND, Farmad watched an American helicopter flash by on either side. He heard a cheer go up over the intercom and saw crew members near the cockpit excitedly pump their fists in the air.

"Pilots are mad. All of them," Farmad whispered.

Two crew members ran back toward him and flipped the side doors open, manning their guns. The air inside the aircraft was suddenly akin to a tornado, and Farmad clipped himself in.

All twelve aircraft reversed course, and there was once again a dogfight. Canons blazed from and at the combatants, no one wanting to fire missiles at such close quarters.

The Arrow elements watched, helpless, unable to do anything, until Arrow 5 suddenly dipped nose down and made a run at the mid-air contest.

"Arrow 5, hold fast, hold fast!" Hartman yelled.

Ryan turned back. Cooper sighed with relief.

"Arrow 6, this is 5, we can't just sit here," Ryan called.

"If we lose the Arrow elements, and someone gets shot down, there would be no one to extract him, and we'll have a repeat of the Sirois situation," Hartman replied. "Not to mention no potential medivac. Just hold your pattern."

"Arrow 6, this is Bullet 13, I'm in the fight," Sirois's voice announced.

McCall searched the sky for him and saw the small aircraft come racing in. "Bullet 13, this is Arrow 42, you are out of Stingers."

"Sweet of you to notice, McCall," Sirois came back. In her mind, she could see his sarcastic grin.

Sirois flew headlong into the brawl, his 7.62mm minigun blazing. A door gunner on one of the HINDs, made the catch, taking a blast from Sirois's guns full in the chest and head, nearly coming apart at the seams.

Farmad shrieked as the air around him was filled with blood and flesh. He freed himself and moved forward again. "Get us out of here!" He reached for his handgun once more, and a crew chief on the HIND drew first. Farmad looked down the barrel of the 9mm handgun, and blinked, his eyelids becoming sticky from the door gunner's blood. The crew chief said, "Understand this, you Persian idiot, we are in this fight because of you. The Americans are here for you, not us. Give me your weapon."

Farmad pulled the CZ85 from his pants.

"Slowly," the crew chief said.

Farmad handed him his gun.

"Now, return to your seat. I will not speak to you again. The next time I will kill you without warning. Move," the crew chief said.

• • •

Sirois's entrance into the fray had thrown off its balance, and like a tire out of round on a freeway, the throng of combatants came apart.

As they loosened up, the firing became less sporadic and more measured.

"This is Bullet 22," a voice came.

Silence.

"Bullet 22, this is Arrow 6, go ahead," Hartman said.

"This is Bullet 22," the voice returned, thready this time.

"Go ahead, Bullet 22," Hartman replied again, anxiety present in his voice as he looked out at the battle and saw what he feared he would. One Little Bird, which at this distance did not appear to have any damage, simply fell from the sky and impacted on the rocks below. The AH-6J burst into flames.

"Arrow, this is Lighthouse, two ship abreast one-niner-zero, five miles, closing fast," Haley called.

Hartman looked out the open cargo door and saw them. Su-27 Flankers from the Syrian Arab Air Force's 826th Squadron, dual tail fins clearly visible.

"This is Arrow 6, fast-movers are here, all Arrow elements, pull in closer to the HINDs or else those fighters will pick us off easily," Hartman ordered.

The four Pave Hawks ran in to close the gap between friend and foe for the Su-27s. McCall and Ryan were glad to finally get out of the cheap seats and get into the fight, no matter how little they might actually accomplish without missiles.

The Su-27s passed over the battling helicopters at nearly the speed of sound, having dropped their airspeed to less than supersonic speed for the run on the slower aircraft. Neither fighter pilot could believe what he saw. Like someone had tied sixteen aircraft together with invisible cables, they climbed and dove, circled and banked, juking in every direction, trying desperately to get a clear shot without colliding with friend or foe.

Suddenly, every HIND broke off at once and came to a mutual heading, frantically climbing, clawing for altitude. The move, for the first moment, caught the Night Stalkers by surprise.

"Stick with them!" Hartman roared into the radio, "They are trying to leave us out here for the fighters!"

"What if they are trying to lure us to altitude for the fighters?" Ryan shouted back.

"Bullet 17 and 26, take up a position on the north side and engage the fighters when they return. Fire and dive. Clear?" Hartman barked.

"Roger."

"Roger."

"Right, Bullet 19, 23, 14. Expend all remaining missiles on those HINDs. Don't wait. I know we're short on missiles, but we won't get another opportunity like this," Hartman said. The three Little Birds soared skyward. They could not catch the HINDs, but the Stingers could. As if on cue, the HINDs dropped flares and broke into two groups of three. The AH-6s fired all five Stingers they had left between them. Sirois watched the missiles climb and turn. Just pure math, he thought, one of the HINDs, at least, will be back. Sirois hoped it was the one with Farmad. Dying instantly in a fireball was too good for him.

Two of the Stingers were fooled by the flares and went off course, harmlessly impacting the ground. The other three found their marks. Almost simultaneously, three HINDS lost their engines and their ability to stay aloft. Three great smoking hulks plunged to earth. The three remaining HINDs, however, turned and faced their would-be killers.

The fighters were coming in again. McCall watched their approach. The Little Birds, which had waited by running a circuit, turned and ran straight at the fixed-wing aircraft.

"Firing Stingers!" Bullet 17 called.

"Firing Stingers," Bullet 26 echoed.

The AH-6Js broke hard right and ran for the ground to find some sort of cover. The Su-27s were not going to give them much of a head start. AA-11 Archer and AA-10 Alamo missiles came streaking at the Night Stalkers. Three missiles turned steeply downward, pursuing the Little Birds running for the deck. Three others raced at the Pave Hawks and the Little Birds just as the HINDs engaged them.

The fighters threw out countermeasure flares like mad. All four stingers passed by the aircraft. One spiraled out, and fell to the ground. The other three reversed course in wide 180-degree turns. The wingman Su-27 broke left, and the lead broke right. Two of the missiles followed the lead plane. Inexplicably, one missile simply broke off the pursuit and went straight down, corkscrewing into the rocks, but the other missile was locked on. Just as it impacted, the pilot ejected, his seat blasting him clear as his plane disintegrated beneath him.

The wingman still had a Stinger on his tail. He rolled and then went vertical with afterburners, rolled again, pulled a double-S, nothing was shaking the Stinger loose. It was closing fast as he dove for the deck, his aircraft vibrated badly as he pushed it hard, diving for his life. The missile was unbelievably close when he pulled up, and he felt the G forces go to work. He gasped for breath. He pulled harder, still saw the ground rushing up at him with unimaginable speed. The nose came up, and the aircraft climbed, the tail and engines missed the ground by a dozen feet. The pilot could not breathe, could not see, his vision went black as his aircraft rocketed skyward. The Stinger could pull more Gs, but it could not anticipate a human's decision. It had to wait until the human acted. By the time the pilot pulled up, it was too late for the missile. It slammed into the ground.

The missiles the fighters had launched, however, were not harmless, they were hungry. Like bolts of lightning, two of the three AA-11 Archer missiles fired at the fleeing Little Birds, Bullet 17 and Bullet 26, in attempting to reach the hot engines, ripped down into their rotors, ripping them off. The two helicopters cartwheeled into the ground below.

The third missile climbed for a moment and then fell back to earth, impacting on the granite.

The other three missiles, two AA-10 Alamos and an AA-11 Archer, soared up at the remaining Night Stalkers. The Pave Hawks broke into pairs to try to evade. McCall followed Ryan's helicopter once more. The HINDs made a strafing run through the pack, hitting Bullet 19 and Bullet 23 with cannon fire. Arsten, flying Arrow 6, banked hard to avoid the HINDs. His wingman, Arrow 33, tried to follow, but was caught in the middle of his turn by the three remaining HINDs. Their cannon knocked the Pave Hawk from the sky and it barrel-rolled to earth. Cooper watched as a crew chief was thrown out through the open cargo door, plummeting to his death, striking the ground mere feet from the exploding Pave Hawk, burning fuel spraying his lifeless body.

"Dammit!" Cooper suddenly screamed into the intercom. "There won't be any of us left! I've had it with this shit! They send us out on these suicide missions over and over like they're trying to get rid of us all!"

"Cool it, Coop!" Ryan barked.

"No, sir, I won't cool it! This is nuts! Let's just go back. All this for one guy? Come on, sir, just turn us around!" Cooper shouted.

Ryan paused, and then in a calm voice, "Sergeant Cooper, I need your help. I need you. You just hang in there, we'll get out of this." Ryan had no idea how, but he hoped he was right. He could hear Cooper inhale as if to speak again, but then the young crew chief said nothing.

"Bullet 14, this is Arrow 5, come around and pick up as wingman for Arrow 6," Ryan called, looking out at the Little Bird.

"This is Bullet 14, good copy, on my . . ."

As Ryan watched, one of the AA-10 Alamo missiles roared right into the small helicopter, just above the windscreen.

"God help us," Ryan whispered.

"Incoming!" Cooper yelled.

The remaining two missiles were locked on to Arrow 5. Ryan gave it full throttle, full collective, and pushed the cyclic forward. He stomped on the left pedal, but the powerful Pave Hawk grabbed so much air with such torque that the helicopter was running forward on its nose but with its tail boom slightly tilted to one side. Cooper grabbed his gun mount with his left hand and clutched at his dog tags and St. Christopher medal with the right. Two giant HINDs turned their cannon on Arrow 5 and ran back at him. Ryan changed nothing. The Pave Hawk was charging full blast at the HINDs, the missiles quickly gaining from behind.

With the HINDs squeezed together, their cannon fire slipped by either side of the Pave Hawk. Cooper felt the huge rounds ripping through the air just a few feet in front of his face.

Still Ryan went on, and still the HINDs came.

"Arrow 5, this is Hartman, what the hell are you doing?"

No answer.

"Major Ryan!" Hartman screamed. The Pave Hawk looked hell-bent to intentionally collide with the larger, armored HINDs as they blasted away at him. In the intercom, Ryan heard Cooper's scream. It started as a low growl and then went higher into a maniacal shriek. In spite of himself, Ryan joined him in it. Everyone on Arrow 5 screamed and braced for impact as the distance to the HINDs became shorter than the length of the rotor blades. The HINDs suddenly parted, breaking and climbing, left and right. The screaming stopped. Then there was shrieking of a different sort.

"The missile is after this one!" Cooper yelled into the intercom as he watched the AA-10 chase the HIND on his side, eventually driving through it, and delivering its high-explosive warhead. The HIND died in mid-air and fell to the ground.

On the other side, Ryan watched the HIND run along the earth, looking for a hiding spot. The HIND hopped over a small ridge, and the missile followed, both out of sight. Ryan expected to see smoke rise, but instead, like a bird of prey in its death throes, the HIND climbed madly into the sky and the missile found it there. The missile slammed into the HIND, and the entire rotor system came away from the aircraft. The HIND fell out of sight. Then Ryan saw the smoke he had anticipated moments before. One HIND left.

"Hey, sir," came Cooper's voice on the intercom.

"Go ahead," Ryan answered.

"Sir, you're nuts, but you kick ass," Cooper breathed. "How'd you know that would work?"

"You think I did that on purpose?" Ryan teased. "Welcome back, Coop."

"Please tell me you did that on purpose," Cooper said.

"You could always go back to dairy farming," Ryan joked.

"Yeah, I just might," Cooper answered.

"Fast-mover's coming back, one-eight-zero!" McCall's voice came over the radio. Ryan looked in that direction just as the fighter opened up with its 30mm cannon. The rounds punched through Arrow 42's rotors and engine. Thick smoke billowed from her exhaust.

"Not again," Ryan said.

"Arrow 42, this is Bullet 13, you've been hit hard!" Sirois called.

"Ya think?" McCall yelled back. She was fighting with the controls.

"So it is true!" Morrison yelled, trying to help.

"Shut up and stop fighting me!" McCall snapped back.

"Dios te salve, María. Llena eres de gracia, El Señor es contigo. Bendita tú eres entre todas las mujeres. Y bendito es el fruto de tu vientre, Jesús," Arroyo whispered, getting good firm hand-holds.

The remaining HIND, seeing that all was not lost, lined up for a run on the two Pave Hawks that were not smoking, Arrow 5 and Arrow 6, and Ryan, unaware, was looking elsewhere.

Ryan shouted into the radio, "The fighter's coming back! Doesn't anyone have any missiles left?"

It was clear the Su-27 meant to finish off McCall's wounded helicopter. Sirois gave his aircraft full throttle and banked to bring himself nose to nose with the fighter. He matched its altitude, raced at it, and both aircraft fired, but before Sirois had gotten even five rounds off, the Su-27 exploded and fell in flames beneath the Night Stalkers.

"Look!" Cooper shouted. "More fighters!"

Two American F-15s roared past and above the survivors below, banking hard and coming around. The three remaining Little Birds converged on the HIND, circling it as it moved very slowly, almost at a hover. A man in civilian clothes suddenly appeared in the side door. Sirois recognized him.

"That's him, that's Farmad. It figures the cockroach would have been on the last helicopter up here. Let's knock it down," Sirois said over the air net.

Farmad appeared to be struggling, and was then thrown from the HIND. His arms flailed and his legs kicked as he fell screaming to the rocks far below. Sirois watched as the Syrian crew chief leaned out the HIND's door, looking down, and then waved to the American aircraft. The doors closed on both sides, and the HIND turned and slowly flew south.

"Arrow 6, this is Bullet 19, please advise."

"This is Arrow 6, all elements, let the HIND go," Hartman said quietly.

"Someone want to find me a soft place to land?" came McCall's voice.

"McCall, are you going to land or crash?" Sirois asked.

"What's the difference?" McCall replied.

"Dammit," Morrison said, shaking his head.

"Arrow 42, this is Arrow 6, what is your condition?" Hartman called.

"Sir, unless I apply full throttle and collective, I begin to spin. It's as if I have full pedal all the time. I'm going to have to land either nearly inverted or rotating," McCall said, "so I need someplace soft."

"McCall, I personally vote for spinning," Sirois said.

"Another brilliant suggestion, thanks, I think I'll take that advice," McCall answered.

"Bullet 13, this is Arrow 5, can you shut up for ten minutes?" Ryan said. "Arrow 42, I think a have a spot for you. It isn't big, but it's nice and flat without obstruction. North of you, a plateau, you'll have to climb to it."

"Sir, this is 42, climbing is not an issue, descending is," McCall called back.

"Arrow 42, this is Arrow 5. Come in on it low, climb, and hop onto the plateau. You might come very close to a climbing landing," Ryan said.

Morrison said into the intercom, "He's as crazy as you are."

"Thanks, I'll take that as a compliment," McCall said, and then into the radio, "Arrow 5, this is Arrow 42, sounds pretty nuts to Morrison."

"McCall, you can do this," Ryan called back. "I'm passing over the plateau now, you see it?"

"Yessir," McCall said, racing around in a large circle at incredible speed, smoke billowing out and creating a black ring around the aircraft. In a much wider circle, and at three times the altitude, the F-15s flew cover for the helicopters.

"Break for the plateau, come in below it, flare to bleed off some airspeed, climb, and hop onto it. Climb to barely above it, skimming over it at a couple feet with much of your forward airspeed killed off, and go to zero lift situation. You'll barely have started to spin when you touch down," Ryan urged.

"Arrow 42, this is Arrow 6, you can do it. Night Stalkers don't quit," Hartman called.

"Okay, okay," McCall answered, "I'm on the way. Just keep Sirois out of my way."

"I'm here Jeanie, you can make it," Sirois said, understanding what she really meant.

McCall did not answer, but said into the intercom, "Arroyo, close the doors, find a seatbelt, and use it."

"Yes, ma'am." Arroyo pulled the large cargo doors closed and picked a spot in the center of the aft seats. He then returned to his praying.

McCall looked over at Morrison and asked, "Ready?"

"Let's go," Morrison said, not returning the look.

McCall straightened the cyclic and then pushed it forward, full collective and throttle. The wounded Pave Hawk leaped forward, nose down, and ran at the plateau. Smoke poured out of the engines.

Sirois could hardly watch.

"C'mon, c'mon, McCall," Ryan whispered to himself.

This was going to be like running a car one hundred miles per hour into a parking garage and getting it into a slot without hitting anything and without slowing down until you turned the ignition off. Her aircraft picked up ever-increasing speed and suddenly flared, slowing its airspeed dramatically. Everyone held their breath as McCall's helicopter went level again. It climbed incredibly quickly, nearly straight up, as if it were attached to an immense bungee cord and was snapping back into the sky. It then had moved forward barely a yard over and above the plateau, when it suddenly lost that tiny bit of altitude and struck the soft earth. The gear sank into the soil.

Inside the helicopter, McCall felt the thud of the undercarriage striking the ground, and then she felt the give of it sinking. For a split second she felt relief, but then the tail rotor pushed them around. She cut the power, but it was too late. The Pave Hawk rolled over its right landing gear just forward and under the cargo door. The tail jumped into the air and the rotor blades chopped into the ground until they tore off. The tail then fell.

There was silence. Hartman, Ryan, and Sirois had watched while what had looked like a perfect maneuver had disappeared in a cloud of dirt and smoke. No one said a word. Then suddenly, from the smoke, Morrison, Arroyo, and McCall ran out into view.

"I'll get her," Ryan said, his Pave Hawk moving down to pick them up.

"Let's get all our people out," Hartman said, and everyone knew his instructions included those who had not survived.

38

Jeanie McCall stood above her father's grave, surrounded by hundreds of other identical white stone markers. She was wearing a navy dress, no sleeves, knee length, with a broad hat to match. She held a clutch purse and a Cuban cigar.

"Well, Daddy, I've been to Iraq. Flew over its deserts, and even landed at Baghdad International Airport." She smiled as she said this.

She knelt, placed the cigar carefully and straightened a small flag planted beside the stone, her face suddenly serious. She would never bring flowers. Since her father's funeral, she hated the smell of cut flowers. Instead she'd bring him one of his old cigars.

She rose and heard hushed voices behind her and looked back. Two older women walked a path beyond a couple of trees, sharing each other's memories. McCall turned back to her father.

"I used to be sad almost every day that we never got to know each other as adults, Dad. That I never got to know who you were to your peers. I think that might be one of the reasons I became a pilot, and I even serve with someone who knew you, but it's the flying . . . it's the missions that have really made me understand who Seth McCall was. I know now why you flew, and why you left us. I always knew what I gave up, but now I understand why. Ryan said you'd be proud of

me. Maybe," she swallowed hard, glanced around, blinked her
wet eyes, "but I wanted you to know how proud I am of you,
and how proud I am to be your daughter." She cried quietly for
a moment, knelt again, and placed her hand in the thick grass.
"I miss you, Daddy. I love you."

   She stood slowly, turned, and walked away.

39

July 15
Adult Behavioral Health Service
3rd Floor, C Building
Blanchfield Army Community Hospital
Fort Campbell, Kentucky

The Minnesota Multiphasic Personality Inventory. It shouldn't be taken more than once in a long while, to ensure the results are valid, but Sirois was taking it again for the second time today. The first go-round, the answers he gave had proven a bit "troubling," so the army was going to have him take it again. After a bit of coaching.

The MMPI-2 is a test, a written psychological assessment, used to diagnose mental disorders. The army had gotten Sirois back after being held hostage and tortured. There was a new program of POW support in place, people for him to talk to, and that was helping, but the MMPI-2 had to be passed for him to remain on flight status. Of course, everyone wanted that. Especially Sirois, so a test that should not be given by anyone other than a specially trained psychologist had been administered by a corporal who also scored the 567-question test, and then decided, after consulting with a harried captain, that he would give the pilot a second chance at proving he wasn't too nuts to fly.

The corporal went over the worrisome questions with Sirois one at a time, indicated the preferred answers, and then readministered the test.

While Sirois worked, the corporal busied himself with shredding the practice-run materials.

Sirois smiled. "You give second chances a lot?"

"If I didn't, just about every person we send out there on these missions would be out of commission half the time," the corporal answered. He did not smile. It was plain that he had once had idealistic and lofty ideas about helping the mentally ill. Now he was rubber stamping warriors, trying to get them back out into the fight for at least one more mission.

Sirois completed the exam, for the second time, in just over an hour. The corporal scored it, stamped it, and placed it in the file. "Congrats, sir, you are no longer cuckoo for Cocoa Puffs. Consider yourself cured, enjoy your whirlybird." His eyes looked sad and tired, and Sirois just wanted out of there.

"Thanks a lot," Sirois said, trying to throw on a cheerful face, but the corporal just turned away. Sirois found the nearest exit, walked down a hallway, through a lobby, and out into the fresh air. He felt like he just barely made it, like a swimmer pulling hard for the surface.

40

July 17
Evening
Pennyrile Lake
An hour north of Fort Campbell

Rick Sirois sat behind her, his arms around her shoulders, their legs extended on the pebbly beach, and the maroon wool blanket spread beneath them. A basket lay open with empty sandwich bags, and two bottles of Czech beer stood between her feet.

Jeanie McCall could feel his soft breath against one ear. He gently rocked them both side to side, as if to a song only he could hear. Waves lapped gently at the shore, and waterfowl moved across the reddened horizon as the sun's last rays faded.

He could smell the pleasant fruit scent of her shampoo, the softness of her skin, the warmth of her back against his chest.

"You know McCall, you'll make someone a great wife someday," Sirois said.

He felt her immediately stiffen; he was unable to easily rock her any longer.

"A wife?" she asks.

"Yeah, you know, you're easy to get along with. You're liberated and stuff, so you can help with the bills, but I bet once you get pregnant and settle down with the right guy, you would really keep a neat house and raise the kids right," Sirois teased, barely able to contain the building laughter. McCall leapt to her feet and spun around to face him.

"Take it back!" she yelled.

"What?" Sirois feigned innocence. "What's wrong?"

She tackled him, tickling. He roared with laughter, half-heartedly fending off her attack, until she sat on top of him, straddling him, holding his wrists down. He could have lifted her body weight with one arm, but this was not a bad position to be in.

"See?" McCall panted. "I kicked your ass, girly man, how about you be the good little wife? You'd make a better wife than I would."

"Yeah," Sirois chuckled, "you're right, I take it back, you would be a terrible wife."

McCall paused. That wasn't what she was hoping to hear either. She let him go, and turned her back to him, sitting between his legs once more. Looking out at the lake, she was a little hurt by his last statement. She knew he was kidding but she became defensive. "I wouldn't want to get married anyway."

"You wouldn't?" Sirois asked.

She laughed, "Nothing personal, I am just not interested in being a wife right now. I have too much to do and see yet." She took a long pull on her beer. Sirois reached casually behind him and pulled a small black-velvet ring box from the basket. Without opening it, he slipped it into his back pocket.

"What are you doing? Still hungry?" she asked.

"I thought I might have been, but I changed my mind," Sirois answered.

"Well, it'll still be there later if you change your mind," McCall said.

"I hope so," sighed Sirois.

41

LTC Jack Hartman pulled up in front of the imposing and beautiful gothic revival building, once a dorm for Georgetown and directly across from Washington National Cathedral. It had been converted into a more-than-comfortable apartment community.

He hopped out of his 1967 Mustang GTO 500 and lifted a bouquet of fresh flowers off the seat. He walked quickly into the impressive lobby area and approached the concierge, hoping to find a painless way of being allowed up to Cat's apartment to surprise her.

"Hi, how are you this evening?" Hartman asked. The concierge, wearing a black suit with a solid black vest over a white shirt, was on the phone. His tie was the only bit of color, and even it was muted. The long slender name tag pinned beneath the lapel on the left side of his chest read, "Lester Boren."

"Excuse me," Hartman tried again. The concierge looked Hartman up and down and decided he was sure Hartman did not live in the building and so held up one index finger, indicating the commander of the 6/160th SOAR would have to wait until he was off the phone.

"Mr. Boren, might I be able to go up to Ms. Catherine Hartman's residence?" Hartman asked in the nicest voice he could still manage.

At this, the concierge immediately responded, "I'm sorry that won't be possible, sir. Please go to the front reception area and have them call her room."

"Well you see," Hartman began, "I'd really rather surprise her and . . ."

"Sir, I've given you my answer. Please move along now," the concierge said, shooing Hartman off with his fingers.

Hartman sighed and looked at the floor. Like a rattlesnake he struck the phone from Lester's hand and grabbed two handfuls of the man's suit jacket. Flower petals fell as he said, "Listen, Les, you're going to be a bit more helpful and a lot less condescending or there is . . ."

"Jack?" Cat's voice called from behind. Jack's grip immediately loosened, and he tried to smooth the concierge's jacket.

"Shall I call the police, ma'am?" the concierge asked hopefully.

"No, Lester, thank you anyway," Cat answered. "Jack, what are you doing here?"

"I know it's unannounced, I just wanted to surprise you," Hartman said, awkwardly holding the molested bouquet.

"Yeah, you surprised me," Cat replied.

He noticed for the first time that she was made up, wearing a black cocktail dress and heels. He looked her up and down and was about to ask when a man stepped out of the elevator. "Sorry, honey, I can't believe I forgot to . . ." He was wearing a tuxedo, nice but not over-the-top, simply black, and he had a civilian haircut. The man stopped, looked at Jack with his flowers, standing with Cat, and tried to decide what was going on.

Hartman looked back and forth between the two.

"Jack, I . . ." Cat offered.

Hartman turned and walked out, tossing the flowers to the tuxedoed man as he went. He sat heavily in the Mustang, threw it into gear, and drove off. It was an eleven-hour drive back to Fort Campbell, and he was already exhausted and way too pissed off to attempt it.

He turned this way and that through the streets, onto Foxhall, Nebraska, Arizona, and Canal. He got on VA-123 until VA-267 and headed west toward Dulles International Airport. He had no intention of abandoning his car and catching a flight, he just needed to put some space between himself and D.C. He exited onto the Reston Parkway, and then turned left onto Baron Cameron Avenue.

"Dammit, how could I be so stupid?" he said to himself. "She doesn't want you back, Jack. You had your shot."

Baron Cameron became Elden, and he pulled into the parking lot of a budget hotel. Stepping out of the car, there were restaurants on one side and a doughnut shop on the other.

"Home sweet home," he said. The night desk clerk stood outside, pacing slowly and smoking, causing the automatic doors to swing open again and again.

"Checking in, sir?" the clerk asked.

"Yeah, if you have vacancies," Hartman replied.

"Sure we do," the clerk answered, and stepped in before Hartman could.

As the clerk ran Hartman's credit card, he could hear a computer modem dialing, and then his cell phone rang. Lifting it, he did not recognize the number.

"Hartman," he said curtly, answering it.

"Jack, it's me," came Cat's voice. "Where are you?"

"Leave me alone, Cat," he said softly. "I don't need you to make me feel better."

"Jack, I'm not trying to cheer you up. In fact you owe me an apology," Cat began. Jack could feel his blood rising into his head.

"An apology?" Jack asked.

"Yes. Meet me at my place around midnight. The concierge has a key for you," Cat said, her tone softening.

Jack was stunned, and came up with the most intelligent response he could muster: "Huh?"

Cat laughed. "See you then, okay?"

Jack collected himself. "Hey, what about the tuxedo?"

"That was my date for tonight Jack, but he's nobody special. If you can handle it, I'll do this little function I have to do with him, ditch the tuxedo, and come back to you before I turn into a pumpkin. Okay?" Cat said.

Again Jack proved himself to be a stellar conversationalist: "Um, okay."

"Great," Cat purred. "See you then."

Jack hung up his phone just as the clerk slid a piece of paper and his credit card toward him. "If you'll just sign here, sir, we'll be all set."

He picked up the credit card, left the paper on the counter, and said, "No, forget it, I think we're all set already." Hartman turned and walked out, the clerk just watching him go.

He hopped back into the Mustang and backed it up. He pulled away, and drove back into the city.

42

Hamed Druha sat quietly in the garden. Farmad was dead, Sayyed Nasballah was missing. He sipped some tea and honestly did not know what to do next. No one really knew that Nasballah was unaccounted for because they had believed Druha when he said his boss was in Iraq, in al-Basra. A man could be hard to reach in Iraq, after all.

Druha took another sip of tea. Suddenly he felt a knife at his throat.

"Where is Nasballah?" a deep voice, half-whispering, asked.

"In Iraq," Druha squeaked.

"Do not lie to me," the voice said and additional pressure was applied to the knife and his throat.

"Wait, wait, in truth, I do not know where he is," Druha said.

"When did you see him last?" asked the voice.

"Just before he left for Tehran. Then he called and claimed to be in Iraq," Druha answered. The knife was removed from his throat. Druha slowly turned around. A man with a badly scarred and pitted face stood before him.

"Who are you?" Druha asked.

The man seemed to consider answering before he did. "I am an associate of the late Khalid Farmad. It is known by our intelligence service that Nasballah betrayed Farmad and us."

"Not possible. Sayyed Nasballah is a great man, a spiritual man," Druha answered.

"He may have been, but the Americans or the Israelis hold him now," the man said, "and we know he has betrayed us, leading to the death of Farmad and the loss of the weapon. In fact you helped him, when he called you and you compromised where Farmad was and where he was going. He called you from Baghdad, from the airport. It was you who unwittingly gave Farmad to the Americans."

Druha was suddenly terrified, "But I did not know! I had no way of knowing!"

"Yes, yes." The man motioned to Druha to remain calm. "We do not think you disloyal, only stupid." There was a pause, a moment of Druha processing the new information. The man waited.

"So it's true? We had a nuclear weapon?" Druha said. He had actually never been directly told about the nuke, not even by Nasballah, but he had heard and seen enough to speculate. It was one of the reasons that he had thought Nasballah would never have betrayed the cause or revealed such critical information. Nasballah had not even told him about the weapon, and that meant he had told no one. At least not willingly.

The man was almost surprised that Druha had not known. The man said, "Yes, but it appears our loss may only be temporary, and Allah may have more than just the one hand next time."

Druha was immediately intrigued and eager to be involved. "How can Hezbollah help?"

"Do you speak for Hezbollah now?" the man asked.

"I speak for the people of Hezbollah," Druha said flatly.

The man smiled. "You speak for our people then. Nasballah was always our puppet," he said. "We can put anyone in charge of Hezbollah. You offer little."

"The people beneath your puppet see me as a familiar face. Perhaps I can speak for them. Without them, there is no Hezbollah," Druha said.

"Be careful to not let your kind offer sound like a threat," the man said, his face darkening, the scars turning darker still, almost a purplish brown. "You have a very large extended family, including a young wife and a little baby."

"It is only an offer," Druha said fearfully. This psychopath was clearly not someone with whom to toy.

As if a switch had been thrown back the other way, the man's face relaxed. "Very well. I have two missions for Hezbollah then. One of repair and one of vengeance."

Druha felt his skin crawl at the man's snakelike speech, hissing his words. The man sat down and began to explain two different tasks for the Party of God.

43

"Allow me to speak with Sayyed Nasballah, prove to me he is alive, and I will tell you where the other nuclear weapons are," Druha said. "It is all I ask. If you have not killed him already, let me talk to him."

"What makes you think we have him here?" asked the CIA interrogator. COL Aksander stood behind him. The office was cool from the air conditioning and the sunlight was being filtered through the sheer blue curtains.

"You are wasting my time. If letting me see and talk to Sayyed Nasballah is too high a price for you to pay in order to learn of other nuclear weapons, so be it," Druha said.

The interrogator considered it for a moment, and then answered, "Very well, but you will have to consent to a vigorous search of your clothing and person. You will have five minutes with him. And then you'll fill us in, correct?"

Druha nodded.

"Right. Let's get this man searched. In fact, I want him x-rayed. Then bring him back here," the interrogator said.

"Wait," Aksander said, "I don't think that's a very good idea. Something's up here."

"Which is why we'll search him, let him play footsies with his buddy, and then hear what he has to say," the interrogator said.

Aksander knew it was a done deal. He squinted at Druha,

as if trying to read his mind. He turned, looked at the CIA man, and then nodded to a couple MPs in the room. Aksander walked out into the Iraqi summer heat.

Druha was immediately taken to the infirmary and strip-searched. The MPs watched as he put on a hospital johnny and was x-rayed from head to toe for weapons or explosives. Nothing suspicious. They searched every inch of his clothing, and then returned it to him. Druha dressed, and they brought him back to the interrogator. Opening a steel door, the interrogator led Druha, flanked by MPs, to a small room. He was put in a wooden chair in the middle of the floor. The MPs backed away and the interrogator stepped out the way they had come in, wanting to get a tape recorder to capture the conversation. Nasballah was led in from a different door, and was seated in a wooden chair across from Druha.

The two men immediately rose and embraced, kissing each other's cheeks. Druha's grip on Nasballah suddenly became fierce, and he began licking Nasballah's face. The MPs looked away in disgust.

Nasballah cried out in Arabic, *"What are you doing?"* Tears streamed down Druha's face. The interrogator returned and dropped the tape recorder, breaking it into several pieces. He rushed forward and grabbed Druha, trying to pull him away. Druha fought to hold onto Nasballah, licking at his face, in his eyes, his mouth.

The MPs followed the interrogator's lead and soon the men were separated. Nasballah and Druha both went sprawling onto the floor. The interrogator and two MPs held Druha down as the man sobbed. The interrogator saw into Druha's mouth as the man wailed. The entire inside of his mouth and tongue were covered in small red sores, many of them open and bleeding.

The interrogator jumped up and moved away. Druha continued to cry.

"Get off him! I think it's smallpox!" the interrogator shouted. The MPs jumped up and away. Druha rolled into the fetal position. The MPs also let Nasballah go, who immediately moved to and knelt beside Druha.

"What have you done to me?" Nasballah asked.

"Hemorrhagic smallpox," Druha sobbed. *"You will surely die, and I before you."*

"But why did you do this?" Nasballah demanded.

"They threatened to kill my family in this way because of your treachery," Druha said. *"Please forgive me, maoulana."*

Nasballah was stunned. He was going to die of this horrible disease. Worse, he knew he deserved to. He stood, straightened, and walked toward the exit. The MPs stepped out of his way, not wanting to touch him again. Nasballah opened the door and stepped out.

"Stop him!" the interrogator shouted. No one knew what to do, but they were sure that they would not touch the man again. He could not possibly have contracted smallpox and become contagious in his own right yet, but the way Druha had coated him with virus-rich saliva . . .

The interrogator watched Nasballah continue his slow walk toward the next door, a door that would lead outside. The door opened, and Nasballah stepped through it and out. The interrogator took a 9mm handgun from one of the MPs.

"Nasballah, stop!" he commanded.

Nasballah never hesitated. In fact, he picked up his step. The interrogator fired two shots, hitting Nasballah in the center of the back, and blood sprayed onto the concrete. It began to bake in the hot Iraqi sun before Nasballah hit the ground.

Druha heard the shots, and his sobbing intensified once more. Mission accomplished.

45

Sirois and McCall sat with the Ryans, talking and laughing.

"So, are you two going to get engaged?" Lydia asked suddenly.

"Aw man," MAJ Ryan groaned. "Sorry, Sirois."

Sirois smiled a sad smile and looked at his hands. McCall just grinned at Lydia Ryan.

"Well, I was just asking," Lydia said.

"You kind of put them on the spot, don't you think?" MAJ Ryan asked.

Before she could answer, Cooper and Arroyo ran up.

"Hey, ma'am, wanna play some football?" Arroyo asked with a big grin. It was McCall's turn to blush and look down. She was not wearing the infamous sundress this time, but instead had on a loose tank top and form-fitting faded jeans. Still, she was a bit sensitive about the last picnic and her football performance.

Sirois stood up, and the two crew chiefs stopped smiling.

"I'll play," Sirois said, glad to be leaving a conversation where marriage had been broached as a topic and happy to lead these two away from McCall.

"Cool," Arroyo shrugged, looking as disappointed as he could. He tossed the football underhanded to Sirois as he and Cooper jogged out to put some distance between them. Sirois threw the ball in a high arc, letting it hang and letting Cooper

and Arroyo fight it out. Just then, a silver minivan pulled up.
The door slid wide and LTC Hartman jumped down. He immediately turned back to the van and stepped back as an elevator
came forward and down, lowering Hill to the grass in a wheelchair. No one breathed. They had heard Hill was getting better,
and to see him like this, to contemplate that the robust athletic
crew chief would spend the rest of his life in a wheelchair, was
heartbreaking. The wheelchair rolled off the elevator and Hartman began to push it. Hill turned and said something to him,
and Hartman quickly released the chair. With his massive
arms, Hill pushed the wheels forward, over the soft earth,
silently approaching them all. Everyone watched, trying to
smile. It was Arroyo who was the first to move. He jogged over
and shook Hill's hand. Cooper followed.

"Welcome back, Hill. I knew you wouldn't miss a chance
for some ribs," Arroyo smiled.

"You saying I eat too much?" Hill asked, looking up.

"For a human? Hell, yes," Arroyo teased.

Hill had yet to smile, and as others approached, something
just felt wrong.

"You think that's funny? You think I'm in the mood for
your stupid wisecracks? You think I came all this way just to
hear your stupid accent?" Hill demanded.

Everyone was suddenly uncomfortable. Their hearts were
breaking for Hill and Arroyo.

"Look, Hill, I was just . . ." Arroyo started.

Hill interrupted, "Well, I did." He grinned ear to ear, and
then, not even very carefully, he stood. A cheer went up across
the picnic ground. Dozens of hands were clapping on both
backs as the two crew chiefs hugged. The nurse and the driver,
wearing all white, helped Hill to sit back in the chair. He had
not taken a step, but he had gotten to his feet by himself.

Someone handed a beer to Hill, who promptly handed it to
Arroyo for safe keeping until he could, as he put it, "park
somewhere." Arroyo motioned to a nearby picnic table, and
Hill moved to it. Arroyo sat with him.

Cooper and Sirois returned to throwing the football, and

McCall and the Ryans welcomed Hartman to their table. But before he sat down he turned to the members of his unit. He cupped his hands to his mouth and asked for everyone's attention. The adults fell silent, and tuned in, but the children never paused their play for a moment. Hartman smiled half a smile at this, and then went on, "I just wanted to say how proud I am of all of you and how glad I am we could be here together today. We honor and remember those we lost, of course. We have been through a rough stretch, and we did not quit. I want to thank you all. You are a credit to the unit and to the army." He raised a can of Diet Pepsi, "Night Stalkers don't quit!"

A cheer went up from the adults as the kids ran in circles around them.

46

August 5
Al-Istiqlal Mosque
Jakarta, Indonesia
Greater Islamic Consortium

"Nasballah is dead, that is the important thing," said a voice in a room of shadowy figures.

Twelve men sat in a circle around a large table. The only lights were recessed lighting fixtures aimed at the walls. None of their faces were clear. They had come from around the world to represent their region and their faction of Islam.

"I question how wise it was to reveal our possession of smallpox in the killing of Nasballah. Was there no other way?" said another voice.

"When it comes to the smallpox, there is little that scares our enemies more than biological weapons. They fear them more than nuclear weapons even. This action not only eliminated the traitor but created fear amongst the corrupt governments of the West." This voice was calm, worn, and old.

"But what is next? We need something to show the great strength of Allah and Islam. A massive blow struck against our enemies to give our people hope, to unite them, so that we might step out of the shadows, and take our rightful place in the world. There are one billion of us, they cannot keep us oppressed forever," came the second voice again.

The older voice replied, "Ah, but many of our own people would be disgusted by a massive loss of life, even infidel life. The average Muslim, unless he cannot feed his family or he lives in a place such as Gaza, believes in peaceful answers. Do not believe our own propaganda about the 'Arab street.' Everyday people who share our faith want peace, not war. Even some Muslims cheered when Saddam Hussein was captured."

"So where does that leave us?" asked an exasperated voice.

"We will be patient. We will wait. We will resist where forced to, but we will bide our time. We will portray ourselves as victims. We will divide them, turning allies against allies. We will convert their college students and turn the youth against their own governments. We will continue to find sympathetic journalists within their media organizations. Then the time will arrive. We will build suspicion between them and then the Hands of Allah will ignite wars between our enemies. We will let them rid us of them," the older voice said.

There was silence for a moment and then a light clapping around the table.

47

Hartman, McCall, and Sirois walked out of the low building into the Kentucky summer air. It was ninety-three degrees, and humid, but Sirois smiled. "At least it's not a dry heat," he said.

"I've never understood that, it's either hot or it's not," said McCall. A breeze blew through the tops of the hardwood trees, the leaves rustling.

"Want to get a beer, sir?" Sirois asked Hartman.

"No, I think I'll pass, thanks," Hartman replied.

"Good, we were just asking out of pity anyway, sir," McCall smirked.

"No need to pity me my solitude, it will be a nice break. Get out of here, go home. Drive slowly." Hartman grinned. "Better yet, take a cab."

Sirois and McCall jogged off and climbed into McCall's Jeep, still without a top even though the forecast promised rain later.

"Hey stranger, you wanna date?"

Hartman turned to the voice. It was Cat.

"What are you doing here? I thought you were in D.C. Why didn't you call ahead? I had no idea you were coming," Hartman stammered.

The tires on McCall's Jeep squealed as it sped off into the quiet streets. Jack Hartman winced, and they both watched

Sirois turn and wave. They almost heard the two pilots laughing as they made a hard right and drove out of sight.

Cat said, "Come on, Jack, take me to lunch. Or maybe the crab rangoon can wait again?" She smiled and took his hand.

Jack followed her to his Mustang. He held the door for her and then ran around to his side. "Yeah, the food can wait," he said to himself. He jumped in, and the powerful car sped away.